LEE BROOK

The Stourton Stone Circle

MIDDLETON
PARK PRESS

First published by Middleton Park Press 2023

Copyright © 2023 by Lee Brook

All rights reserved. No part of this publication may be reproduced, stored or transmitted in any form or by any means, electronic, mechanical, photocopying, recording, scanning, or otherwise without written permission from the publisher. It is illegal to copy this book, post it to a website, or distribute it by any other means without permission.

This novel is entirely a work of fiction. The names, characters and incidents portrayed in it are the work of the author's imagination. Any resemblance to actual persons, living or dead, events or localities is entirely coincidental.

Lee Brook asserts the moral right to be identified as the author of this work.

Lee Brook has no responsibility for the persistence or accuracy of URLs for external or third-party Internet Websites referred to in this publication and does not guarantee that any content on such Websites is, or will remain, accurate or appropriate.

Designations used by companies to distinguish their products are often claimed as trademarks. All brand names and product names used in this book and on its cover are trade names, service marks, trademarks and registered trademarks of their respective owners. The publishers and the book are not associated with any product or vendor mentioned in this book. None of the companies referenced within the book have endorsed the book.

First edition

This book was professionally typeset on Reedsy.
Find out more at reedsy.com

For Olivia—
Our very own prem baby.
We love you so much.

Contents

Chapter One	1
Chapter Two	8
Chapter Three	20
Chapter Four	27
Chapter Five	36
Chapter Six	45
Chapter Seven	52
Chapter Eight	58
Chapter Nine	63
Chapter Ten	72
Chapter Eleven	80
Chapter Twelve	86
Chapter Thirteen	94
Chapter Fourteen	102
Chapter Fifteen	108
Chapter Sixteen	116
Chapter Seventeen	124
Chapter Eighteen	128
Chapter Nineteen	135
Chapter Twenty	138
Chapter Twenty-one	147
Chapter Twenty-two	158
Chapter Twenty-three	167
Chapter Twenty-four	175

Chapter Twenty-five	182
Chapter Twenty-six	188
Chapter Twenty-seven	193
Chapter Twenty-eight	195
Chapter Twenty-nine	203
Chapter Thirty	210
Chapter Thirty-one	218
Chapter Thirty-two	226
Chapter Thirty-three	233
Chapter Thirty-four	243
Chapter Thirty-five	252
Chapter Thirty-six	259
Chapter Thirty-seven	266
Chapter Thirty-eight	270
Chapter Thirty-nine	278
Chapter Forty	288
Chapter Forty-one	295
Chapter Forty-two	300
Chapter Forty-three	309
Chapter Forty-four	313
About the Author	321
Also by Lee Brook	322

Chapter One

Penny Haigh got off the bus on Pontefract Road and turned around, passing by the BP garage and heading towards Škoda, where she knew she could turn right onto Thwaite Lane. The sun had already set, and the dark October evenings were already drawing in. It was Halloween next week, Penny's favourite holiday.

She continued down the narrow lane, the floodlights flooding the compounds to her left with light, making her feel safe until she reached an area of the road where the foliage deepened, and the streetlights stopped.

Deciding to walk on the road instead of on the path parallel to the dense foliage, Penny could hear the water to her left. She was getting close to her destination now, and through gaps in the metal fences, she could see the dark, fast-flowing water.

Soon, Penny passed by the boathouse and then the Sea Cadets, knowing she would quickly have to turn the bend at the end of the lane and head over the bridge.

A silver Renault was parked to her right, blocking access to the trail that, as a child, Penny had spent many hours walking up and down with her mum and dad. Penny heard a noise and stood stock still. She turned quickly, looking for any movement in the shadows but finding nothing.

After finally satisfied she was alone, she crossed the red-bricked bridge, looking at the graffiti in the low light. It was then that she noticed that the yellow barrier wasn't up, which was unusual for that time of night. Usually, she had to get back onto the path to pass, but she continued walking on the road, oblivious to the person watching her, waiting.

The usually bustling car park was empty, and the lights from the streetlights caused shadows that made Penny uneasy. She knew all she had to do was turn left around the bend, past the gate, and along the path to reach her final destination: the Stourton Stone Circle, but something made her stop.

Thick foliage crept upon her, compelling her to adhere to the path's centre. It only relented as she glided past a once-pristine metallic container, now adorned with graffiti, much like the bridge on the opposite side. Suddenly, a bird's cry sent a shiver down Penny's spine.

She pivoted toward the sound and blinked, but the woods were vacant, except for the swaying trees. For an instant, a chill coursed through her. She saw something. Something strange.

Could it have been the silhouette of a person silently observing her?

Penny stood motionless.

No.

The silhouette shifted, revealing its true identity—a sapling swaying in the breeze.

Penny could see the boathouse and the Sea Cadet's roofs to her left, the rushing of water the only sound she could hear.

It meant she couldn't hear the rushing of footsteps coming up behind her.

In the distance, Penny could only just see the start of the

CHAPTER ONE

circle but could feel the force it gave off, energising her. It was a special place to her, a special place to her people.

There were no lights on this stretch of path, the only light coming from the moon above and the businesses to her left across the river. It wasn't the first time Penny Haigh had decided to meet at the stone circle for a midnight tryst, and she hoped it wouldn't be her last.

* * *

The man stood stock still, his mobile phone out in front of him, eagerly awaiting the woman's emergence from the bus. It was a late October evening, around eight o'clock, and the moon was out, shining in the clear night sky. While daylight lingered longer each evening, the sun had already set, leaving only traces of light accompanying the encroaching darkness.

The bus pulled away from the kerb, and suddenly, there she was, the raven-haired beauty he'd been waiting for, looking lovelier than ever.

A sly smile crossed the man's face as she immediately turned around, headed past the garage, and turned right onto the path that would eventually take her to the Stourton Stone Circle.

Excellent, he thought. He felt a surge of excitement watching her adhere to her weekly routine.

He kept a vigilant eye on her as she progressed down the lane. Signs proclaiming CCTV was watching him were stuck to the metal fences that lined the road—the glow of floodlights cast eerie, elongated shadows on the surrounding area.

Her pace quickened as she passed the compounds to her left, her yellow coat snugly enveloping her slender figure.

Having meticulously researched her route, he maintained

a safe distance, knowing there was really only one way to her final destination. That was until she reached the bend near the City of Leeds Sea Cadets, and she paused, looking at the silver Renault parked to her right, blocking access to the trail that, as a child, he had spent many hours exploring and murdering.

Luckily, he had remained far enough away to avoid detection, knowing she would follow the lane over the bridge and towards a desolate car park before doubling back on herself and heading towards her final destination.

Eventually, the pair reached the car park, and the man had to huddle beneath the trees, watching as she stopped and assessed the area around her.

Had she seen him?

No, she couldn't have.

He was being too paranoid and for no reason.

The path towards the stone circle was lined by thick foliage, and whilst he could have waited for her in there, ready to ambush her, he preferred stalking her. It made everything more real, more exciting. It made him feel something he hadn't felt in a long time.

He could have taken her at any point since leaving the car compound, pulling her into the foliage where he'd spent much of his youth, but the boathouse and the City of Leeds Sea Cadets posed a risk. Whilst at the stone circle, surrounded on three sides by an impenetrable canopy, he could do whatever he wanted to his victim without prying eyes.

She was almost there, nearing the point where the path opened up, and the stone circle came into view, where the bordering trees grew more expansive, and the undergrowth thickened, so he quickened his pace when suddenly a bird's cry caused his prey to pivot toward the sound.

For an instant, a chill coursed through him as he stood stock still, waiting for her to see him.

But she didn't. The gods were smiling upon him. It was fate. It must have been because the conditions were perfect, seemingly ordained. He had been granted the ideal opportunity and was determined not to let it slip through his fingers.

His heart raced, matching his quickening pace. He glided between the trees to their left and into the foliage. She was so close there that he could almost smell her perfume as he moved stealthily through the bushes. He almost succumbed to the anticipation, nearly jumping out at her immediately.

Instead, he forced himself to wait, to calm his nerves, and continue to stalk his prey.

That was when *he* appeared.

* * *

"Give me all your money. Now!" said a voice, causing Penny to jump. The person had snaked their arm around Penny's body and cupped her mouth with his hand.

Penny froze.

The person removed their hand. And then she heard the sound of soft laughter.

"Pete?"

"Sorry babe, I couldn't resist."

She turned around and thumped him in the arm. With a stern grin she playfully scolded Pete. "You fucking prick!"

Laughing, Pete rubbed his arm where she had thumped him, but Penny couldn't help but laugh along with him, relieved that it was just a prank.

With a shrug, Pete chuckled and said, "I had to make it

interesting, didn't I?" He pulled her into a warm hug to make amends.

As they embraced, Penny felt a surge of affection for her mischievous new partner. They continued towards the stone circle, enjoying each other's company, with Penny keeping a wary eye out for any more unexpected surprises from Pete. But that soon became a distant memory as they got even closer to the stone circle, marvelling at its construction.

But the night's shadows had entirely enveloped them now, and unbeknownst to them, someone had been watching their every move.

Suddenly, Penny couldn't shake the feeling of being watched. She whispered to Pete, "Do you feel that? Like we're being followed?"

Pete glanced around, his smile fading. "Maybe it's just your imagination, babe."

But suddenly, a rustling in the bushes nearby made them both jump. Out of the darkness emerged a figure wearing a hooded sweatshirt and a mask, concealing their face.

The stranger stepped closer, blocking their path. He pointed at Pete and spoke in a low, menacing voice. "If you don't want to get hurt, leave now!"

Penny's heart pounded, and panic welled up inside her, but she had Pete by her side and decided she wasn't going to let fear paralyse her.

Pete stepped in front of Penny protectively and demanded, "Who are you? What do you want?"

The man wearing the mask laughed, a chilling sound that sent shivers down Penny's spine. "I want her," the stalker replied, pointing at Penny. "And if you know what's good for you, you'll step aside."

Pete didn't back down. He reasoned with the stalker, "Look, we don't want any trouble. Just leave. We'll call it a prank gone wrong."

The masked man's response was swift and unexpected. In a sudden burst of agility, the masked figure lunged at Pete, knocking him to the ground.

Penny screamed, but before she could react, the man had grabbed her, cupping her mouth with a gloved hand. "Don't fight, my love. Don't scream. If you do, he dies."

She nodded her understanding and tried to relax her body, hoping this was just a prank gone wrong.

Chapter Two

George woke and glanced at his phone. It was only five-thirty in the morning. Isabella and the baby were nowhere to be seen, and now that he was wide awake, George knew he wouldn't get back to sleep, so he decided to go downstairs and grab a coffee.

As he walked into the kitchen, he looked around for Izzy and the baby, who was nowhere to be seen again. He frowned as he clicked on the kettle, waiting for it to boil. George pulled out his phone and fired off a quick text.

He received an instant reply.

Just taking Rex out for a quick walk xxx

Olivia Jane Beaumont had struggled to sleep since coming home from the hospital. Now that George's paternity leave was over, Izzy did her best to ensure he had enough sleep to carry out his work as a Detective Inspector.

The problem was that his body could sense that Izzy and Olivia weren't in the room. Like something primal, from the days when they lived in caves, a sense no doubt dulled by technology but still in the back of his mind.

The kettle beeped, and he pulled out a mug. Then, after pouring the water over the coffee bag, he went and perched on the edge of the sofa and switched on the TV.

CHAPTER TWO

Leeds was leading the Championship. He'd not managed to watch the match at the weekend, but it was apparently a cracker. The Rhinos hadn't made it to the Grand Final that year but had an OK season. It was hard being a Leeds fan.

Thinking about sport made him think about Johann Gruber, the disgraced footballer, who they had arrested and charged with multiple murders earlier that year. Gruber had denied everything from the get-go and still, to this day, denied being the killer.

And George was beginning to believe him.

Isabella pushed open the back door that entered the kitchen, looking tall and model-like, her brunette curls cascading, accentuating her dimples, and Rex sauntered in. The DI helped his fiancée with the pram and then handed her the coffee he had made for himself and started on a new one for him.

Izzy blew the coffee and took a sip, smiling at George. She had a slightly rosy complexion, and her breathing was heavier than usual. "Morning, gorgeous," she said. "You're up early."

"I missed you both." George shrugged and grinned. Then Rex came bounding over. "I missed you too, buddy." He patted Rex on his head and then ruffled behind his ears. He then looked at Izzy. The dark circles under her eyes were evidence she hadn't slept much. "You OK?"

"I think I did a bit too much on the way back," she said, running a hand through her curls. At the concerned look on George's face, she added, "I'm fine. My scar's fine, too."

The recovery from the caesarean section had been brutal, and because she'd spent ten days in the hospital recovering, she felt like a whale when she finally got out.

Of course, she hadn't looked any different, George thought. She was probably thinner than before her pregnancy, but

Isabella was still worried about her figure.

And George understood. He'd put on a lot of weight since the accident and, for a time, had worried Isabella wouldn't love his new shape. But George needn't have worried. Sometimes, he even felt like she loved him even more. "Thank you for trying to help me sleep in," he said. "I'll cook us a nice tea tonight." He grinned, and Izzy cracked a smile.

"Not going to happen, George Beaumont," Isabella said, shaking her head. "I'll cook."

"I guess that's wise," George agreed.

Whilst George wasn't the world's worst cook, Isabella was exceptional, as she was with most other things. Isabella Wood was talented in so many ways.

As Isabella was about to retort sarcastically, George's phone rang.

George glanced at the number and then frowned. "DI Beaumont."

"Sorry to bother you so early, boss." It was DC Jason Scott, one of his detective constables.

"What's wrong, Jay?" he asked, glancing at the clock on the wall. "I'm in at eight, so I won't be long."

"We've got a suspicious death, boss. A woman has been found in Stourton, near Thwaite Mills."

"What do we know so far, Jay?" George glanced at Izzy and mouthed, "There's been a murder."

"Not much, boss. Someone out jogging found the body," Jay said. "It's near some pagan worship thing."

"Pagan worship thing?"

"Yeah, that's all I know, boss."

"Right, OK. I'll meet you there, yeah?" George knew where Thwaite Mills was as he'd been there various times as a kid.

"Shall I get DS Mason to meet us there, too, boss?"

George thought for a moment. "Nah, I fancy stretching my legs today. Luke can run things from the station."

"Tell me about the murder," Izzy said.

"A woman's body has been found near Thwaite Mills."

"Is that all you know?" she asked.

George nodded, noticing the expression on her face. She couldn't resist a murder. It was killing her not being at work, but then, one look at Olivia, and all was right with the world. She was an incredible mum, and he and Olivia were lucky to have her.

"Just that a jogger found the body. I'm going to meet Jay there now."

* * *

It took twenty minutes to get to the crime scene, and the DI was pleased to note that a cordon was in place and several uniformed officers were strategically placed, ensuring no one could enter the area. The road meant George could park the car close to the scene, just before the outer cordon, after which he got out and walked up to the officer guarding the cordon.

"Good morning, Candy," George said to the police constable. He noticed Jay hadn't arrived yet and wondered how the tension would be. He was sure Jay and Candy hadn't worked together since the split. "What personnel do we have?"

"Just uniform, sir. CSI is on the way."

"Who set up the scene?"

"I did, sir," she said.

George nodded. Candy was an officer who could always be depended on. In fact, he wanted to get her out of uniform and into plain clothes, but he had two DCs already.

"I've also kept the log as usual." She held it out, and George nodded but didn't take it. "Shall I sign you in?"

"Please, Candy." He stepped closer. "DC Scott's on his way. Is that going to be OK?"

"Of course, sir. We are both professionals."

George knew Candy was, but the jury was still out considering DC Scott. "Where's the body?" he asked.

"She's through there." Candy pointed to a gap in the trees where George could see a small clearing.

"And the person who found the body?"

"The jogger is with PS Greenwood by the car, sir."

"We'll take a look at the scene first, and then I want to interview him," he said aloud.

Candy nodded, and George headed towards the inner cordon, using the stepping plates to reach the clearing.

He cast his eye around the surrounding area. The place was secluded.

The woman, who appeared to be in her twenties, was draped across a stone altar surrounded by stone carvings, arms and legs spread-eagled to remove her dignity. He averted his eyes and moved to change the angle, an attempt to stop him from feeling hideously voyeuristic.

The body had been arranged carefully. Foul, violent-coloured bruises smeared the porcelain skin of her throat and arms. As George trod carefully, ensuring he left a wide berth around the body, he could see the traces of broken blood vessels beneath the skin on her face and the speckled bruises on her slender throat. Someone with large hands had choked her to death. Her long, dark hair fanned out behind her in a graceful arc, and matted blood crusted her temples. And the girl's eyes, which had once been a warm coffee colour, were now as they stared unseeing at the October sky, cold and lifeless.

George noticed the animals had started to do their work, which led him to estimate that she had been dead for only a few hours. Her body looked rigid but not as stiff as some he had seen before, which meant rigor mortis had set in, but only fairly recently.

The DI read the plaque and learned it was still used by a local pagan group for worship, which was what Jay was talking about on the phone. He shook his head as he read the final paragraph. 'We hope you enjoy your time here and ask that you treat these stones with respect and dignity.' There was nothing respectful or dignified with how the woman died or, indeed, was posed.

"I'd say the scene's staged, boss," came a voice from behind George. The DI nodded slowly but kept his eyes on the woman. DC Scott added, "Look at how she's been left."

"What does it suggest to you, Jay?"

"Are her clothes missing?" the DC asked.

"Aye, but CSI may find them," George explained.

"Then whoever did it was careful," Jay said. "She's naked, and her body looks arranged. Bruising to the neck and arms suggests she was strangled and then moved. Any sign of sexual assault?"

"No idea until Dr Ross gets here, but it looks like a homicide with ritualistic overtones to me, Jay."

"I'd agree with that, boss." The pair of detectives moved closer to the body. "What the hell is that?"

George narrowed his eyes and stepped closer. "Stab wound to the neck. It looks as if the blood has been cleaned up."

"But that must have gushed and gushed," said Jay. "He looked around the scene, eyeing the grass for signs of blood. "There's no blood anywhere on the ground."

George nodded. "Weird, isn't it?"

"That it is, boss, and even weirder that she's posed. Why?"

The DI shrugged. "Perhaps she meant something to the killer—"

"Morning. I was going to say good morning, but it appears to be already a terrible one," a familiar voice said.

George turned to find Dr Christian Ross, the pathologist, striding towards them.

"Morning, Dr Ross," George said as he stepped aside to let the pathologist through.

"My first impressions are that it looks ceremonial," Christian Ross said, and George nodded. "I hate these bloody ritual killings. It's terrible enough that a person has been killed without the killer having to make a song and dance about it, too." He shook his head furiously. "It adds insult to injury."

"That it does," said George. "We'll leave you to do your work and come back later. I've got a jogger to interview."

"Come to the morgue, George, and I'll give you every bit of information I can."

"Thanks, Dr Ross."

They approached the man standing with PS Greenwood, dressed in jogging gear.

The DI pulled out his warrant card and flashed it in front of the jogger's face. "I'm Detective Inspector Beaumont, and you are?"

"Joseph Stevens."

"Is this your usual route and usual time of day?"

"It is." He glanced at his watch. "I jog before work, which I am currently late for. When can I leave?"

The DI narrowed his brows. Joseph appeared incredibly composed for someone who had just discovered a dead body.

"And what job are you late for?"

"I'm a primary school teacher."

"At which school?"

"You wouldn't know it."

"Try me."

"Look, can I please go?"

"Why are you avoiding my question?"

"Because I already told him everything," Joseph said, pointing at PS Greenwood.

George stood his ground. "And now it's time to tell me everything."

"No wonder the West Yorkshire Police has such a shitty reputation."

George said nothing. It wasn't the first time, nor would it be the last. He had a job to do, and people like Joseph seemed to think they were above the law.

"Fine, I work at Hunslet Carr."

"I know the school."

"I'm sure you do."

George nodded at Jay, who understood the meaning and pulled out his PNB.

The DI looked Joseph in the eye and said, "Explain to me in detail the events of this morning, please."

"I live in an apartment at Victoria Riverside, so I run along the river to the watermill and back again." He shrugged. "Naturally, I didn't make it to the watermill today."

"Because you found the body?" asked Jay.

"Saw her from the corner of my eye. It was her hair. The

black contrast against the white skin." He shivered.

George asked, "Then what?"

"Well, I wanted to see if she was alive, so I stepped closer, but once I saw the marks around her neck and the stab wound, I retreated and called nine-nine-nine. They told me to wait until you lot arrived."

"Did they ask you to check the body for any signs of life?"

"No, when I explained about the wound and the marks, they told me to stay away from her."

Jay added, "While you were running, did you see anybody?"

"No. There was no one around. There never is, which is why I run at this time."

"Did you see any cars parked up?" asked George. "Or notice any cars that aren't usually in the vicinity?"

"No, I didn't see anything, nor did I hear anything, either. I wear headphones when running and listen to music. Sometimes, I listen to TED Talks, especially if I need them for my teaching."

"Have you noticed anything different during the last several days? If you visit this location daily like you say you do, have you noticed anyone loitering around?"

Joseph gave his head a shake. "No, nothing unusual that I can remember has happened." He frowned. "Sorry."

He wasn't going to much use to them then, not unless he was the killer. The best thing they could do now was order him to attend the station to give a formal statement, a DNA sample, and fingerprints.

"Here's my card," the DI said, explaining how he wanted Joseph to attend the station tonight.

"So, I can go now?" Joseph asked.

"Yes, but make sure you attend the station tonight."

Joseph nodded and began stretching, no doubt intending to jog back to his apartment. PS Greenwood would have driven him home, of course, but he didn't appear to be the kind of person who would accept help.

George and Jay headed back to their cars. Once out of earshot, Jay said, "Considering what he'd seen, he seemed remarkably calm."

"I should have told him to take the day off," admitted George. "It'll hit him later on, I'm sure of that."

"I just wish he'd have been more helpful," Jay said. "We've got nothing."

George nodded towards the stone circle in the distance and said, "Maybe Dr Ross has something for us, or maybe CSI has arrived."

They returned to the Stourton Stone Circle, where Christian concentrated on his work.

"Back so soon, my boy?"

"Aye, Dr Ross, we hoped you'd found some identification."

The pathologist turned and grinned. "That's Lindsey's job."

"Where is she?"

"Over there." He nodded towards the surrounding wooded area where people in white Tyvek suits wandered around.

"Found anything interesting?"

"A stab wound which was cleaned. And signs of strangulation." He pointed at the marks on her arms. "The killer forced her onto the altar and then strangled her. And before you ask, I'm unsure whether she was strangled to death or whether the wound on her neck killed her." He smiled. "Come to the morgue later, my boy, and I'll provide you with the cause of death."

"Thanks, Dr Ross. Any idea on the time of death?"

"According to my preliminary findings, the deceased would have passed away between one and four in the morning. I'll be more specific when I get her back to the lab."

The DI thanked the pathologist and headed towards CSI, taking a wide berth around the body and following the common approach path that Lindsey or one of her team had created.

"Have you found any identification yet, Lindsey?" George asked.

"And a good morning to you too, DI Beaumont," she said. The DI could see her smile reaching her eyes despite wearing a mask.

"You know me, always straight to the point."

"We've found various items of clothing scattered around the woods. There's a phone in her jeans."

"Have you photographed it all?"

She nodded. "Yes. You can take it if needed, but I believe it's locked."

Lindsey bagged up the phone, did all the relevant paperwork, and handed it to George.

"Found anything else?"

"Nothing yet, but as soon as we do, you'll be the first to know."

"Thanks, Lindsey."

George pulled out his phone and rang Detective Chief Inspector Alistair Atkinson. He picked up on the fourth ring, his monotone voice insulting George's ears as he provided information and took orders from his boss.

Eventually, the DI said, "I'd appreciate it if we could hold off on telling the media anything for as long as possible, sir, as I haven't had an opportunity to inform next of kin yet."

"That's fine, but I'll speak with Juliette Thompson to get a preliminary statement ready to be sent out by this afternoon." The DCI huffed. "These things have a habit of leaking on their own, otherwise."

"Understood, sir." George turned to the young DC. "Come on, DC Scott, we'd better get back to the station and get IT to recover the victim's details from her phone."

"Assuming it's hers," Jay said.

Chapter Three

"Right, everyone," George said, calling his team to attention. The noise in the Incident Room was overwhelming, but they soon quietened. "We've just come back from the Stourton Stone Circle. Our victim, a woman, was left in the open, arranged into a display atop the altar. She was strangled and appeared to have been stabbed. No attempt was made to hide the body."

He pointed at the image of their Jane Doe, a close-up of her face, that DC Scott had tacked onto the Big Board. "We have no ID, but we do have a phone," George said. "DS Williams, I want you to take this to DS Josh Fry in IT. I believe it's locked, so we need to break into it and check the images to confirm it's the victim's phone. Get onto the providers with the IMEI number whilst Josh does that because we need her name and any next of kin. Ensure there's a full download of texts and calls so we can see if there's anything about her plans for last night. Dr Ross has given us an approximate time of death between one and four this morning, so we need to know what she was doing before. That, and we also need to inform her family as soon as possible."

"Yes, sir," Yolanda said.

DS Fry was the department's research guru. If you wanted

anything found, then he was the one to do it. George admired his skills greatly but missed having him on the team. He'd fought long and hard with Detective Superintendent Smith to keep Josh on the team, but ultimately, his wishes had been ignored.

"In the meantime, Luke, I want you to oversee door-to-door enquiries with PS Greenwood and his uniforms. There are a lot of businesses in the area that will most likely have CCTV, so take DC Blackburn with you. And get uniform to check the bins for a murder weapon."

George pointed at the map on the Big Board. "I want you to concentrate on this area and then work your way out, but don't go any further than this radius, OK?" George sighed. The DCI had been moaning at him to keep to budget recently, so he needed to be careful what his team spent money on.

George then pointed at the image taken of the scene. "The scene was clean, which could indicate she was murdered elsewhere and then dumped, but Dr Ross said she was strangled after being dragged and placed on the altar, so I'm stumped."

Jay raised his hand, and when George nodded at him, the DC said, "Did Dr Ross say he couldn't say for sure the cause of death?"

George nodded again.

"This is a bit morbid, but maybe the killer stabbed her in the throat and then collected the blood?" Jay looked embarrassed as he said it, so he stayed quiet and shut his mouth.

"Keep going, Detective Constable," said George, "I'm interested in your theory."

"I'm sure once the body has been removed, and CSI has thoroughly inspected the scene, they'll find blood spatter expected from a throat wound," Jay explained. George nodded, trying to give his young colleague confidence. "I also think that the wound will have been inflicted post-mortem, especially if the killer collected the blood, so I think strangulation will have been the cause of death."

"Sounds plausible to me," said George. "But why collect the blood? And why clean her up?"

"It's all very ritualistic, especially with the altar and the stone circle." Jay shrugged. "I'm no expert, so we should probably speak with one."

"That's your job then, Jay," said George. "Find us an expert. Hell, find us people involved with the stone circle. Do what you can and get us a result."

A movement caught George's eye, and he looked up to find DCI Atkinson staring at him. "Are you here to see me, sir?"

"Yes. We need to set up that press conference."

"But we haven't even identified her yet, sir," George explained. He stifled a sigh that he knew would get him a bollocking; it just pissed him off just how officious the DCI was being. "I think we should get Juliette to put out a brief statement and sort out a conference later."

Alistair was like an old World War grenade with its pin pulled. You weren't sure whether he was going to blow or not. Every time you spoke to him, it was a risk.

"I'm in charge, DI Beaumont, and I want this murder solved ASAP. In my expert opinion, we need help from the public."

The pin had definitely been pulled. Did George continue to back himself, or did he retreat from the grenade and accept what his boss told him?

In the end, there was nothing to consider. "We'll receive all the help we can get from the public from our door-to-door enquiries, sir. I really advise against a press conference until we have more information." He wanted to add, "And that's my expert opinion," but didn't.

"What can you tell me about the enquiry so far?"

"We have a theory that our victim was forcibly dragged to the altar, where she was strangled to death. After that, the killer stabbed her in the throat and collected her blood. Then, the murderer cleaned up the wound and arranged the victim's body."

"What a load of tosh, DI Beaumont!" shouted the DCI. "Why on earth would you think that?"

DC Scott physically recoiled, but George stepped towards the DCI. "It's very much ritualistic in nature, which makes the collection of blood, cleaning of the body, and posing of the body, not a load of tosh." He raised his brows, challenging his senior to say something.

"And a pathologist has confirmed this?"

"Not yet, sir, no. As I said, it's a theory."

DCI Atkinson scoffed and shook his head. "I need more than just ridiculous theories on ritualistic shenanigans, Beaumont."

"Well, there's no point speculating yet, is there, sir?" said George. "Once we have more information from Dr Ross and Lindsey Yardley, we can move our investigation along." He pointed towards the door. "DS Williams is with DS Fry now. He's attempting to unlock a phone we found at the scene, and Yolanda is on the phone to the providers with the IMEI number so we can identify the victim. Once the briefing is over, DS Mason is heading out with PS Greenwood and DC Blackburn to conduct door-to-door enquiries around the scene, focusing on businesses as they will have CCTV we can look through." He paused. "But as I said before, until all that is done, there's no point in worrying the public."

The DCI stepped forward and locked eyes with George, his attempt at trying to intimidate the DI. When the DI didn't shift his gaze, Alistair turned away, obviously angry but not wanting to get into anything. To George, that was one of the wisest moves DCI Atkinson had ever done.

"DI Beaumont, we'll have the press conference this afternoon at five sharp."

George shrugged and said, "I might not have anything else to tell you then."

"Yes, you will because I'm not negotiating with you; I'm ordering you. Find something. And solve this ASAP."

George said, "I think you're being unreasonable."

"I don't care; it's an order. Be at my office by a quarter to five sharp, and you can brief me and Juliette Thompson." The DCI's phone rang as he turned to walk away. "DCI Atkinson," he said, but suddenly, he stopped in his tracks. "What, a ball pein hammer and a Phillips-head screwdriver?" He paused. "You're sure?" He paused again. "Holy fucking shite!" George watched the DCI nod his head as Alistair listened to the person on the other end of the line. "In Bingley?" Another pause. "OK, sir, thank you for letting me know."

The DI watched as a shaky DCI Atkinson left the Incident Room without bothering to close the door.

The atmosphere was tense, and George found he had no motivation to get on with the investigation, wondering who had called the DCI and what they had discussed.

But all that changed from one look at the death mask staring back at him from the Big Board. It made him extremely angry, both towards the DCI and the person who had taken that poor woman's life. His fists balled tight. He needed to calm down.

CHAPTER THREE

George had a wicked temper, one he tried extremely hard to control.

"I hope you don't mind me saying, son, but that man has a right stick up his arse," said Luke.

George grinned, and his team mirrored that grin. "That's your boss you're talking about, DS Mason," he said with a wink. "I better not hear you speak that way about him again, even if you are only stating the truth."

"Fair enough, sir," Luke said in jest.

"Right, does everybody know what they're doing?" George asked just as Yolanda re-entered the Incident Room.

"Sir," she said, "I know who the victim is." She headed for the Big Board and tacked on an image of a beautiful, porcelain-skinned woman with long, dark hair and intense brown eyes. "This is Penny Haigh, an only child aged twenty-three who lived with her parents at Hillidge Square in Hunslet."

George's clenched fists spasmed with emotion, but he managed to take a calming breath. Jay winced. The DI wondered whether the young DC was thinking about the two parents who no longer had a daughter.

"Great work, Yolanda," George said. "I want you to start a background search. Look at her friends, family, work, social media, and finances. The usual, OK?"

"OK, sir."

"Also, Yolanda, find out if our victim has been reported as missing and let me know ASAP. It could mean the killer kept her prisoner somewhere if she's been gone a few days."

"Yes, sir," she said.

"I'll inform the family now." George turned to Yolanda. "So make sure you look and see if she's been reported missing because I don't want to look like an idiot."

"No problem, sir."

"Right, Jay, you're with me," George said with a sombre tone. The muscles in his face were tight as if anticipating the awful news they were about to deliver.

Chapter Four

Jay pulled the squad car up outside the house on Hillidge Square in Hunslet, taking a vacant parking space. The house was an end terrace with a neat and tidy garden. The burgundy-coloured door looked recently painted.

Jay rang the bell. George's head was hurting. He felt tense. He never really enjoyed this part of the job and remembered the last time he was in this area. It had been during the Bone Saw Ripper case, and he'd had to be prescribed medication because of his struggles.

An older woman with a tense face appeared at the door, her eyes narrowed. "Yes?"

"Mrs Haigh?" Jay asked.

"Yes," she repeated, though this time, not a question and looking puzzled.

"I'm Detective Constable Scott, and this is Detective Inspector Beaumont." The pair held out their warrant cards. "We'd like to come in and have a chat if that's OK?"

"Is it about the neighbours and the noise complaint I put in?" she asked. "I really didn't expect someone to come around straight away and certainly didn't expect detectives. It's them on the corner, they're always having—"

"No, it's not about a noise complaint," George interrupted.

"Is your husband here?"

"Yes. He's in front of the TV, where he always is." She blew away a single strand of greying hair that fell in front of her eyes. "Is everything OK?" She bit down on her bottom lip.

"We would like to speak to both of you together," George said gently. "Is it OK that we both come in?"

Jay was making mental notes, impressed by his boss' skill in handling such difficult circumstances. Whilst George was a tough man, it appeared he never faulted in his compassion, despite having had to take on the terrible task of delivering devastating news to fragile families.

"Sure, OK. I'll fetch us some drinks if you want to make yourselves comfy in the living room." She ushered them into the house and opened the door to a substantial living room with a huge television in the window. "Tea? Coffee? Water? Anything?"

"White tea with two sugars," replied Jay. "Thanks." The young DC took in the décor. The walls were painted terracotta, and the carpet was brown. The grey sofas that flanked the armchair Mr Haigh was sitting in looked comfy, so Jay sat down. It was all very tidy in keeping with the exterior of the house.

George followed his DC after advising Mrs Haigh he'd have the same as Jay but stopped when he saw a photo of the victim in her graduation gown on the fireplace. In the picture, her parents flanked her with huge smiles. The fireplace was littered with photos, but as expected, they all contained just the three of them. The news he was going to provide was going to destroy them.

The DI took a deep, calming breath, trying to relax the muscles in his body as his physio had instructed, but he struggled with the breathing technique. He wanted a coffee, knowing that it would calm him, but the caffeine wouldn't do his headache any good.

After a few minutes of waiting in silence, Mrs Haigh appeared with a tray of drinks. Mr Haigh had switched off the TV when the detectives had entered, a tall, slim man with a shock of white hair and pale, blue eyes. He, too, looked to be in his early seventies. Mr Haigh had eyed the detectives but said nothing until his wife had appeared. "What's all this about then?" he asked, looking at each detective in turn. He raised his brows and said, "Well?" when neither detective said anything.

"We've here to speak to you about your daughter, Penny," George said.

Mr Haigh narrowed his brows. "Is everything OK?"

"Has there been an accident?" Mrs Haigh added.

George took a deep breath. "A body was found this morning in the woods in Stourton, and we believe, from the identification she carried, that it's Penny." He paused. "We are very sorry for your loss."

Mrs Haigh let out a whimper, but Mr Haigh remained frozen, staring at them as if he hadn't understood what had been said.

The detectives remained silent, allowing the news to sink in. They hadn't reported Penny missing, and George needed to find out why.

"What happened?" Mrs Haigh eventually asked.

"We can't share much this early on in the investigation, but we're treating her death as suspicious. We're waiting to hear back from the pathologist for confirmation about what took place," George said.

"Are you sure it's Penny?" Mrs Haigh asked. "She hasn't

gone anywhere near the woods since she was a child. Surely, it's got to be a mistake."

"We're sure it's Penny, I'm afraid." George paused for a few seconds. "Do you feel up to answering some questions?"

Mrs Haigh looked up at her husband, who was blinking away tears. "Yes," she eventually said, nodding.

"What were Penny's living arrangements?" George asked.

"She recently moved back here after splitting up with her boyfriend," said Mrs Haigh.

George nodded, wondering whether they had an aggrieved ex-boyfriend on their hands.

"Do you have his name and his address? We want to speak with him," George said.

"Caden Clark," said Mr Haigh. "As his name suggests, he's a bit of a prick." The poor man was still blinking away the tears.

"He still lives in Morley, where he lived with Penny," Mrs Haigh eventually explained after struggling through sobs and moans.

George nodded. He'd get the address before they left, but he wanted to press on with the questioning. After Mrs Haigh had calmed down a little, George asked, "When was the last time you saw Penny?"

"Last night when she got in from work," Mr Haigh explained, sniffing.

"What did she do for work?" asked George.

"She was a waitress," Mrs Haigh said. "She worked at an Italian restaurant on Pontefract Road. Because of her studies, she only worked from noon until five." Mrs Haigh began to cry harder. "She was always trying to get us down for dinner because they always had an offer on during her shifts."

"How did she seem last night when she got home from

work?" Jay asked.

"Happy," said Mrs Haigh. "It's Halloween next week, her favourite time of year."

Mr Haigh made a huffing noise as if he didn't quite agree with something. George turned to him. "Is everything OK?"

"Penny was a pagan," Mr Haigh explained. "That's what my wife meant, but for some reason, she has to sugar-coat everything."

"A pagan?" asked Jay. He turned to George, who narrowed his brows.

"Wait a minute, she was found in Stourton, you say?" asked Mr Haigh, and George nodded. "That's where that stone circle is she visits. It sounds silly, but our Pen believes in magick. With a C and a K. It's something to do with rituals and spiritualisation rather than the magic with a C on the end like witchcraft and stage shows, or that's what Pen said."

"And was she part of a group?" asked George.

"Oh, yes. Pen was always on that bloody Facebook group, chatting away." Mr Haigh frowned. "It's why Caden split with her. He didn't respect it or something. Or that's what she said."

"What's the Facebook group called?" Jay asked.

With a shrug, Mr Haigh said, "I'm not sure." He scratched his chin. "Leodis Pagan something, I think."

George nodded. The Facebook page would be on her phone if what Mr Haigh said was true. It could be a coincidence that the stone circle was where she was left, but George didn't believe in coincidences. Plus, all the talk of magick and rituals made him feel uneasy. "Did Penny attend events at the Stourton Stone Circle?" asked George.

"We're not sure," Mr Haigh said, cutting off his wife, who

was just about to talk. "She intended on going, I'm sure, but I don't know whether she ever attended any."

George turned to Mrs Haigh. "You said she was happy last night when she returned from work. Other than it being Halloween next week, could there be any other reason?"

Mrs Haigh looked at her husband, who narrowed his eyes. It was clear to George that she knew something. "Anything you say may help us find your daughter's killer, Mrs Haigh." He then turned to Mr Haigh. "Anything at all, sir. Let us be the judge of what's important or not."

"All we ask for is honesty," added Jay with a bright smile on his face.

Mr Haigh nodded at his wife, who said, "We think she was seeing somebody new. Somebody from that Facebook group."

Bingo. He'd get Yolanda on that ASAP, as no doubt they would have been in contact. "And she met with this person last night?" George asked.

Mrs Haigh shrugged and shook her head. "We don't know."

Mr Haigh said, "I think she did go out with him. Peter, something." He strained his brain to think. "Sorry, Peter, something. Check that Facebook page. He's part of her group."

"Did you ask her where she was going?" asked George.

"And when she didn't come home, didn't you worry?" added Jay.

"Penny's twenty-three and had a new boyfriend." Mr Haigh shrugged. "I just assumed she'd stayed at his and went to work this morning."

"Do you think—do you think this Peter killed—killed our daughter?" said Mrs Haigh.

"We are following certain lines of enquiry, which leads me to this question. What were you two doing between eight last night and six this morning?"

"You don't think we had anything to do with it, do you?" asked Mr Haigh.

The DI said, "I'm sorry, but it's a routine question, I'm sure you understand."

Mr Haigh nodded his understanding. We were here all night. Susan cooked curry for us, which we ate at eight. We watched TV until midnight like we always do. We went to bed together. I fell asleep because of my pills, but I think Susan was reading." He turned to his wife.

Susan Haigh nodded. "Roger's right. I cooked curry, which we ate in front of the TV. We watched some shows we'd recorded and then went to bed at midnight. I was reading my new crime novel on my Kindle, and like Roger said, he fell asleep."

With his pen poised, Jay asked, "What time did you fall asleep?"

Tears began streaming down her face. "I don't—I don't remember. Between one and two."

After giving her alibi, she'd broken down fully now, and Mr Haigh held up his hand. "I think we should stop this for now."

"Understood," said George, standing up. "We'd like to take a look at Penny's room if that's OK with you?" Mr Haigh nodded. "And when you feel up to it, we'll need someone to formally identify Penny for us."

"Yes," Mr Haigh said. "When do you need me to go?"

"Today or tomorrow would be fine, Mr Haigh," said George. He got up and ambled towards the senior man. "Here's my card. Give me a ring when you're ready, and I'll arrange for someone to collect you."

"I want to come too," Mrs Haigh said. The tears had abated,

revealing red, puffy skin under her eyes.

Shaking his head, her husband said, "I don't think that's a good idea."

Mrs Haigh got up and grasped her husband's hands with her. "I need to see my little girl one last time."

George nodded. "As soon as the pathologist has more for us, we'll let you know. In the meantime, we will provide you with a Family Liaison Officer. We're very sorry for your loss."

"We don't need one," said Roger.

"I appreciate that, Mr Haigh, but we've already allocated Thomas Forde. Tom. It's standard procedure in cases like this. FLOs are trained to provide support and information to you during this difficult and emotional time."

Tom Forde was a jolly man who was as wide as he was tall. George couldn't understand how Tom could be jovial all the time, assuming his personality might be an attempt to create a more approachable and comforting presence during a challenging time.

Having strong interpersonal skills to help families navigate the complexities of a murder investigation and the following legal processes was part of an FLO's skill-set. Tom certainly was strong in that area.

They left the house, having found nothing of worth in Penny's bedroom, and walked down the path to where their cars were parked. "I hate this part of the job," George said.

"I know what you mean, boss; it's like we've now completely wrecked those lovely people's lives."

George stopped. "We didn't ruin their lives; the killer did, Jay." He ground his teeth. "That's why we need to find him, and fast!"

"It still doesn't stop me from feeling like shit, boss," Jay said.

"And it never will, Jay," the DI explained. "All you can do is understand that you delivered such sensitive news in the most sensitive of ways." He continued walking towards the car. "And then you find the fucking bastard that did it!"

Chapter Five

When George arrived back at Elland Road, the shared office was bustling. He called his team into their Incident Room for a quick briefing and said, "Jay and I have just come from the parents of our victim, Penny Haigh," he said. "We learnt that Penny was a pagan who was part of a pagan group on Facebook." He turned to Yolanda. "DS Williams, I need you to look into it as a matter of urgency."

"On it, sir," she said. "I'm guessing that's why she was left at the stone circle."

George nodded. "That's certainly an obvious link. That, and her parents think she was seeing somebody from the pagan group, so find out who that was, OK?"

Jay wrote 'Caden Clark' on the Big Board and 'wrote ex-boyfriend' next to it. The Haighs had provided Clark's address in Morley, which Jay wrote underneath. The young DC then wrote 'Peter' and 'new boyfriend?' on the board.

"As you can see, we have both a current and an ex-boyfriend we need to speak with," George explained. "They split because Penny became a pagan. He stayed in Morley, and she moved in with her parents. I'm heading out soon to interview him. As for Peter, we know nothing about him, so that's down to Yolanda to figure out more." The DI turned to Luke as Yolanda

CHAPTER FIVE

stood up and left the Incident Room, no doubt heading to see DS Joshua Fry on the IT floor.

"Anything in the bins?" George asked the team.

"SOCO found nothing," Tashan explained, and George nodded.

The DI asked, "Have you found anything on the CCTV footage around the woods?"

"Not yet. It's hard because of the lack of cameras around there."

George frowned. "Lack of cameras?"

"Leeds City Council couldn't afford to put cameras up by the river, and the local businesses all use dummy cameras," Luke explained. "They have signs up, but they're warnings, rather than real. We're still looking though, and PS Greenwood is still out with his uniforms, but I'm not hopeful."

"Shit." George sighed. "Keep checking. It's probably someone who knows the area well. But they'll make a mistake; killers always do." He turned and looked at the Big Board. "Forensics and pathology get in touch yet?"

He was greeted by shaking heads when he turned back around. "Shit." He sighed again. "Right, Tashan, you speak with Lindsey Yardley. I'll go to the morgue and see Dr Ross. DS Mason, please do a background check on Caden Clark and find out everything. I will see Dr Ross first, and then I'll visit Clark."

"I think you might want to go and brief DCI Atkinson first, though, sir," Tashan chimed in.

"Why's that, Detective Constable?"

"He keeps going on and on about the press conference." DC Blackburn shrugged. "He's been in about five times asking for you. He seems really stressed."

"Right, OK, I'll go and see him now. Jay, please do your research on rituals while I'm up there. You're with me once I'm back, OK?"

"Aye, boss, no bother."

The DI went upstairs to DCI Atkinson's office and knocked on the door. He called out for him to come in.

"You wanted me, sir?"

"Not you, just an update, Beaumont."

George explained what information he'd gleaned from the Haighs and his plans for the rest of the day.

"We're not sure of the cause of death until we hear from the pathologist, and I have DC Blackburn getting onto forensics."

"So you have fuck all then?"

"No, sir, not fuck all." George frowned. "We have three leads now."

Alistair matched George's frown. "The ex-boyfriend, the new boyfriend, and the pagan group?"

"Correct."

"And what about the jogger, Beaumont? And her parents."

"The jogger will be in to give a statement later. If you want, take the statement and grill him for all I care." George winced at his words. He hadn't meant for them to sound so harsh. "Her parents are innocent. I'm sure of it."

"They alibied each other?"

George nodded.

"And you found nothing in her room?"

"Correct," George said.

Atkinson shook his head but said nothing.

Silence hung heavy in the air, so George broke it. Shattered it, even.

"Are you OK, sir? You seem stressed.

CHAPTER FIVE

"I'm fine, Beaumont, I just wish you had a fucking lead."

"I heard you on the phone earlier. Ball pein hammer and a Phillips-head screwdriver. Bingley. Ring a bell, sir?"

"What's your point, Beaumont?"

"Has a new Ripper victim come forward or something?"

Atkinson hesitated, and George saw it. The DCI sipped his tea, most likely pondering how much he could share. "This needs to stay between you and me for now, Beaumont. Are we clear?"

George had never been invited into the DCI's confidence before. "Of course, sir."

"We have a copycat on the loose in Bradford."

When George heard the news, his heart started to race, and a lump appeared in his throat. A copycat Ripper in Bradford? It sent shivers down his spine, and he couldn't help but think about the dark days of the past when the original Yorkshire Ripper had terrorised the region.

DCI Atkinson continued, his voice low and grave. "This isn't something we're taking lightly, Beaumont. The details are chillingly similar to the original Ripper killings, and we need to catch this imitator before they strike again."

George nodded, his mind racing with thoughts of the gruesome crimes that had plagued Yorkshire in the 1970s. He had studied those cases during his training, but nothing could prepare him for the shock of facing a new wave of violence echoing that dark history.

"What can I do to help, sir?" George asked, his determination overriding his initial shock.

Atkinson leaned in, his gaze unwavering. "Just keep quiet whilst I dig deep into the original Ripper case files."

George knew now why the DCI was so stressed. A task

like that would be daunting, but George also understood its importance. "I'll not tell a soul, sir—"

"Not even Isabella, please, Beaumont."

George nodded. "Are you sure I can't help?"

"No," Atkinson replied. "We're working with your mate, Mark Finch. We also have officers and detectives who were around in the seventies." He paused. "If you can think of anybody else with knowledge of the original case, then let me know, as it would be invaluable."

As George left Atkinson's office, he felt a mix of emotions—fear, curiosity, and a burning desire to bring this copycat to justice. He knew that the West Yorkshire Police were once again stepping into a dark and treacherous path that would test their investigative skills and their courage. The shadow of the Ripper had returned, and whilst George wanted to help, he knew he had to capture the shadow that was haunting Leeds.

Heading back to the Incident Room, his phone rang. He looked down to see Dr Ross' name. "DI Beaumont."

"When are you coming over, my boy? I've some preliminary findings for you," Christian said.

"Now, actually, Dr Ross," he said.

After ending the call, George called Jay and asked the DC to give him five minutes and meet him in the car park. He headed downstairs, then, to collect his jacket, which had his car keys in it.

* * *

By the time George reached the car park, Jay was standing by the Merc, waiting for him. They got in, and the DI sped off towards the morgue at St James' Hospital.

"How's Isabella and Olivia?"

"They're doing very well, Jay; thanks for asking."

"Bet you're knackered, aren't you?"

George grinned. "You know how good Isabella is at everything, don't you?" he asked, and Jay nodded. "Well, she's an even better mother."

Jay grinned but said nothing more, the silence deafening. "How's the research going, Jay?"

"Not great, boss," he said. "Vampires keep coming up, and witches. A couple of serial killers from America and Germany." He shrugged. "I still think it's ritualistic, especially now we know she was a pagan."

"Did you happen to find an expert?"

"Aye, there's one at the University of Leeds. He hasn't taken any of my calls, but I've emailed him."

"It might be that we have to show up unannounced," the DI said as he pulled into the hospital.

Once inside, they walked down the corridor and towards the morgue. Naturally, they expected George, so Dr Ross' assistant walked them through after providing protective clothing.

"What's wrong?" George asked Jay.

"I hate this place," Jay said.

"I don't think anybody in their right mind enjoys the place, Jay," George said with a grin.

"It's the smell, I think."

George clapped him on the shoulder. "I'd like to say it gets better, but it doesn't."

Just then, they entered the lab. "Oh, the smell does become bearable, I promise you," Dr Ross said with a chuckle.

"Good afternoon, Dr Ross," Jay said.

"Good afternoon, son." He frowned. "Sons?" He shrugged.

"Follow me; I've laid her on the slab for you."

Dr Ross pointed at the wound on Penny Haigh's neck. "That's not the cause of death; the strangulation is."

George looked at Jay and nodded. Despite the circumstances, the young lad had a grin on his face.

"The entry wound is smooth and measures thirteen millimetres across and sixty-three millimetres deep. The murder weapon had a sharp tip and was non-serrated."

He thought about the size of the wound and the fact it lacked serration and was caused by a sharp tip. "What are we thinking? A long, thin knife?" George asked.

Dr Ross frowned. "I'm unsure, actually, because of the profile." George matched his frown. "I'm going to send the images to a blade expert to see if they can help."

"OK, thanks, Dr Ross. Anything else?"

"She was raped atop the altar whilst being strangled to death," Dr Ross explained. "Then she was unbound and stabbed, and it appears from my conversations with young Lindsey the blood was collected."

"Jesus Christ, I was right," said Jay.

"What did you say, son?" asked Christian.

"Jay had a theory that the wound was caused post-mortem with the intention to collect the blood," said George. "It appears he was right."

Christian said, "I suppose all you need now is to know why?"

"Any ideas?"

The pathologist shook his head.

Jay asked, "Did he leave anything behind?"

"No trace of semen, but that's to be expected as he wore a condom," Dr Ross explained. "I've found lubricant from a popular brand condom. There was nothing under her nails, but that's to be expected, considering her hands were tied to the altar. Oh, and her ankles, too."

George thought back to that morning. She was displayed like a cross with her arms outstretched. Her pale skin had been purple and black around her wrists and ankles. Why hadn't he realised before she'd been bound?

The more he thought about it, the more he was convinced she wasn't displayed like a cross. Her legs had been spread-eagled, which George had assumed was to remove her dignity. Perhaps that's why he'd missed the bruising on her wrists and ankles because he'd averted his eyes.

Idiot, he thought. He couldn't keep missing vital clues like these.

"He put her through hell before killing her as per the bruising to her arms and shoulders," Dr Ross said, returning George from his thoughts. "As I said before, the cause of death was asphyxiation. Strangled because of the bruising to the neck and windpipe." He paused. "What else..."

"Do you know what was used to restrain her?" George asked.

"Nylon rope," he said, confident.

"Why so confident?"

"Her right wrist still has a few fibres embedded into the skin. He'd bound her extremely tightly."

"Were there any signs of a struggle?" George asked.

Dr Ross nodded. "The marks on her wrists and ankles aren't uniform, indicating she struggled a lot. I've sent off samples to toxicology to see if she was drugged because it doesn't appear she was forcefully knocked out."

"Any idea when the restraining marks were made?"

"I do have an idea, son," Christian explained. "It means I can give you an idea of how long it was between her death and the time she was restrained."

"Excellent. Anything else?"

"Just that he used bleach to clean up her skin," said Christian. "Lab's looking into a brand, but it'll no doubt be one of the popular ones." He paused. "Once I have more, I'll send you the report."

"Thanks, Dr Ross," said George, turning to leave, but Jay stood still.

"What kind of monster does this to someone?" Jay asked.

"A monster that you and I are going to find, Jay," said George. "Come on, DC Scott. Let's go find this bastard!"

Chapter Six

Detective Inspector George Beaumont and Detective Constable Jay Scott pulled up to the Topcliffe Mead in Morley, the sun sinking below the horizon and casting long shadows across the tranquil landscape. The area surrounding the east of Morley, not far from the White Rose Centre, was surrounded by farmland.

George's unmarked Merc halted, gravel crunching beneath the tires as they surveyed the scene. The house they were looking for soon appeared: a semi-detached property with solar panels on the roof.

The pair got out, and once they got through the gate and up the steps, they found themselves staring at a tall, gaunt man in his late twenties with dishevelled brown hair and a haunted look in his eyes.

Was Caden Clark a man burdened by guilt, or had he heard about Penny and had been mourning? That was why they were there.

"Mr Clark, I'm Detective Inspector Beaumont, and this is Detective Constable Scott," George said and both detectives flashed their warrant cards. "We'd like to come in and ask you a few questions about Penny Haigh."

At the mention of Penny's name, Caden's eyes darted nervously. "I'm fucking devastated, me," he said, stepping aside to let them in.

"You've heard about Penny's death, then?" George asked as he entered. The house was dimly lit, with walls still adorned with photographs of happier times when he and Penny were still together. The house smelled strongly of sweat and held a heavy silence, only broken by the occasional rustle of the trees outside.

The detectives took seats on the sofa, leaving Caden to the chair, and then George began the questioning. They intended to extract essential details about Caden's relationship with the victim, his activities on the night of the murder, and any potential leads or information that could assist the detectives in solving the case.

"We understand you were in a relationship with Penny Haigh, Mr Clark," he began gently, his tone a mix of empathy and authority. "Can you tell us about your relationship with Penny? When did you two start seeing each other, and when did you break up?"

Caden nodded, his eyes glistening with unshed tears. "Erm, we started seeing each other about three or four years ago after I split with my son's mother. But we broke up a while ago. It was quite messy and pretty unexpected."

"We're sorry to hear that," Detective Scott added, trying to establish rapport. "Can you tell us about the last time you saw or spoke with Penny?"

Caden sighed, running a hand through his unkempt hair. "It was about three weeks ago. We met for coffee to catch up. Things didn't end well between us, but I never wanted it to end. And, of course, I never wanted any harm to come to her. We argued, but I swear, I didn't do anything to hurt her."

Jay scribbled notes as Caden spoke. "Where did you meet for coffee? What did you argue about?"

"At the White Rose Centre," Caden explained. "We had a coffee. I told her I wanted her back and didn't care about her stupid pagan obsession." Caden winced. "The fact I called it stupid is why we argued. She said I'd never understand and not to get my hopes up about us getting back together."

"What was the reason for the messy breakup?" Jay pressed.

"Because of all that pagan bullshit," Caden said. "We were talking about kids, but she kept banging on about naming ceremonies and stuff." He twisted a lock of hair between his fingers. "I said I didn't want a child with her if she was going to bring it up as a pagan, and so she told me to go fuck myself and left."

"Did Penny have any enemies or people who might have wanted to harm her?" George asked. "Were there any recent disputes or conflicts you know of in her life? Is there anyone who might have had a motive to harm Penny?"

"No, Penny was pretty much loved by everyone," Caden explained. "She had a good family, good friends, and a pretty good life." He shrugged. "I guess she was thriving without me." He held his face in his hands. "I'm such a fucking dick!"

George asked, "Where were you between eight o'clock last night and six o'clock this morning?"

Caden hesitated for a moment before responding. "I was at my mum's house last night. We had a family dinner. My young son can vouch for me; he stayed over last night. I didn't even know Penny was gone... not until Roger and Susan called me earlier."

George frowned. He really wished the Haighs hadn't contacted Caden. "So you didn't have any contact with Penny on the day or night of her murder?"

"No."

George gave Caden a stern look. "We'll find out if you're lying to us, Caden," he explained. "If we find messages on her phone, you'll be in trouble."

"I'm not lying to you, I swear."

Finally, George asked, "Is there anything else you can recall about your relationship with Penny or any information that might be relevant to the investigation?"

"I'm sorry, but no. Nothing."

"What about anyone from her course?"

Caden shook his head. "I'm sorry."

Before leaving, Detective Inspector Beaumont handed Caden a business card. "If you remember anything else or have any information that might help our investigation, please don't hesitate to call." He went to leave, then turned on his heel. "Oh, and don't go anywhere because no doubt we'll need to come and visit you again."

As they drove away from the house, the detectives were left with more questions than answers. It appeared Caden had his secrets, and Penny Haigh's murder was far from solved. But they knew they had to keep digging, searching for the truth before the killer killed again.

* * *

Back at the station, George pulled the team together in their Incident Room. "Caden Clark is a dead-end," he explained. "He was home with his son all night, so couldn't have been involved in Penny's murder."

"There's nothing on Penny's phone to indicate they were

in contact, either," Luke said, "though that doesn't mean he didn't get somebody to murder her."

"True, but I don't think he has a motive," George said. "We'll keep an eye on him, but I'm not convinced he's involved."

"You're the boss," said Luke with a grin.

"I hear you've found CCTV footage, though?" George asked.

Luke nodded. "PS Greenwood and his uniforms came through for us," he explained. "Yolanda's in Incident Room Five, going through it."

"What have we got footage-wise?" George asked.

"We have footage of Penny getting off the bus and turning around before turning right onto Thwaite Lane. Then we see her again, though only partially when she passes the City of Leeds Sea Cadets."

"Is that it?"

"Let an old man get there, son," Luke said, and George grinned. "We see her passing over the bridge, due to the change in height, and then again in the car park. But yeah, that's it."

"Got any footage from the bus?"

"Working on it, son."

"Thanks, Luke." George then looked at Tashan. "I want you to help Yolanda look at previous days, weeks, and even months for Penny Haigh."

Luke tacked a map of Penny's route on the Big Board. "Thanks, Luke." George then addressed the room. "That's Penny's route. Take copies of it. I desperately want to know if anyone was following her." The DI had secured convictions based solely on video evidence in many cases he worked on, yet George knew that studying CCTV footage was a very tedious job. Despite it being arguably one of the most critical tasks, nobody liked it, as they'd invariably be shut away in a darkened Incident Room for hours on end, surveying footage from different cameras. "Thank you." He looked between Tashan and Yolanda. "Both of you."

* * *

"Sir," Yolanda exclaimed, her voice laced with excitement. She was a seasoned female police officer George trusted to review CCTV footage, and her expertise proved invaluable in cases like this, where there were no witnesses. George had collaborated with her in the past and appreciated her eccentricity.

George casually tossed his jacket onto his chair and followed Yolanda out of his office, entering Incident Room Five, where two large monitors displayed paused CCTV footage side by side.

"What's caught your eye, Yolanda?" George inquired.

She gestured towards the setup. "This is a map of Stourton. I've marked cameras one in blue, two in red, and three in green. Camera two captured this image." She pointed to the right monitor, displaying a blurry figure standing in the background beside a car, dressed entirely in black. "They chose a poorly lit spot, but that's definitely someone observing Penny."

George's heart quickened. The surge of adrenaline was always inevitable. "Is that a Renault?"

Yolanda nodded. "I've spoken to Josh to see if he can enhance the image so we can get a reg."

"Good work." He paused. "Anything else?"

Yolanda said, "Watch this."

George and Yolanda watched Penny Haigh cross the bridge

in grainy black and white. "It's in black and white, sir, but the image quality and angle are superior."

"Is that all we got?" George asked.

"Keep watching."

George did, and a moment later, the pair watched as a dark-cladded figure followed Penny across the bridge.

"I also have this," Yolanda explained.

She pulled up another file and pressed play. It was a blink-and-you'd-miss-it moment, a blurry shadow sprinting across the scene. She paused it, then rewound it until she captured the blur.

"It's impossible to make anything out, sir. The person is just a silhouette dressed entirely in black. They clearly knew what they were doing. That's assuming this person is the culprit."

George nodded.

"I'll keep examining the footage. Maybe I can capture a clearer image of this person."

"You've been incredibly helpful, Yolanda. Keep searching, and let me know if you find anything else."

Yolanda settled back into her seat, donned her headset, and began typing away. "You can count on me, sir."

Chapter Seven

George was a few minutes late when he hurried upstairs to meet DCI Atkinson to prepare for the press conference. As usual, he was on the phone, his voice booming through the door as the DI reached his office. From experience, George knew it would be better to wait until the DCI had finished before knocking on the door and walking in.

"You're late, Beaumont," he said, glancing at his watch. "Hurry and fill me in on what we've got so far."

"The victim is twenty-three-year-old Penny Haigh, who lived with her parents at Hillidge Square in Hunslet. According to her phone, she was seeing a new man named Peter Chase Haarmann, who, according to her parents, she met on Facebook via a pagan group. She went out last night, but they didn't ask where."

"And when she didn't return, did they not question where she was?"

"They explained that Penny was twenty-three and had a new boyfriend." George shrugged. "Roger, Penny's father, assumed she'd stayed at his and went to work this morning."

"Have you interviewed Peter Haarmann? The most likely offender in these cases is someone close to the victim."

George desperately tried not to roll his eyes. Haarmann was

high on their list, but they couldn't find him. According to every power they had at their disposal, Peter Chase Haarmann didn't exist, so it was clear to George that he was using a fake name. He told the DCI as much.

"Well, what about the ex-boyfriend?" Alistair asked.

"We have interviewed him, and he was at his mother's having a family dinner. His mother and father gave a statement confirming when he arrived and left. And then he was home all night with his young son."

Alistair clenched his jaw. "Is there anyone who can verify that?"

"Only his son, but with him only being four, he isn't the most reliable witness. Obviously, we're still going to keep an eye on him."

"OK," the DCI said. "Have you been to the victim's workplace?"

"No, not yet. The plan is to go after the press conference. Penny worked at an Italian restaurant on Pontefract Road."

DCI Atkinson cocked a brow. "Shouldn't you have been there already?"

George drew in a deep breath. "With respect, sir, you wanted to have the press conference this afternoon; otherwise, I would have been there right now. Once we've finished, I'll speak with her boss. I should be there now, really, because this is the time she usually finishes her shift, and one of their regulars might be able to help." He paused. "Having the conference now is impacting my investigation."

DCI Atkinson held up a hand. "OK, fair enough."

George said. "Thank you, sir."

"What are we going to tell the press?" he asked.

"In my opinion, as little as possible." George bit his lip.

"We need the public to be vigilant, but we don't want to scare them."

"What has Dr Ross told you?"

"So it appears DC Scott's theory that you branded 'a load of tosh' was actually highly relevant," George explained. The DCI narrowed his eyes, but George continued. "Cause of death was asphyxiation. She was strangled. Dr Ross found bruising to the neck and windpipe." He paused. "He put her through hell before killing her as per the bruising to her arms and shoulders we saw at the scene." He paused again. He didn't want to explain what the killer did to Penny before killing her, but the DCI needed to know. "She was raped atop the altar whilst being strangled to death. Unfortunately, there was no trace of semen, but that's to be expected as he wore a condom."

"Anything else?"

"She was bound to the altar before being raped and killed," George explained. "And after death, the culprit removed the bindings and put her into a very specific position. Then he stabbed her in the neck with something thin and long that had a sharp tip and was non-serrated. Any ideas what it could be?"

"Dimensions?" asked Alistair.

George looked down at the notes DC Scott had made. "The entry wound was smooth and measured thirteen millimetres across and sixty-three millimetres deep."

The DCI shrugged. "Boning knife?"

"Maybe. Dr Ross is consulting with a specialist. Anyway, I suggest we keep everything quiet apart from the fact that a young woman was killed."

"I do know what should be kept quiet and what should be shared," the DCI said abruptly.

George frowned. Why was George in charge of the investigation if the DCI wanted to micromanage everything? It made no sense.

The DCI checked his watch. "OK, we've got to go." He stood up, put on his jacket and did up the buttons. Then, they left his office and walked silently to the conference room. Juliette Thompson, their PR officer, was waiting, and she opened the door for them to walk in. It was packed.

George took a deep breath as the trio seated themselves behind the long table at the front of the room, facing the cameras at the back and the reporters in the front.

"Good evening," Juliette said, "and thank you all for coming. I will pass you to Detective Chief Inspector Atkinson for the briefing."

Atkinson leaned over and said into his mic, "Thank you, Juliette." He nodded in her direction, then closed his eyes and contorted his face into something resembling an Easter Island statue. "Unfortunately, a young woman's body was found in Stourton in the early hours of the morning, and we are treating it as a suspicious death. Please get in touch with us if you noticed anything unusual in that area last night from around ten." He paused. "Thank you."

"What's the name and age of the victim?" a reporter called out.

"Out of respect for the family, we're not releasing her identity at present. Next question."

"How did the victim die?" another reporter called out.

George glanced at Atkinson. What was he going to say? Would Alistair stick to what he'd asked?

"I'll pass you over to Detective Inspector Beaumont. He is SIO and will answer any further questions." He nodded at George.

"We are awaiting information from the pathologist," George lied. "Next question."

"Do you have any leads?" a female journalist in the front row asked. She had red hair and wore massive, hooped earrings.

"I'm not going to jeopardise the investigation by sharing details with you, but we're following several lines of enquiry." He paused. "Anyone with information is asked to contact me, or DS Mason, at the Leeds District Homicide and Major Enquiry Team quoting reference 16354910377 or online via live chat. All contact will be treated confidentially. That's it for now. Thank you."

"Do we have another serial killer on our hands, George?" the female journalist asked.

George frowned. "What makes you think that?"

"You seem to attract them," she explained.

"We are not," he said firmly. "Thank you all for coming. We'll keep you updated with the investigation as it progresses."

George was about to stand up when another journalist, who was balding, tall and thin with a dark moustache, said, "I have a question for Detective Chief Inspector Atkinson."

"OK," said George, frowning.

"Why are you trusting such an important investigation to a man who is quite clearly not fit for the job?" the journalist said.

"Excuse me?" asked Atkinson.

"Detective Inspector George Beaumont cracks under pressure," the journalist explained. "Two murder suspects have died under his watch, and then there was the accident he was in earlier this year." He looked down at his notes. "I've seen a copy of his medical file, and I wouldn't trust him as far as I could throw him." He pointed at George. "Look at the man; he's clearly not fit enough. And as for his reputation, I—"

"That's enough!" shouted Atkinson, standing up. "Detective Inspector Beaumont's reputation is impeccable, and anybody questioning him can also question me and my boss, Detective Superintendent Smith." Alistair turned to George. "DI Beaumont has our full support. Next question."

"But clearly sleeping with his colleague, his deputy—"

"Enough!" interrupted Atkinson. "He nodded at the uniforms flanking the room. Get him out of here!"

The trio left the room together, with Juliette leaving the two men to chat.

"I'm sorry about that, Beaumont, but I meant what I said." He gripped George by the shoulder. "We all believe in you, OK?"

Alistair hadn't ever been that nice, and George had to fight a frown. He said, "Thank you, sir."

"Don't let pricks like that get you down, OK? Get this case solved ASAP so you can fucking shut him up, yeah?"

"Yeah, thank you, sir."

"About that serial killer bullshit, what do you think?" the DCI asked.

George pondered for a moment. "I think what I said, sir. I'm not expecting a serial killer." But deep down, he'd only said that to reassure his boss. As far as he was concerned, the nature of the murder didn't strike him as a crime of passion or a one-off. The fact the murderer had displayed his victim on an altar in the centre of a pagan stone circle meant the possibility was high that there was more to come.

All George could hope was to stop the bastard then.

Chapter Eight

The detectives arrived at Capri, the Italian restaurant where Penny Haigh had worked as a waitress. The sun had long since set, glowing warmly on the cosy eatery's exterior. Inside, the aroma of garlic and tomato sauce filled the air, mingling with the soft hum of diners enjoying their meals.

The detectives approached the hostess stand, where a young woman with a friendly smile greeted them. Her complexion was fair, and she had a natural, fresh-faced beauty that needed minimal makeup to enhance.

George felt eyes upon him as the young woman asked, "Good evening, how can I help you?"

At the bar stood an athletically built man in his early thirties. He had neatly groomed dark hair and a well-trimmed beard accentuating his chiselled jawline. He was staring at them. Or the young hostess. George couldn't decide.

Ignoring the barman, the detectives flashed their warrant cards, and George introduced them. "I'm Detective Inspector Beaumont, and this is Detective Constable Scott. We're here to speak with anyone who worked with Penny Haigh. Is there a manager or a colleague who could assist us?"

The hostess nodded and motioned for them to follow her. She led them into a back room where a middle-aged man dressed in a neatly pressed shirt and tie sat reviewing a stack of invoices. He looked up as they approached.

"Detectives, I'm Tony Ricci, the manager here at Capri. How can I assist you?" Tony inquired, his voice carrying the hint of an Italian accent.

Detective Scott spoke, "We're investigating the murder of Penny Haigh, one of your waitresses. We want to ask a few questions about her and her time here."

Tony's expression turned sombre, and he nodded. "Of course, Penny was a valued member of our team. Her parents called me earlier. Such a tragedy. Please, fire away."

Detective Beaumont started the conversation, "Can you tell us about Penny's employment here at Capri? How long had she been working here, and what was her role?"

Tony responded, "Penny had been with us for about two years. She was a dedicated waitress, always punctual and with a friendly demeanour. Our customers loved her."

Detective Scott said, "Did Penny have any issues or conflicts with co-workers or customers? Anything that might stand out?"

Tony hesitated momentarily, then replied, "Penny was a professional, and we never had any significant issues. Occasionally, minor disputes with difficult customers would occur, as is common in the restaurant industry, but nothing unusual."

Detective Beaumont asked, "Did Penny ever mention any personal problems or concerns to her colleagues or supervisors?"

Tony thought for a moment. "Not that I can recall. Penny kept her personal life private. We knew she had some ups and downs in her personal life, but she was always professional at work. Naturally, we know about her breakup with Caden."

Detective Constable Scott inquired, "Has anyone reported anything unusual on the day of Penny's murder or in the days leading up to it?"

Tony shook his head. "No, nothing out of the ordinary. It was business as usual. Penny worked her shift and left. We were all shocked when we heard about what happened to her."

The detectives thanked Tony for his cooperation and contact information in case they had more questions.

"May we have your office for an hour or so, Tony?" George asked. "I'd like to speak with some of your staff."

"Sure, no problem. I'll get Sofia first, another waitress, somebody who worked closely with Penny."

It turned out Sofia Fontana was a petite woman in her late twenties with a warm and friendly smile. She had long, chestnut-brown hair tied back in a neat ponytail, no doubt to keep it out of her way while working. Her hazel eyes sparkled with a mixture of kindness and enthusiasm when she spoke about Penny. "I worked with Penny for about a year," she explained.

George said, "Tell us about Penny."

"Penny was a hard-working and reliable colleague, always willing to help out during busy shifts. And she was a proper laugh, too."

"Can you recall any conflicts or unusual behaviour from Penny in the days leading up to her death?"

"Not really, only Caden, really," Sofia explained. "But I wouldn't say you need to be concerned. They broke up amicably, according to Penny."

Carlo Esposito, the head chef at Capri, had worked alongside Penny for the entirety of her employment, a man in his late forties with a sturdy build that reflected his years of experience in the culinary world. He had a shaved head, which emphasized his robust facial features, including a well-maintained salt-and-pepper beard. His dark eyes gleamed with an intensity that only DSU Smith could match.

When asked whether he knew of anybody who could have a problem with Penny, Carlo said, "No. Penny was a friendly waitress who often joked with the kitchen staff and, unlike some of the other waitresses, respected the work the kitchen had to put in."

Carlo confirmed that Penny had a few regular customers who adored her service. He didn't notice any unusual interactions or behaviours from her before her murder.

Elena Testa, the hostess who had greeted them, was next, a woman in her mid-twenties with a slender, petite frame that George had noticed the barman hadn't been able to keep his eyes off when she'd greeted them earlier. She had only recently started working at Capri and hadn't known Penny for long but described Penny as reserved but professional. "I'm sorry," she said, "but I haven't observed any conflicts or received any complaints about Penny's service."

And finally, the barman, Lorenzo Lombardi, entered the office. When asked how long he'd known Penny for, he explained, "I've known her for two years."

"And how would you describe your relationship?" asked George.

"A professional one." He shrugged, showing off pearly whites that met his friendly, brown eyes. The Italian appeared approachable but also charismatic. "She would sometimes confide in me about her challenging personal life, including her breakup with Caden." Lorenzo ran a manicured hand through his short hair, his crisp white dress shirt stretching against his tattooed biceps. The man obviously spent every hour he wasn't working in the gym.

"And did she confide in you about any issues?"

Lorenzo asked, "Such as?" He rolled up his shirtsleeves, showcasing his forearm tattoos.

"Can you recall any recent unusual occurrences or threats that might have been related to Penny's murder?" George asked.

"Sorry, no. She was a lovely, attractive girl, well-liked among her colleagues."

So, George and Jay left, concluding that no immediate red flags or conflicts could point to a motive for her murder within the restaurant. Nevertheless, they knew that further investigation was required to uncover the truth about what had happened to Penny and identify any potential suspects or leads outside her workplace.

Chapter Nine

George awoke to his phone ringing, and as usual, Isabella was nowhere to be seen. He trained his hearing but couldn't hear Olivia babbling, Rex barking, or the TV going.

"DI Beaumont."

"George, it's Jim Smith," the Detective Superintendent said. "There's been another murder," he explained.

Shit. "Where?"

"Stourton Stone Circle again."

"Again, I thought we had officers in the area, sir?" George asked.

"We did, but there's not enough budget to keep them in the area at all times." The DSU paused. "It appears the murderer let themselves in through the tape."

"Right, sir, I'm on my way."

"OK, Beaumont, I've already contacted forensics and pathology, and uniform at the scene has set up a cordon. Who do you want as your deputy."

"DS Mason, but he's better off at the station. I want DC Scott with me at the scene."

"OK, I'll call him now." He paused. "Report to DCI Atkinson as usual."

George was about to ask if that was wise considering how

busy he was with the copycat, but luckily stopped himself. Instead, he was about to hang up when Jim Smith said, "Oh and George, nice to speak to you."

"Thanks, sir."

The DI texted Isabella, telling her he was heading for work and got in the Merc.

On the way, he thought about his conversation with Mark Finch last night.

Just as he was about to leave his office, George's phone buzzed in his pocket, and thinking it must have been Isabella, he said, "Hi gorgeous, I'm sorry, I'll be home soon."

A hearty laugh echoed through the phone, emanating from deep within and unmistakably belonged to a man, not Isabella. "George, it's Finchy," he said, his Scottish accent flowing through the speaker. "I was calling to let you know that I'll be late to the pub, but I've just seen your press conference, so I wanted to know if you wanted to reschedule."

"Thanks, mate," George said to his oldest friend, the University of Leeds tenured Professor of Criminology and highly regarded criminal profiler. They had known each other since childhood, their friendship dating back to when they were mere boys. George's parents used to take him to Scotland to visit his grandparents during school holidays, and Mark was always there, waiting by the door. George cherished many fond memories, most of them beginning with him leaving his suitcase with his grandpa and then venturing into the nearby woods with Mark. The separation had been painful when George's family relocated to Leeds just before he turned five, leaving Mark behind. "I appreciate it."

"Bit of a sick murder by the sounds of it," Mark said.

"What have you heard?" George replied.

CHAPTER NINE

"Enough," Mark retorted. "You need my help?"

"Are you charging?" George replied with a laugh.

"Not for old friends."

"Ah, go on then. You've twisted my arm."

"Find out as much as you can about the victim," Mark said. "Most killers aren't serial killers. They find their victims through opportunity. They have no plan, it just happens, and they shit themselves and try to cover it up. The crime scenes are messy, with lots of evidence. Was the scene messy?"

"No, and to tell you the truth, we barely found any evidence."

"Then you're definitely looking at someone who has killed before, George, or has been planning this for a while." Mark paused. "I'd look into her in detail, looking at CCTV for anybody following her. Look into her friends, her family, everything. It's the people who show up the most you need to prioritise."

"We're already doing all of that."

"I thought you would be, mate, I know not to teach you to suck eggs," said Mark. "All I'll say then is if he planned this murder meticulously, he probably already has his next victim in mind." Finchy paused. "You only have one body, though, so you don't have a pattern yet," Mark explained. "So, I can't tell you much."

"Right, OK."

"But what I can tell you is that your victim will have been selected for a reason." Mark paused. "It's Penny Haigh, right?"

George went to answer but held back, wondering how Mark knew. "How did you know that?"

"Her parents called me after you left this morning," Mark explained.

"Why would they do that?" George asked, confused.

"Because she is... No, she was a student of mine," Mark admitted.

Why hadn't someone informed George of this? He thought back to who he had asked to do background checks. Was it Yolanda or Luke? It didn't matter; they should have told him.

"I can't talk to you about the case then, Mark; I'm sorry."

"Yeah, I didn't think you would be, which is why I wanted to be honest with you, mate."

George remembered he'd hung up on his mate and had stared at a wall for half an hour before Isabella had brought in his tea.

Eventually, George made his way back to the woods in Stourton. The area had been cordoned off, and Police Constable Candy Nichols stood guard at the entrance. George approached, nodded a greeting and signed himself in.

"Who discovered the body?" he asked.

"Unfortunately, we did," Nichols responded. "PC Hammond and I were on patrol earlier and were asked to check the area." She frowned. "Since hearing about the murder, kids have been sighted in the area. Unfortunately, that's when we came across it."

The DI was impressed. For such a relatively new officer, Nichols appeared surprisingly composed after witnessing such a scene. George recalled vividly his own first experience at a murder scene. It wasn't a pleasant memory.

He desperately wanted to get her into plain clothes and wondered how to proceed. She was a resource the force wasn't fully utilising.

"What time was that?" George asked.

"A few minutes past eight this morning, sir."

CHAPTER NINE

"Anything of note?"

She shook her head. "There's no visible blood or anything particularly gruesome down there."

"Alright. I need a report from you and PC Hammond as soon as possible."

"Yes, sir."

The sound of a car engine interrupted their conversation – it was Jay.

George walked over to greet him. "Morning, Jay."

"What do we know about the victim, boss?" Jay inquired. He tried his best to keep his eyes off Candy but failed miserably.

"Nothing at this point. We'll gather more information when we investigate further."

After suiting up, they ventured into the woods, sticking to the footpaths until they reached a clearing with the stone circle in the centre. The victim lay on the altar, naked and spread-eagled, exactly how Penny Haigh had been left.

In fact, George had to double take. The woman looked identical with her porcelain skin and dark, flowing hair.

"Bruising to the neck, arms, wrists and ankles again," George observed as he closed the distance. "And a stab wound to the jugular."

"Same as before, then?" Jay suggested.

"Looks that way." He'd forgotten to ask if forensics and pathology had been called, but he needn't have worried about Candy.

"Step back, please, lads!" the pathologist called from behind them.

"Good morning," both detectives greeted Christian as he approached.

"It's not though, is it, lads? This appears awfully similar

to the last one," Christian remarked. "In fact, it's exactly the same as your other victim," the pathologist explained. "See the lesions on her wrists and ankles; I can already say she was bound." He pointed at the neck. "Signs of strangulation." And then at her arms and shoulders. "She was forcibly moved."

"I'm guessing you'll find signs of sexual assault?"

Dr Ross shut his eyes. "No doubt."

"Good morning, DI Beaumont. Dr Ross. DC Scott."

The trio turned to find Lindsey Yardley already suited and booted, her team following behind her. "Shall I proceed as I did yesterday?" she asked George.

George nodded. "The DCI asked me to remind you about our tiny budget."

"So, no print collection other than ones on the body?" she confirmed.

"Correct, and if you find anything substantial, contact me immediately so I can get clearance for any fast-tracking."

The detectives stood back and watched pathology and forensics work. They were undoubtedly like a well-oiled machine because of Lindsey's qualifications. She often covered for Dr Ross in the morgue when and as required, as if being groomed for his position. Rumour was he was retiring soon.

"We need to identify the victim to inform the family," George said aloud and to no one in particular.

Lindsey pointed towards her CSIs, who were looking through the foliage. "That's our priority, DI Beaumont."

"I've found a bag," SOCO Hayden Wyatt said. The blonde American called the photographer over, who took photos before disturbing the scene.

"Check inside the bag. If there's any ID, it should be there," Jay suggested.

"Give us ten minutes, please," Lindsey advised.

Ten minutes later, Lindsey approached, holding up various exhibit bags. "In the victim's purse, I found a driving licence and what appears to be a name badge for a pizza restaurant. Her name was Joy Pritchard."

George inspected the licence through the plastic bag and passed it to Jay. "Do you recognise her?"

Jay frowned. "No, I don't. Why would I?"

"You love pizza," George said. "You're always banging on about going out for pizza, so you may have recognised her." The DI turned to the CSI manager before Jay could retort. "Thank you, Lindsey; ring me if you have anything." He then turned to the pathologist. "Dr Ross. We need to locate and inform her family. Please give me a call after you finish the post-mortem."

Christian cracked a grin. "You, er, don't want to know the time of death, son?"

"Of course I do."

"Sometime between midnight and six this morning," he replied. "I'll be more specific once I get her back to the lab."

"Thank you," George acknowledged before making a move to leave.

"Wait, I'm not done," the pathologist grumbled.

"Sorry, Dr Ross, what is it?"

"There was a note tucked into her... her vagina."

George recoiled, as did Jay and Lindsey. "What the hell, from the killer?" George asked.

"That's for you to decipher, son. That lovely SOCO over there took a photograph, and it's now in an evidence bag," Christian passed it to George, who peered at it through the transparent bag.

It was handwritten, meaning they had handwriting to analyse. "What a cocky bastard."

"My thoughts exactly, son," said Christian.

"What?" asked Jay.

"It's handwritten, so unless the killer got somebody else to write it, which is obviously a risk, we can analyse it," George explained.

"You mean to share this with the public?"

George nodded. "The quote may mean something to someone. If our killer didn't write it, the person who did may come forward." He held the bag close to his chest. "This is exactly what we needed." The DI smoothed the exhibit bag and read, "I have no remorse. I never felt any misgiving in my soul; I never thought that what I did was bad, even though human society condemns it. My blood and the blood of my victims must be on the heads of my torturers. The punishments I have suffered have destroyed all my feelings as a human being. That is why I do not pity my victims."

"What the fuck?" asked Jay, mirroring the thoughts of the others.

"Turn the bag over, son," Christian said.

George did as he was told and read, "There will be more. But probably not here. Catch me if you can."

"Cocky bastard," said Jay.

Ignoring him, George pulled out his phone. The threat of more was too much to ignore, and they needed to make a headway. He called DS Mason, who was back at the station.

"Now then, son," Luke answered.

"Our victim is Joy Pritchard; she works at Pizza Express, though I don't know which one. Call their head office and get her family's contact details ASAP."

CHAPTER NINE

"No bother, son. Bye."

"Wait, I need you to contact PS Greenwood and get his uniforms back out. And get Yolanda on CCTV. We're looking for anything that matches up with the first murder."

"Cars and that?"

"Exactly."

"On it."

"And have a look into any possible links between the victims."

"OK. Anything else."

"For now, no. Bye, Luke."

Jay said, "Wait, boss, we need to analyse this."

"Luke, are you still there?"

"I am."

"The killer left a handwritten note. I'll ring DCI Atkinson to clear the budget now, but we'll need a graphologist."

"I know just the person," Luke said. "When are you coming back with it?"

"After you've found me next of kin details and I've visited the victim's family."

"Tashan has the information you requested; I'll put him on."

"Hello, sir," said DC Blackburn. "Pizza Express were horrified but happy to provide details. She worked at the Clarence Dock branch and lived with her husband and two children at Richmond Hill Approach."

"Thanks, Tashan; let Luke know Jay and I are heading there now." He ended the call. "Jay, we're off to Richmond Hill."

Chapter Ten

"I hope someone's in," George remarked as they pulled up outside the semi-detached property, which, like all the others on the street, bore an identical, red-bricked design.

The pair got out of George's Merc, having left Jay's car in Stourton, and Jay rang the doorbell. Within a minute, a man answered.

"Are you Shane Pritchard?" George asked, already dreading the conversation ahead.

A worried expression greeted them. "Yer. Who're you?"

"I'm Detective Inspector Beaumont, and this is Detective Constable Scott." The pair extended their warrant cards for Shane to see. "We'd like to come inside to speak with you for a moment."

"Is this about Joy?" Shane asked, and when neither detective said anything, he added, "I called you lot earlier to report 'er missing and gave the officer her details." He narrowed his brows. "I didn't expect to see you so soon because the officer said something about her not being a priority because she didn't have any health or mental health issues." He paused. "Has something happened, then?"

"I think it's best if we speak inside, Shane," George said.

"Fine, I've had to call in sick because of the kids," Shane

explained as he led them into a messy living room. "Sorry about the mess; I wa' getting the children ready for school when you rang the bell. They don't know about their mummy, as I didn't want to worry them, so I told them she had to go out early." His jaw clenched, accentuating the lines around his eyes.

"Where are they now?" George asked.

"Upstairs brushing their teeth."

"How old are they?"

"Seth is six, and Gwen is four. Let's talk in 'ere so they can't hear us." He gestured to the sofa. "Please sit."

George found he couldn't meet Shane's gaze. Those poor kids had now lost their mother at such a critical time in their lives.

"Do you want a drink or owt?" Shane asked.

"Are you OK answering some questions?" George asked, and Shane nodded. "When was the last time you saw your wife?"

"Last night. She left at half three, as usual, and went to work. When I woke up this morning, she wasn't 'ere. Normally, she doesn't come 'ome until after we've all gone to bed 'cos it's well after eleven by the time they clean down and everything. She..." His voice faltered.

George took a deep breath. He despised this part of his job. "I'm very sorry to inform you that we've found the body of a woman we believe to be Joy."

His face drained of colour. "Are you sure?" he whispered.

"Do you have a recent photograph of her?" Even though he'd seen the pink licence, he wanted to be absolutely sure.

"There's one on the windowsill. We only got married last month."

George walked over and studied the family photo, instantly

recognizing Joy. "I'm sorry, but based on this photograph, it does appear to be Joy. We will need you to come to the morgue to make a formal identification. I'm very sorry for your loss."

George returned to the sofa and remained silent while Shane stared vacantly into space.

With tears falling from his eyes, Shane eventually said, "Joy's gone. What do I tell the children? What happened?"

"We're still investigating, but we're treating her death as suspicious for now."

"You mean... murder?"

"Yes."

"How did she die?"

"We're awaiting the pathologist's report. All we can say at this point is that she was found at the Stourton Stone Circle."

"But that's..." He furrowed his brow. "That's where you found that other body."

"That's right." George didn't want to discuss it further until they had more information from Dr Ross.

"Was her car there? She drives a blue Mokka."

"There were no cars nearby, so she likely didn't drive herself." That was all George was willing to disclose, but it meant they had something to go on. He pulled out his phone and texted Luke, asking him to find the reg plate and see if ANPR had picked the Mokka up at any point last night or this morning. "Do you have anyone we can contact to be with you during this difficult time?"

"No. None of our family lives nearby. We've only been here for just over a year. We moved here for my job."

"What do you do?"

"I'm a diesel mechanic, and the company I work for needed me to move here because apparently Leeds didn't 'ave one."

George nodded. "Would you be willing to answer a few more questions?"

"Yes, I think so," he said, swallowing hard and sitting up, attempting to compose himself.

"You mentioned that Joy was at work last night. What was her job?" He pulled out her notebook and pen. He already knew from the badge, of course, and the fact that Pizza Express had been the ones to provide next of kin details, but easing spouses into the more intricate questions was something George found necessary.

"She's been working at Pizza Express near the armouries for the past six months. She works lates to fit in with my early morning work."

George's heart ached for those poor kids. Their lives would never be the same.

"How many nights a week did she work?"

"Three nights a week. She's also doing a part-time degree at the university. Uni of Leeds. She has online lectures once she's dropped the kids off. Since COVID, they gave the students the options, apparently."

"What was she studying?" Jay asked.

"Criminology. She..." His voice trailed off, and he stared at them, his eyes distant. "What am I supposed to do now? What the hell can I do without her?"

George wondered whether Joy was on the same course as Penny, studying under Mark Finch. He said, "I'm going to arrange for a family liaison officer to come and stay with you as your point of contact with the police. Any questions you have or any information you need about the investigation, they will be the person you turn to."

Did Shane understand what he was saying? George both

understood and suspected much of this was overwhelming Shane due to the shock. In many murder cases, the culprit was someone known to the victim, often someone close. But if it was him, what was his link to Penny Haigh? Was it the course? Did that mean then that the murderer was on the course, too?

"What about the children? What the hell am I supposed to tell them?"

George wanted to demand that Shane shield them from the inevitable turmoil that would follow once people learned their mother had been murdered. But, of course, he couldn't tell him that. Instead, he said, "They need to know, but I'd keep them home from school. It may take some time for them to process. But they'll need your support." He paused. "Are you religious?"

"Joy was," Shane said. "And the kids believe in God." He frowned. "Why?"

"Tell them that mummy has gone to heaven and that she's waiting for them there. Tell them she will be watching over them and to live long, kind and fruitful lives."

George was sure Shane wasn't listening, but he'd made his point and needed to move the conversation on. "We'd like to take a look at your bedroom and Joy's laptop to see if there's anything that might assist us in our investigation if that's alright with you," George said.

"OK." Shane's voice sounded robotic, and his eyes appeared vacant.

They made their way to the desk in the corner of the living room, which was impeccably organized, with only textbooks on it. "Do you mind if we take Joy's laptop?" George inquired.

"No," he replied. "But I want it back."

After putting on gloves, George pulled out an exhibit bag,

one of many he kept in his pocket, and placed the laptop into it. Then, the pair followed him upstairs. As they reached the top, his daughter emerged from her bedroom.

"Are you OK, Daddy?"

"Just stay in your room for a minute, Babe."

"Who is this, Daddy?" she asked, eyeing George.

"I'm George, and this is Jay." He decided not to mention she was a police officer.

Shane shot him a thankful glance. "Get Seth to put the Fire Stick on for a bit," he told his daughter.

He then led them into the bedroom, and they conducted a brief search. The room was modern, with white furniture, and the bed was against the back wall. George winced when he noticed that only one side of the bed was messy.

After a fruitless search, they returned downstairs. George stepped outside and called Luke.

"I need you to arrange a family liaison officer for Shane Pritchard and his family."

"OK, son."

Returning to the living room, Jay was still with Shane Pritchard. He needed to ask one crucial question, however uncomfortable it might be.

"Shane, can you please tell me what you were doing between nine last night and six this morning?"

Shane recoiled. "You can't possibly think I had anything to do with this?"

George shook his head. "We ask everybody, Shane. The more people we eliminate, the better."

Shane rubbed his eyes furiously and said, "I was 'ere with the children 'cos they're too young to be left alone."

"Is there anyone who can confirm you were here?"

"Seth and Gwen, but they were in bed by nine."

"And you didn't leave the house at all?"

Shane looked insulted. "No, I would never leave the children alone." He hesitated for a moment. "My ma called around ten, and we chatted for about twenty minutes. You could ask her. Besides that, no one can confirm I was here the whole time." A tear slid down his face. "Joy. My Joy," he moaned, burying his head in his hands.

"Shane," George said gently. He looked up at the DI. "Can you think of anyone who might have wished harm upon your wife?"

"No. Everyone loved Joy."

The doorbell rang.

"I'll get it," Jay said.

When Jay opened the door, Detective Sergeant Cathy Hoskins, the Family Liaison Officer, stood on the doorstep. Cathy was in her early forties and highly experienced, excelling at her job. When Jay escorted her into the living room, George was relieved to see her.

"Hello, DI Beaumont. I live in the area, so it didn't take me long to get here."

"Shane, this is Detective Sergeant Hoskins, Cathy. She's your Family Liaison Officer and will be with you throughout the investigation. If you need anything, she's the person you speak with, OK?"

Absent-mindedly, Shane nodded, and George turned to Jay. "Jay, take Mr Pritchard upstairs and get him to identify Joy's belongings, please," he ordered. "CSI will be over soon to take samples, but having a list will ensure they're in and out."

"After you, Mr Pritchard," said Jay, before both men headed upstairs.

CHAPTER TEN

The DS and DI headed into the kitchen to ensure privacy. "Nice to see you, Cathy," George said. He pointed to the ceiling. "The husband is in shock, and there are two young children, aged six and four, who are unaware of their mother's situation. I've had a brief conversation with the husband, but we'll rely on you to gather any information you believe will be helpful and pass it on to me." George didn't need to explain further; Cathy understood her role perfectly.

"Of course, sir."

"The husband had actually reported his wife missing to the station when he discovered she was gone this morning. However, whoever spoke to him didn't connect it to our case. I'll look into that when I return to the station."

"He only noticed her missing this morning?" Cathy inquired. "That's unusual."

"She had been working at Pizza Express last night, and he had gone to bed before her expected return."

"OK, that explains it."

"We need to leave now. Cathy, please schedule a time for Shane to make a formal identification, and we'll be in touch later."

"Will do, sir."

George and Jay left and returned to their car.

"What's our next step?" Jay asked.

"Pizza Express, where Joy worked."

Chapter Eleven

George found a parking spot right outside. Although it was six o'clock, only a few people were in there. Then again, it was a Tuesday.

They walked up to the greeter. "Is the manager in?" George asked the tall, thin man.

"That's me," he said, smiling. "Jared Simmons."

George held out his warrant card, and Jay followed suit. "I'm Detective Inspector Beaumont, and this is Detective Constable Scott. We'd like a word with you in private."

From the corner of George's eye, he saw a man get up from the booth he was sitting at and clapped a young, blonde woman on the shoulder. She wore a Pizza Express uniform, the red apron matching the shade of lipstick she wore. Her eyes were dark blue, like the British seaside.

"Is everything OK?" she asked Jared. She had a lot of dark makeup around her eyes.

"Can you take over for me, please, Lucy?" Jared asked. "These detectives have a few questions for me."

"I can, but we're a bit short-staffed, that's all," Lucy said, pouting. "Joy hasn't shown up."

"That's who we're here to talk to you about," said George.

Shocked, Jared said, "Then we'd better head into my office."

CHAPTER ELEVEN

Once the trio were alone, with George and Jay sitting opposite Jared, the DI turned to the manager. "As I said, we'd like to speak to you about Joy Pritchard."

"Joy? What about her?"

Jay kept focused on his face, wanting to assess how he took the news of the death.

"Unfortunately, she was found dead this morning."

His eyes widened. "Dead? What the hell happened to her?"

"That's what we're investigating. She was found in Stourton."

He frowned. "I saw something on the TV last night, but Joy worked last night." He rubbed his eyes.

George thought Jared was a portrait of dedication to his job, a symphony of fatigue and determination, the bags under his eyes his battle scars.

"So, there's been two deaths in Stourton then?" Jared eventually figured out. "I can't believe it. She was fine last night." He gripped the desk, his knuckles turning white.

"I need to ask you some questions," said George.

"Yes, of course." He let out a long sigh. "What a shock."

"We've been informed that Joy worked last night," said Jay.

"Yes," he confirmed. "Her shifts were on Monday, Wednesday, and Friday evenings, from four 'til eleven. She was an exceptional employee. Both the customers and the staff held her in high regard. It's hard to believe she's gone."

The manager appeared genuinely sincere to George, and there were no immediate red flags to raise his suspicion.

"Can you recall any noteworthy incidents from last night that might aid our investigation?" asked George.

He ran a trembling hand across his lips. "No, it was a typical Monday evening."

"Was it crowded?" George probed further.

"Not particularly. We had a few regulars, and there were a couple of unfamiliar older women from a book club who stayed briefly early on, but that was about it."

"Did anyone seem unusually fixated on Joy?"

"No more than usual. Monday nights are quiet, and we usually use the time to clean and restock."

"Did Joy mention anyone acting strangely towards her recently?" George questioned.

"No, she didn't, and I didn't observe anything out of the ordinary either."

"Did she ever discuss her family? Any issues with her husband or relatives?"

"Joy didn't confide in me that way." He shrugged. "We weren't friends, not that she wasn't friendly, but she was a dependable, reserved worker. She was always polite to customers. Even though she hadn't been here long, she quickly became one of my best staff members." He cleared his throat. "Our relationship was entirely professional."

From the corner of Jared's eye, he could see Jay furiously scribbling notes. "What's he writing?"

"Probably what you've just said, Mr Simmons," George explained. "What time did Joy leave?"

"After we finished cleaning, the restaurant cleared out, so probably between quarter past eleven and quarter to midnight," he replied, checking the wall clock.

"How did she get home?"

"I assume she drove herself." Jared looked out of the window of his office. "Her car doesn't appear to be outside."

It wasn't. Jay had already checked. Was Jared hiding something?

"Where did she usually park her car?"

"There in the car park, hence why you saw me looking just now."

"You mentioned regulars; how regular are they?" George asked.

"Erm, there's Jordan," Jared said. "He was with Lucy when you arrived."

George thought back. "The one that scarpered pretty quickly?"

Jared nodded.

Jay asked, "Does he come in regularly?"

"He's in here three or four nights a week since his wife left him about a year ago. Poor guy can't cook for himself. He—" Jared hesitated.

"What's the matter?" George asked.

"Jordan had a thing for Joy, actually. But—"

"When you say 'thing,' what do you mean?" George probed.

"He would always show up on the nights Joy was scheduled to work, and I sometimes noticed him staring at her. But he's harmless. He's been a customer for years, a nice guy. I can't imagine him doing anything like… you know…"

"Sometimes, it's the ones you least suspect," George remarked.

"Did he ever give her any gifts?" Jay asked, considering the possibility that obsessions could escalate if they were reciprocated.

"During her third or fourth shift, she worked on Valentine's Day and received some flowers. They were delivered here, and she was certain they weren't from her husband. We joked about it, and she didn't seem overly concerned. I did wonder if they were from Jordan but didn't investigate further." He shook his head. "Maybe I should have."

"Why did you decide not to?" Jay asked.

"It's not uncommon for customers to develop feelings for the staff. It's part of the job. It's not my fault the wages are crap."

"So she flirted with customers for tips?" asked Jay, and Jared nodded.

"They all do."

"OK, did anyone else seem 'infatuated' with Joy?" George asked, making air quotes with his fingers.

"Not to my knowledge."

"Do you know much about Joy's family?"

"No, her husband looked after the children while she worked. I think she was quite bright, though, studying for a university degree. As I said before, our relationship was entirely professional."

So you keep saying, thought George. "We're aware of her studies. We'll go back into the restaurant and speak with Jordan. May we bring him through here?" George requested.

"Yes, of course."

Once they'd left the office and arrived at the restaurant floor, they realised Jordan was nowhere to be seen. Jay and George exchanged a concerned look.

"Where's Jordan?" Jared asked Lucy.

"He suddenly decided to leave and didn't say why. He didn't have pudding, which was very unlike him," Lucy replied. "And he paid by card, instead of cash."

"Did he mention if he'd be returning?" George inquired.

"No. He didn't even finish his pizza before he left."

"That's highly unusual," Jared remarked. "Jordan usually stays and has dessert. He's often the last to leave, especially during the week when it's less busy."

George motioned for Jared to step aside, out of earshot from Lucy.

"Do you know where he lives?" George asked.

"Er, yeah, Richmond Hill," said Jared. "I only know because I had to give him a ride home once when he had too much to drink." He paused. "It's the blue door on Kitson Street, closer to Pontefract Lane than Kippax Lane."

George said, "Thanks." Then he asked, "Do you know his last name?"

"Rathmell. Jordan Rathmell."

"Thank you. We might need to speak with you again later. If you remember anything in the meantime, please don't hesitate to contact us." George retrieved a card from his pocket and handed it to the manager. "I understand you may want to discuss Joy's passing, but for the sake of her family, please refrain from mentioning that her body was found in the woods, as we haven't released her name yet."

"Sea Scout's honour," said Jared.

Chapter Twelve

"He left because of us," George remarked as they exited the restaurant, frustrated with himself for not noticing how much their presence had affected him earlier on. "Let's head to his house. It's not far away."

Before driving away, George took out his phone and called Tashan, hoping the officer hadn't left for the day.

"Hello, sir," the young officer answered.

"I'm glad you're still there. I want you to investigate a Jordan Rathmell, who lives on Kitson Street. He's a potential suspect. We're on our way there now. Call me when you have any information."

"Yes, sir. It won't take long."

Upon arrival, they approached the terraced house and knocked on the door. There was no response, so they knocked again. In his peripheral vision, George noticed somebody approaching, a blue plastic bag swinging from his hand. He'd been to the offy for booze.

"Don't look, but Jordan's over there," George whispered to Jay. "Crouch down behind this car so he can't see us until he gets closer to his front door."

They remained out of sight and waited until Jordan put his key in his blue door. George stepped out of the shadows, and

CHAPTER TWELVE

Jay followed. Jordan stared at them, his mouth open.

Was he about to flee? He could try, but they would catch up to him. Or Jay would; he was pretty quick. And young, too.

"Stay right there," George called out as he moved toward him, closing the distance.

"What do you want?" Jordan asked.

"A word with you, Jordan. Inside," George replied.

Jordan glanced behind George, and the DI braced himself to run if the suspect attempted to escape, but Jordan seemed to think better of it.

He unlocked the door and led them into the living room, where they sat on a faded dark blue sofa. He sat opposite them, still holding the plastic bag.

"Cosy night in?" asked George, nodding at the bag.

"Nowt wrong with that, is there?"

"No. Why did you leave the restaurant?" George inquired.

"I was thirsty," he held out the bag.

"Nothing to do with us being there?" George locked eyes with him, and Jordan lowered his gaze. "Plenty of booze at Pizza Express."

"It's expensive there."

"It's apparently not stopped you before."

Jordan frowned. "Alright. Yeah. I left because you were there," he admitted.

"Why?" George pressed.

"I thought you were coming for me."

"For what?" George couldn't believe Jordan would confess to killing Joy.

"Because I had a right fight with my ex last night, and she threatened to call you lot as usual!" He shrugged. "I thought you'd come to arrest me."

"That wasn't why we were there or why we're here now. We want to talk to you about Joy Pritchard."

"Joy?" He frowned. "Why?"

"Her body was found this morning, and we're treating her death as suspicious."

His face turned ashen. "Joy's dead?" he said slowly.

"Yes. I want to know more about your relationship with her," George leaned forward, scrutinizing his face for signs of genuine distress.

"I didn't have a relationship with her."

"You were attracted to her, though, weren't you?" George said.

His cheeks turned pink. "I don't know what you mean," he muttered.

"We understand you were attracted to her and sent her some flowers on Valentine's Day. Is that correct?"

His head shot up. "Who told you that?"

"It doesn't matter. Did you, or did you not, send Joy flowers?"

"I liked her," he admitted, picking at his nails.

"Even though she was married, you still thought it was okay to pursue her."

"I didn't pursue her."

"What did you do, then?" George asked, locking eyes with him.

"She wasn't happy in her marriage," he replied, sitting up straighter, a defiant look in his eyes.

"What makes you say that?" George thought it was a very different story from what they'd been told so far. Perhaps the husband wasn't as innocent as he initially made out.

"Because of stuff, I'd overhear her talking to the other staff about."

"What kind of stuff?"

"It's not really relevant, is it?"

"I'll decide what's relevant," George said.

"They hadn't had sex once since moving to Leeds because he was always asleep when she got home." Jordan shrugged. "She thought he was cheating on her."

It appeared George's instincts had been right, then. The staff at Pizza Express weren't being entirely honest with him.

"Do you know where she lived?"

"No comment," Jordan said, clamming up.

"Have you been following her?" Jay pushed.

"No comment."

"Would you like to come with us to the station?" George asked. "We can stay here, but I'm getting bored of you saying no comment." He stood up and took a step toward him.

"What's the point? I have nothing to tell you."

"I don't believe that for a minute, so I will give you a choice." The DI paused for effect. "You can either come with us voluntarily, or I'm going to arrest you, and then you'll leave here in handcuffs for all the neighbours to see."

In George's experience, threats like that invariably led to a suspect taking the easiest option. In truth, he'd rather no one saw Rathmell being arrested in case they used their phone to record it and then forwarded it to the press. YappApp was the bane of George's life.

"Do I have a choice?" he asked, standing. George shook his head. "What about a solicitor? Do I need one?"

"That's up to you. You're entitled to have one present if you wish. Do you have one?" George asked.

"Do I look rich enough to have a solicitor on speed dial?"

he asked, his jaw clenched. "If I had one, I'd have used them in my divorce and not had to agree to all the conditions and demands my ex made."

"If you'd like one with you during questioning, we can arrange that. We have duty solicitors available."

He shrugged. "I'll let you know when we get there."

"I'd also like to search your house," George said.

"Why?"

"As part of our inquiries. You can give us permission, or we'll get a search warrant, meaning no corner of your home would be left untouched. It's up to you."

He didn't doubt they'd get one, but he'd rather not wait. With Jordan's permission, Lindsey and her team could begin searching immediately.

"I've got nothing to hide," he said.

"Are you giving your permission?" he checked.

"Do I have a choice?"

"Yes. But I'll get a warrant."

"I don't care. Do what you like." He gave an angry sigh.

"Give me the key, and then we'll take you to the station."

"How am I going to get home?" he asked as they left his house.

"I'll arrange for an officer to escort you back here after we've finished with the questioning."

* * *

They left Jordan in an interview room to stew and headed upstairs to the HMET floor. George headed to DCI Atkinson's office first to share the news.

"I'll meet Lindsey at Rathmell's house," Alistair said. "You interview him."

"Are you sure, sir? I know how busy you are with the copycat case."

"It's fine, Beaumont," Atkinson said. "He only has one kill to his name; yours has two."

The DI entered the shared office to a buzz of excitement and intrigue among the team. Clearly, they'd heard the news of Jordan Rathmell's arrest and the new developments surrounding the case.

"Tashan, have you found anything on him yet?" George inquired, eager for any additional information to help build their case.

"His full name is Jordan Calvin Rathmell, and he's got a record for sexual assault ten years ago—he still denies it to this day, apparently. He gets PIP due to deteriorating mental health and is on Universal Credit," Tashan provided.

George said, "He told us he's divorced but is trying to get back with his ex. They argue a lot, and she tends to call us, apparently. That's why he did a runner when we went to the restaurant, believing we were there to arrest him."

"Guy's paranoid," Luke said.

"He is, and I want to know why." George paused and then looked at Yolanda. "I want you to check out the CCTV footage around Pizza Express to see if we can see when the victim left and if there was anybody close by at the time," George instructed, focusing on gathering more evidence. "If we can get Jordan in the footage, we'll be able to charge him easily enough." He turned to Jay. "Jay, I want you looking into the pagan side of things, still. We need to speak with somebody involved in the stone circle."

"On it, boss."

"Luke, you're with me," George said, directing Luke to accompany him for the upcoming interview with Jordan Rathmell.

"Tashan, find out Joy Pritchard's car details and let Yolanda have them. Then, put the reg through ANPR and create a timeline for us. We want to know the time she left work and where she went. Luke and I will interview Jordan now," George instructed, efficiently delegating tasks among the team members.

Before heading into the interview room, George clarified to Luke that his role would be as backup, allowing the DI to take the lead in questioning Jordan Rathmell. Luke was used to being George's sounding board in an interview room, often using his banter to relax the interviewee and then applying pressure when necessary.

* * *

Inside the interview room, Jordan Rathmell appeared tense, his gaze fixed straight ahead. George initiated the recording and began the interview with the usual spiel.

As the questioning progressed, Rathmell's emotions started to surface. He admitted to regularly following Joy Pritchard home in his car, claiming it was to ensure her safety. However, his explanation for his actions raised suspicions, and George continued to probe for more information.

The interview revealed that Rathmell had been infatuated with Joy Pritchard, but it seemed his feelings were not reciprocated.

The tension escalated when George questioned him about his actions on the night of Joy's death. Rathmell admitted to

CHAPTER TWELVE

drinking heavily but denied following her that night. However, George sensed he was holding back information.

The interview was temporarily suspended when a uniform banged on the interview room door to pass a phone to George. DCI Alistair Atkinson was on the other end to report a significant development at Rathmell's house.

George's heartbeat quickened with anticipation, knowing that this development could be a crucial breakthrough in the case.

"Interview terminated," George said as he turned off the recording. "You can stay here for a bit," he told Rathmell, his mind racing with the possibilities of what they might find at Jordan's residence.

As he and Jay prepared to leave the station, the team's excitement and determination to solve the case were palpable, and George couldn't help but feel a sense of camaraderie among his team members. They were determined to uncover the truth behind Joy Pritchard's death, and every piece of evidence brought them one step closer to justice.

Chapter Thirteen

George and Jay hurried to Jordan Rathmell's residence in response to the urgent call from the DCI, filled with eager anticipation. They hoped to uncover vital evidence that could provide insight into the death of Joy Pritchard.

George parked the Mercedes behind a patrol car, and as they exited the vehicle, Atkinson approached them from the house.

"I hope this is worth it, sir," George remarked. "You interrupted our interview."

"I believe we may have a lead. You'll see that when you see what we've discovered," Atkinson replied.

"Are you saying you've found something to link him to the murder, sir?" Jay inquired, wearing a sceptical expression. He wasn't sure Rathmell was their killer, especially if the two murders were linked because they hadn't made a link to Penny Haigh yet.

"You look confused, Detective Constable."

"I am, sir." He didn't want to say it aloud. Still, the sophistication and control implied by the murder's execution, such as the placement of the body on the altar, pointed to someone with differing qualities to Rathmell. He hadn't even said this to George yet.

"How about we take a look before jumping to conclusions,"

George suggested.

They followed Atkinson upstairs to the bedroom, which was modest and sparsely furnished. It contained a wardrobe, a chest of drawers, a dressing table, and an unmade bed.

"We nearly missed this," Atkinson said, approaching the wardrobe. The DCI bent down. "See? The floor panel is moveable." He lifted the panel, which revealed a space hidden in the floor. "This is what we found in there." Alistair handed over five Exhibit bags, three with photos of Joy; the other two contained a pair of lacy underwear in each.

"Do these belong to Joy?" George inquired, raising his brows.

"I'd wager they do," Atkinson replied confidently.

"Excellent find, sir. Has Lindsey photographed?"

"All is in hand, Beaumont," the DCI explained.

"Did you come across anything else of interest?"

The DCI shook his head. "This should be sufficient for an arrest."

They left Atkinson and returned to George's Merc.

"I'm still not convinced it's him, boss," Jay voiced as they drove away.

George frowned. "Why not? He had the motive, the means, and the opportunity."

"Is that right?"

"Yes, it is, Jay. Jordan was infatuated with her, and she didn't reciprocate. We've seen that scenario countless times."

Was George grasping at straws because Atkinson had pushed for a swift resolution to the case? Jay thought so.

"I just don't think the man is clever enough to plan one elaborate murder, never mind two," Jay explained.

George grinned. "Fair enough, Jay." He scratched his

bearded chin. "What do we do next?"

"We need to find a link between Penny and Joy. The murderer will also share that link."

The DI nodded. "I agree."

"Will you interview him again when we return to the station?" Jay asked.

"After we brief the team, yeah."

* * *

Upon entering the Incident Room, George called the team together. "Listen up, everyone. We may have a lead involving Jordan Rathmell, who is currently in custody."

"Nice one, son, what did Atkinson find?" Luke asked.

"Photos and various items that appear to have belonged to Joy Pritchard. I'm going to re-interview him with Jay." He turned to his other DC. "Tashan, what additional information do you have?"

"In addition to the sexual assault charge, the police were called to Rathmell's house many times during his time with his wife, as he admitted, but no further action was taken. He has no social media presence at all, and financially, as expected, there isn't much in his bank account." He paused. "I'm waiting for complete statements to see what he spends his money on.

"OK, great, Tashan." He turned to Yolanda. "What about the CCTV?"

"I didn't see Rathmell's car following her when she left the restaurant last night," she explained, "but I'm still waiting for footage from other cameras. I'm also still looking at footage of Penny Haigh. And I'm still trying to sort you a timeline using ANPR."

CHAPTER THIRTEEN

George nodded. He knew they were stretched, but there wasn't much he could do. "So you saw Rathmell leaving Pizza Express?"

"Yes, sir, he stayed in his car after leaving the restaurant, then when Joy left in her Mokka, he left about ten minutes later."

The DI raised his brows. "Did he drive in the same direction?"

"Yes, sir."

"They do both live in Richmond Hill, boss," said Jay.

George nodded. The young DC was right, but why did Rathmell wait for Joy to leave instead of leaving straight away?

The DI voiced that concern to his team and then looked at Jay. "Jay, I'm gonna speak to Jordan again. You're with me this time."

"OK, boss."

* * *

Leaving the incident room, they headed toward the interview room, where a uniformed officer awaited them. "Any issues?" George inquired.

"No, sir. He hasn't moved."

"Thank you."

Upon entering the room, George activated the interview equipment. "Interview resumed. Detective Constable Scott is taking over from Detective Sergeant Mason." He looked at Jordan. "I need to ask you again whether you want a solicitor," he explained.

"I'm fine for now."

Jordan's demeanour had changed since Jay had last observed

him at the house on Kitson Street. Jordan's eyes now held a visible tension that wasn't there before, as if he was suddenly aware of the seriousness of the situation. That, or the man was possibly concealing something.

Jay also noticed Rathmell's arms were folded tightly across his chest. The DC was no body language expert but knew that when a suspect's arms were tightly folded across their chest, it often indicated a defensive or guarded stance. Was he trying to shield himself from the detectives or maintain a barrier between himself and them?

Rathmell could just have been nervous, of course. Even innocent people were anxious when interviewed by the police. He'd seen the combination of tense eyes and folded arms many times during his career, and it could easily mean Jordan was feeling nervous or uncomfortable.

It could also mean the man was hiding something.

Detective Inspector Beaumont maintained his professional composure. "Very well, Jordan," he acknowledged. "We'll proceed without a solicitor for now. If you want one, all you have to do is say so, OK?"

"OK."

"Jordan Rathmell, I'm arresting you under suspicion of the murder of Joy Pritchard. You do not have to say anything. But, it may harm your defence if you do not mention when questioned something which you later rely on in court. Anything you do say may be given in evidence." George paused. "Do you understand?"

Jordan stared at them unblinkingly.

"Do you understand?" George repeated, louder this time.

"What?"

Neither detective said anything.

CHAPTER THIRTEEN

"You dickheads have got this all wrong. I do understand what you're saying, but it's fucking insane."

"As we've repeatedly said, you are entitled to legal representation. We can assign a duty solicitor for you, or you can choose your own. Would you like one now?"

Jay glanced at George. The determined expression on his face made it clear that George wanted to be convinced of Rathmell's guilt. But for Jay, time would tell.

"I don't have one, as you know. You'll have to call the duty solicitor."

George said, "I'll arrange that. In the meantime, one of my officers will escort you to the custody sergeant, who will process you and chaperon you to a holding cell."

"Tell me what's going on? Why did you decide to arrest me?"

"When we searched your house, we found incriminating evidence in a hidden compartment in your wardrobe," George said. "We'll share this information with the duty solicitor when they arrive."

Jordan's face lost colour. The fight seemed to drain from his body, and he slumped in his chair. "Just because I have some photos and things belonging to Joy doesn't mean I'm the one who murdered her."

"We will discuss this further when your solicitor arrives. Come with us to the custody sergeant."

"I'm innocent. I didn't do it," Jordan protested as he followed them out of the interview room.

* * *

In the Incident Room, George thought back to the scenes. "Why the Stourton Stone Circle? And why leave them out in the open and not even attempt to hide them?" he said aloud.

"Clearly, the killer wanted the two women to be found, boss," said Jay. "Anybody who knows the area knows it's a popular spot."

George nodded. "So it's obviously something symbolic or significant," the DI explained. He turned to his team, but a knock at the door interrupted him.

Detective Sergeant Joshua Fry entered a stack of sheets in his hand. "Hello, sir, I've something I think you're going to like."

"What is it, Josh?" George asked.

"I got into Penny's Facebook. These are printouts of her messages—"

Tashan's phone began to ring, interrupting the DS.

"Sorry, Sarge, this is important."

DC Blackburn put the phone to his ear and left the Incident Room.

"As I was saying, these are printouts of Penny's messages," Josh said. "They make for interesting reading."

George quickly scanned the pages and raised his brows. "It appears Jordan Rathmell was trying to get Penny Haigh to meet him."

"Of all the things I thought was going to be on those pages, that wasn't it," remarked Luke.

Josh said, "It's certainly interesting, isn't it?"

George scanned through the messages. It became apparent that Jordan Rathmell was persistent in pursuing Penny Haigh. He'd sent her numerous messages, some of which were increasingly desperate and pleading. On the other hand, Penny's responses were consistently polite but distant, indicating that she was not interested in pursuing a romantic relationship with him.

"It's clear that Penny wasn't reciprocating Jordan's advances," George observed. "But why was he so insistent? Is this why he murdered her?"

Luke chimed in, "I suppose Jordan became so obsessed with Penny that it's possible he killed her, aye. You know how some people can't handle rejection."

Jay nodded in agreement. "Obsession could lead to jealousy and anger. If he found out that Penny was seeing someone else, it might explain his persistence."

"Right, Luke, I need you to keep digging into Jordan's background. Let's find out more about his motivations and whether he had any connection to the victims beyond his pursuit of Penny and Joy."

Luke nodded and left the Incident Room to continue investigating Jordan Rathmell's life, looking for any clues that might tie him to the Stourton Stone Circle murders.

"Sorry about that, sir," DC Tashan Blackburn said as he re-entered the Incident Room. "That was the bank. They've provided Rathmell's bank statements." Tashan headed towards the computer and clicked on the projector. "Like the DMs, they make for pretty interesting reading."

George turned his attention to the screen, where Tashan began to display Jordan Rathmell's bank statements. The statements revealed a series of transactions that raised further questions about Rathmell's involvement in the case.

Rathmell's bank statements revealed that he spent the evenings Joy worked at Pizza Express and the afternoons at Capri, where Penny worked. The women's shift patterns were pinned to the Big Board, and the transactions matched up.

Chapter Fourteen

The discovery that Jordan Rathmell's bank statements aligned with the work schedules of both Joy and Penny sent a chill through the Incident Room. The pieces of the puzzle were falling into place, and it was becoming increasingly clear that Rathmell had a disturbing connection to the two victims.

George studied the Big Board, where the women's shift patterns were pinned alongside Rathmell's transactions. "This can't be a coincidence," he muttered. "He was clearly tracking their movements, but why?"

Luke chimed in, "Maybe he was stalking them, boss. Obsession can lead to dangerous behaviour." He added, "And if he was present at both locations, he had the opportunity to observe them closely. He could have been learning their routines, getting to know them."

Just then, Detective Sergeant Yolanda Williams entered, their CCTV expert. "Sir, I've been looking at the CCTV of Capri and Pizza Express, and you'll never guess what I've found."

George grinned. "I bet we can. But go ahead."

Yolanda cocked a brow and mirrored George's grin. "It turns out Jordan Rathmell was a regular at both Pizza Express and Capri."

The pieces of the puzzle were fitting together with unsettling

CHAPTER FOURTEEN

precision.

"Are there any specific interactions or behaviours that stand out in the CCTV footage?" George asked, trying to contain his growing sense of unease.

Yolanda nodded. "Yes, sir. In several instances, Rathmell engages in conversations with Joy and Penny during their work shifts. Clearly, he wasn't just a random customer; he had a personal interest in them."

DS Williams sat down at the computer and loaded up the video files. She pressed play after the detectives gathered around the screen.

The footage revealed a series of interactions between Jordan Rathmell and the two victims, Joy and Penny. At Pizza Express, they watched snippets of Jordan Rathmell, who was shown entering the restaurant during Joy's evening shifts. He appeared calm and composed, taking a seat in one particular booth. George figured that was because that specific booth was in her section. He watched as Joy, the waitress, greeted him with a friendly smile. They engaged in conversation for several minutes while she took his order.

As the clips continued to be loaded up and watched, it became evident that Jordan was a regular customer, only visiting on Joy's workdays. Their conversations appeared amiable, with Joy occasionally lingering by his booth, their conversations resulting in laughter.

However, in some clips, there were subtle hints of discomfort on Joy's face, suggesting that Jordan's conversations might have taken a more personal or intrusive turn.

It was clear that Joy flirted with Jordan for the tips and that the man had taken her 'flirting' at face value.

"I've got the Capri footage to show you next, sir," Yolanda

explained.

The CCTV at Capri showed a similar pattern. Jordan Rathmell frequented the Italian restaurant during Penny's afternoon shifts.

Penny was also seen engaging in conversations with Jordan. Their interactions ranged from casual chit-chat to more intense discussions. Though in some clips, Penny could be seen glancing nervously at the clock as if eager to finish her shift and escape the conversation. That, and much of the footage, hinted at moments of tension, with Penny appearing increasingly uncomfortable during some interactions.

The detectives noted the timestamps of these interactions, the body language of the victims, and Jordan Rathmell's demeanour. It was clear from the footage that Rathmell had a persistent interest in both women, and some of their interactions had been strained.

George couldn't help but feel a growing sense of unease. The CCTV footage added another layer of complexity to the case, raising questions about Rathmell's motives and the extent of his involvement with the victims.

Jay leaned closer to the screen. "OK, boss, after seeing that footage, I'm worried," he explained. "In fact, that footage is pretty damning, isn't it?"

"I think we need to go back to Pizza Express and Capri so we can find out what those conversations were about and whether the staff can shed light on Rathmell's motives."

* * *

Leaving Capri and Pizza Express until later that afternoon, George decided to pay pathologist Dr Christian Ross a visit.

CHAPTER FOURTEEN

They pushed open the double doors, and straight away, the antiseptic smell invaded his nostrils. When they arrived at the lab, they poked their heads into the office area, but no one was there. Then they walked into the main area where Christian was peering at a body on one of the stainless-steel tables in the middle of the room.

"Hello, Dr Ross," Jay said.

"Now then, lads, how are we?" Christian asked.

"We're stressed and frustrated as usual," George said, laughing. "So, I'm gonna cut to the chase. On the way over, DCI Atkinson has told me I have a press conference coming up. We've identified the victim as Joy Pritchard. She went to work at Pizza Express last night and didn't return. What have you got for us?"

"Actually, I was going to call you later, but as you're here now, you can come and look." Christian beckoned them over.

The woman's petite body was doll-like on the large table, and her raven-coloured hair hung limply around her shoulders. The crimson stab wound in her neck starkly contrasted her porcelain skin.

Swallowing hard, George asked, "What is it?" It shocked him how somebody could tragically end this poor woman's life.

"This time, the stabbing occurred much earlier—"

"Ante-mortem?" George interrupted.

"No, son, peri-mortem. At or near the time of death. I still believe she was strangled to death, especially after cutting her open. But he must have stabbed her in between strangling her," the pathologist explained. "Judging by the angle of entry, the killer was left-handed." Dr Ross held his right hand up towards George's neck and then, with his left hand, pretended to stab George in the jugular. "The wound isn't as deep because of the crossing of arms, but I'm confident it's the same murder weapon."

"Have you—"

"No, my contact hasn't identified the weapon yet," Dr Ross interrupted with a grin.

George nodded. "Why the change?"

"You mean, why did your killer stab Joy peri-mortem when he stabbed Penny post-mortem?"

"Exactly."

Christian gave the DI a toothy grin. "I'm afraid that's your job, not mine, son." He pointed to the purple pressure marks shaped like fingertips on her shoulders and upper arms. "She was bashed around like poor Penny was before death," Dr Ross said.

"Can you get any fingerprints from the body?" George asked.

"No. The marks are consistent with the person wearing gloves. They are most likely latex, as they're thin enough to leave a complete finger mark without the actual prints. Hence the bruising."

"Was there any sexual abuse?" George asked.

"Blood around the anus suggests she was raped. And like with Penny, I've found traces of lubrication inside her vagina."

"Same brand as before?" asked George, and Dr Ross nodded.

It was the most popular brand, so it wasn't as if they could go to every shop that sold them and ask for CCTV. Their killer may not even have bought them from Leeds, may not have bought them at all. That, or he could have purchased them online or got somebody else to buy them for him.

Again, they had more questions than answers, and George could feel the frustration causing his body to overheat.

"Were there any signs of struggle?" Jay asked.

"There was nothing under the nails. But because of the crossing of hands during the stabbing and strangulation, I'm hoping for fibres." The pathologist paused. "If I find any, I'll let you know and send them off." He paused again. "Oh, there was debris on Joy's body consistent with it being dragged," Dr Ross explained. "Whilst still slim, she was older and more muscled than Penny, so weighed slightly more. She may also have resisted harder, as we found nothing on Penny's body resembling the debris on Joy. I've sent that to Calder Park labs for you for analysis."

"Any DNA or prints on the note?" asked George.

"It's too early for DNA, son, and no prints yet either. They're working hard for you, George, trust me."

George nodded. "Anything else?"

The pathologist shook his head, so the pair left the lab and made their way down the corridor. "Capri or Pizza Express first?" he asked Jay.

But that's when Jay's phone rang, and they immediately changed their destination.

Chapter Fifteen

Coniston Avenue in Headingley, where Leodis Pagan Group coordinator Diana Rubadue lived, presented an inviting facade, a charming semi-detached house that set itself apart from its neighbours on the street in a most appealing manner.

Beneath the ground floor windows, vibrant flower-filled window boxes added a touch of natural beauty. The door, painted a glossy navy blue, boasted gleaming brass fixtures.

After knocking and waiting momentarily, the front door swung open to reveal a young man in an orange hoodie, denim jeans, and eye-catching yellow socks. His brown, spiky hair was tipped with blonde.

Jay held up his identification as he spoke, and the young man's eyes widened. "We were hoping to speak with Diana Rubadue. I'm DC Scott, and this is my boss, DI Beaumont."

The young man tilted his head thoughtfully. "My mother is in the garden," he stated. "You can either wait inside while I fetch her or join her in the garden."

George replied, "The garden is fine."

"I'm Fred," the young man introduced himself, holding the door open wide for them to enter. "I assume you don't bring bad news?"

Jay reassured him, "No, nowt like that. Your mother is

expecting us. I called ahead. She's assisting us with an investigation."

Fred nodded, and they followed him into the spacious living room. The interior of the house exceeded their expectations, boasting an open-plan layout with leather sofas surrounding a sleek chrome and glass dining table. Four black leather chairs flanked each side of the table. The polished wooden floors and white-painted walls provided a modern ambience, quite different from what George had imagined.

On the way over, Jay had read out some of the research he'd done on paganism.

"Paganism in the United Kingdom," Jay had said, "is a diverse and multifaceted movement encompassing many beliefs and practices. It is often seen as a revival or reconstruction of pre-Christian indigenous religions practised in the British Isles before the arrival of Christianity. In recent decades, paganism in the UK has experienced a resurgence and is now a recognised and legally protected religious belief."

"Wow, did that hurt to say?" George had asked with a laugh.

"Just reading it from an article I found," Jay had explained.

The young DC continued, "Paganism in the UK has its roots in the ancient Celtic and Druidic traditions that existed in the British Isles before the Roman and Christian periods. These traditions were largely suppressed with the spread of Christianity, but they never entirely disappeared. In the 20th century, interest in these ancient belief systems was revived, leading to the modern pagan movement."

It's why they were visiting with Diana Rubadue, as she was effectively in charge of the Leodis Pagan group that Penny Haigh was part of and who held rituals at the Stourton Stone Circle.

As a result of what Jay had told him, George had expected the house to be flooded with nature rather than the sleek and modern design it displayed.

Fred led them to a set of French doors that opened onto the garden, calling for his mother. As George stepped outside, he observed Diana Rubadue—a woman in her fifties who was greying gracefully, her loose, unruly waves cascading down her shoulders, a testament to her life's experiences—rising from a flower bed, extending a welcoming hand.

She wore a flowing, earth-toned skirt made of natural fibres that swayed gracefully with her every movement. A loose-fitting, embroidered blouse adorned her upper body. Over her clothes, she draped a richly coloured shawl with symbols of her faith intricately woven into its fabric. A pendant in the shape of a crescent moon hung at her neck, symbolizing her reverence for lunar energies.

Around her wrists, she wore multiple bracelets crafted from various materials: polished stones, wooden beads, and intricately woven fibres. These bracelets were not just ornaments but talismans, no doubt each with its own significance in her practice.

After introductions, Fred reappeared behind them, bearing coffee. Both detectives accepted a cup, and then Fred shut the doors, leaving them alone with his mother.

George couldn't help but appreciate the garden's rustic charm, an unexpected oasis amid the heavily polluted city. The verdant greenery and continued blooming of flowers struck him as quite unusual for the time of year. "Thank you for seeing us, Diana," George said.

"It's my pleasure," Diana said. She met George's eyes with her own. Whilst they both had green eyes, Diana's were a

CHAPTER FIFTEEN

deep and soulful shade of forest green, sparkled with a serene wisdom that came from years of observing and revering the natural world. She held an intense and knowing gaze, hinting at the depth of her spiritual connection.

To George, she was intimidating, but kind. She was not somebody to be trifled with.

"How can I help?" she asked.

"We're sorry to tell you this, but Penny Haigh was murdered yesterday," George explained.

Diana nodded her head. "I'm aware." She took a deep breath. "Her parents called me. I shared the news with everyone."

Turning to George, Diana inquired, "How much do you know about the religion?"

George admitted, "Not much, to be honest."

Diana explained, "To outsiders, paganism may seem strange, but it's no different from some other religions." She paused. "Various traditions and belief systems characterise modern paganism in the UK. Some of the most prominent pagan traditions include Wicca, Druidry, Heathenry, and various Celtic and Norse paganism forms. Each of these traditions has its own rituals, deities, and practices."

"I'm so sorry, but I've no idea what Wicca, Druidry, or Heathenry is," George said.

Diana grinned. "Not many people do." She shrugged. "Most believe it's all about witchcraft, and modern TV doesn't help in that regard."

George could imagine. The amount of people who tried telling him how to do his job was staggering. They believed they could watch one murder show and suddenly become an expert. And the authors were the worst. They often bullshitted their way from the beginning to the end, hardly getting anything right and nearly everything wrong.

"I can certainly explain those to you, Detective." She paused, and George assumed she was trying to figure out how to explain everything clear enough so that the detectives could understand. Wicca is perhaps the most well-known pagan tradition and is often associated with witchcraft. Wiccans worship the Mighty Goddess and God and follow a set of rituals and festivals, usually centred around the cycles of the moon and the seasons."

George nodded.

"And then you have Druidry, another significant pagan tradition in the UK. It draws inspiration from the ancient Druids and focuses on nature spirituality, the worship of deities associated with the land, and a reverence for the natural world."

"I'm guessing they're not festivals like the one at Bramham Park," said Jay. He wasn't being serious, but Diana smiled at him.

"No, paganism in the UK is marked by the celebration of seasonal festivals, often called 'Sabbats' or 'Wheel of the Year' festivals. These include celebrations like Samhain—Halloween to you, which is next week—Imbolc, Beltane, and Lammas, which correspond to various points in the agricultural and astronomical calendar." Diana paused, taking in a deep breath. "I have to ask, how did Penny die?"

George mimicked Diana, inhaling the garden's fresh scent. He wondered how much to share. "She was bound to the altar and then strangled," George explained. "After she passed, the culprit stabbed her with something sharp and collected her blood." He looked at Diana, whose face wrinkled in disgust. "Does any of that sound like paganism to you? Is it one of your rituals?"

"No, definitely not. And it doesn't sound like paganism at all, not in the slightest," Diana said. "In fact, it's the opposite of what we all believe." She shook her head, still not quite able to believe what happened. "Pagan rituals often involve the use of symbols, magick, and nature-based symbolism. I include a lot of meditation, divination, and the casting of circles for sacred space." She paused. "There's nothing at all violent. Nothing but peace."

"I'm sorry if I offended you," said George.

"Not at all, Detective; I just wanted you to understand the abuse we receive as pagans, and the world has misconceptions about us. Paganism in the UK is generally inclusive and welcoming of people from diverse backgrounds, sexual orientations, and gender identities. It emphasises personal spiritual experience and often promotes a strong sense of community." She paused and grinned once more. "We're like a big family, and like a family, it's important to note that paganism is not a monolithic belief system, and individuals within the pagan community have a wide range of beliefs and practices."

"I don't follow," said George.

"The pagan community in the UK continues to evolve and adapt, with a growing interest in ecological and environmental issues and a commitment to preserving and celebrating the natural world." She took another deep, calming breath. "What Penny's murderer has committed is the complete opposite, antithetical, and absolutely contradictory to what we believe in."

"Did you have much to do with Penny?" asked Jay.

"Of course," Diana explained. "We have many roles, such as

Treasurer, Chief First Aider, secretary, Public Relations officer and even a Keeper of the Stones. Penny came to me because she wanted to get more involved, so we were training her to become Treasurer once Nicole decided to retire, if that makes sense?"

By this point, they'd been chatting for over an hour, and Fred arrived with more coffee, distributing the cups.

"Can you share anything else about Penny?"

"Only that she was interested in our handfasting ceremony and asked if I'd be because I am an independent civil celebrant, able to conduct a ceremony for her and Caden."

"What kind of ceremony was that?"

Diana smiled mischievously. "Paganism is legally recognised as a religion in the UK, and pagans have the same rights and protections as followers of other established faiths. This recognition has helped pagan communities gain acceptance and rights, such as the ability to perform legally recognised marriages and conduct religious ceremonies." Diana licked her lips. "Handfasting is a word we use to describe a marriage rite between two people who wish to make a public commitment to each other in a way that is spiritually meaningful to them." A sudden stray tear fell from her eye. "I remember when Penny asked me about it because she wanted to broach the subject with Caden." She shrugged. "Alas, they broke up not long after."

"And is that legally binding?" asked George.

Diana shook her head. "No. Unfortunately, as the law currently stands in England, Pagan celebrants and venues cannot meet the requirements of the State and the Registrar General, so handfasting has no legal status here. In short, they still have to get married legally at a registry office."

CHAPTER FIFTEEN

"That's a shame," said Jay.

"I agree, but the rules will catch up eventually, as they always do. Though it'll probably be too late, as always."

"Can you tell us anything else about Penny?" asked Jay.

"I'm sorry, but no, other than that, she was a kind-hearted, lovely young woman with the world her oyster." She closed her eyes and inhaled deeply. "She was taken far too early."

"What about Peter?" George asked.

Diana frowned. "Peter?"

"Do you have somebody named Peter in your group?"

"Of course we do. Peter is a very common name," Diana said.

"And did this Peter spend a lot of time with Penny?"

"It depends on which Peter you're talking about," she said.

"Whichever one spent the most time with Penny," George said. He didn't like playing games with Diana, but it appeared she was insulted by the suggestion there was a murderer within her group.

Jay pulled out his PNB and flicked to the correct page. After skimming it, he looked at Diana and said, "Penny's parents told us that on the night she died, she was going out with a man named Peter, who was part of your group. We naturally want to speak with him and ask him some questions, as he may be the last person, other than the killer, to see Penny alive."

Chapter Sixteen

"What did you think of all that then?" DC Jason Scott asked George as the DI manoeuvred the Mercedes down Coniston Avenue, away from Diana Rubadue's house. It was unusual for Jay to turn the conversation contemplative. Unfortunately for the young DC, he couldn't help but mull over the tangled web of their current investigation.

"It's a lot to take in, isn't it? But at least we knew the killer wasn't attempting a pagan ritual."

"But what is he attempting, boss?" Jay asked.

"I guess once Jordan admits to everything, he'll tell us, won't he?" George said with a grin.

The DI thought about their suspect. Jordan Rathmell was a man who left an impression, though not necessarily a positive one. He stood about five foot ten, with a somewhat stocky build that had lost its youthful vigour as he approached his forties. His once-chiselled features had succumbed to the wear and tear of time and the consequences of a less-than-healthy lifestyle.

His thinning, greying hair, once a dark chestnut, now clung desperately to his scalp, and his unkempt beard tried, in vain, to mask the wrinkles that etched deep lines on his face. Jordan's hazel eyes, once lively, had dulled over the years, and they held a sly, calculating look that made people uneasy in his presence.

Jordan's wardrobe choices leaned towards the shabby and uninspired, with a penchant for ill-fitting suits that seemed like hand-me-downs from a bygone era. He often smelled faintly of stale cigarette smoke, a testament to his vice of choice.

Perhaps the most unnerving aspect of Jordan Rathmell was the way he carried himself. He had a habit of leering at women, and his eyes would linger just a second too long, making them feel uncomfortable. Though not unpleasant, his voice held an unsettling charm that he had likely used to manipulate more than a few people in his life.

Overall, Jordan Rathmell presented an image of a man whose best days were behind him, a man who had succumbed to the darker impulses of his character. His appearance and demeanour combined to create an aura of suspicion, making it easy to believe that he might be capable of more than he admitted.

"There's more chance of it being this Peter," Jay said.

"Even if it is, we can charge him for unlawful entry. I'm convinced his prints will be on the keys we sent off."

"You don't think it's wrong to keep him locked away at the station if he's innocent?" asked Jay.

They pulled up to a set of traffic lights, and George turned to his left and stared at the young DC. "Jordan Rathmell is not an innocent man, Jay," George explained. "He's a forty-year-old man chasing after young women because they flirted with him for tips." The light turned green, so George floored the Merc. "Don't forget he was done for sexual assault, too."

"Which he profusely denies, boss."

"He denies everything, Jay." George shook his head. "That man doesn't have an honest bone in his body."

"But what if we're missing something, boss?" Jay asked, his brow furrowed. "I mean, Jordan Rathmell might be a creep, but he might not be our murderer. We can't ignore any leads, can we?"

George sighed, gripping the steering wheel a little tighter. "Then get me a lead I can use that takes us away from Rathmell, Jay," George said. "I know we can't afford to tunnel vision on Jordan, but we need more evidence, something concrete to tie him to this case or clear his name."

The Mercedes cruised through the busy streets, the city's rush-hour ambience setting a solemn mood inside the car. George couldn't shake the feeling that they were still chasing shadows.

"Remember, we're here to find the truth," George said with determination. "Whether it's Rathmell or someone else, we must ensure justice is served. But we go where the evidence takes us, and at the minute, it's taking us to Jordan Rathmell."

Jason nodded, feeling the weight of the responsibility they carried. "I just hope we can wrap this up soon. We're only two days in, and it's already been a hell of a case, boss."

* * *

With an intent to gather more about Peter, who might have been connected to Penny's life and murder, Detective Inspector George Beaumont and Detective Constable Jay Scott returned to Capri.

"Nice to see you again, detectives," Elena Testa, the hostess, said. "Do you need Tony?"

CHAPTER SIXTEEN

"Please," George said. She nodded and went to inform Tony Ricci, the restaurant manager, of the detectives' arrival. Tony joined them shortly after and agreed to help facilitate the interviews with the staff regarding Peter.

Soon, they began speaking with Penny's co-workers, starting with Sofia Fontana, Penny's fellow waitress.

Detective Beaumont asked Sofia, "Do you know anyone named Peter who might have been associated with Penny?"

Sofia furrowed her brows, thinking for a moment. "Peter... Peter Thompson, you mean? He's a regular customer here. He's been coming in for years."

Detective Scott said, "Can you tell us more about Peter Thompson? How often did he visit, and what was his relationship with Penny like?"

Sofia replied, "Peter's a friendly guy, always orders a glass of red wine and the Spaghetti Bolognese. He and Penny sometimes chatted when he came in, but I wouldn't say they were close. Just the usual friendly banter. We try to get tips."

The detectives then spoke with Carlo Esposito, the head chef.

"Carlo, do you know anyone named Peter who might have been associated with Penny?" Detective Beaumont inquired.

"I know of one or two Peters who come to the restaurant," he said. "She's a waitress, so they all interact with her."

"Does anybody specific come to mind? Is there anybody who would give her a bit more attention than the other servers? Anyone who would ask for her to serve them specifically?"

"You're referring to Peter Thompson, aren't you?"

"You tell us," said Jay.

"OK." Carlo nodded. "Yeah, Peter's a regular. He sits at the bar while he eats, usually on weekends. He and Penny would exchange a few words, but nothing unusual. But I know out of

Penny and Sofia, he prefers Penny."

George asked, "Any idea why?"

"No idea, detective. Sorry."

Detective Scott asked, "Did you ever notice anything odd or suspicious about Peter's interactions with Penny?"

Carlo thought for a moment before replying, "No, not really. He seemed like a typical customer." He shrugged. "She was a pretty girl; maybe he had a crush?"

The detectives continued their inquiries, speaking with Elena Testa, the hostess, and Lorenzo Lombardi, the barman, and received similar accounts about Peter Thompson. He was a regular customer, but his interactions with Penny seemed ordinary and friendly.

Tony Ricci, the manager, also confirmed that Peter Thompson was a well-known patron but didn't have any additional information to provide about him or his connection to Penny.

As the interviews concluded, it appeared that Peter Thompson was a regular customer at Capri, and while he had some interactions with Penny, nothing stood out as suspicious or unusual. Nevertheless, the detectives noted his name and decided to conduct further inquiries to determine if any relevant information might link him to Penny's murder.

With frustration growing as their leads regarding Peter had yielded little information, George decided to shift the focus and inquire about Jordan Rathmell.

The detectives spoke with Lorenzo, the barman, first. "I don't remember names very well; do you have a picture?" he asked.

George pulled up Jordan's mugshot on his phone and showed it to the barman. "Maybe, I'm not sure. He's not one of the friendly regulars, that's for sure."

Next, they spoke with Elena, the hostess, who recognised Rathmell's picture and knew he'd been in the restaurant recently but couldn't say whether he even talked to Penny or not.

Sofia, Penny's server friend, furrowed her brows when George asked her about Jordan, thinking for a moment. Eventually, she said, "Jordan Rathmell... doesn't ring a bell, sorry."

Detective Beaumont followed up, "Can you recall if Penny ever mentioned a person named Jordan, even in passing?"

Sofia shook her head. "No, I can't say I ever heard her mention that name."

Again, George showed her an image of Jordan. "He looks familiar, but not enough that I could put a name to a face, sorry."

The detectives finally spoke with Carlo, the head chef.

"Carlo, have you ever seen or heard of Jordan Rathmell at the restaurant?" Detective Beaumont inquired.

Detective Scott added, "Did you ever notice Penny having any unusual interactions or conversations with someone named Jordan, even if it was outside of work?"

Carlo thought for a moment. "No, the name doesn't sound familiar to me, sorry." He shrugged. "And outside of work, I don't know much. Penny was a professional, and her personal life wasn't something she discussed openly at work. I can't recall anything specific."

Eventually, they got around to interviewing Tony Ricci, the manager, who unfortunately also confirmed that the name Jordan Rathmell did not ring a bell, and there were no records of such a person visiting the restaurant.

When George showed a screenshot taken from CCTV and the mugshot, Tony said he knew who they meant, but he must have made the bookings under different names and paid in cash.

As the interviews concluded, it appeared that Jordan Rathmell was not a familiar figure to the staff at Capri, and there were no apparent links between him and Penny Pritchard.

Before leaving, George asked Tony for copies of the restaurant bookings so they could look into what names Jordan had used instead of his own.

* * *

George now shifted his focus to Pizza Express, where they hoped to gather information about Joy Pritchard and her potential connection to a man named Peter. They were greeted by Jared Simmons, the manager, and Lucy Moss, one of Joy's co-workers.

"Good afternoon," Detective Beaumont greeted them. "Yes, we're back. We'd like to speak with you and Lucy, Jared, and anyone else who worked closely with Joy. We have some questions about a man named Peter who may have been an acquaintance of Joy."

Jared Simmons, a tall, thin man, nodded in acknowledgment and motioned for the detectives to follow him. Lucy Moss, a young woman in a Pizza Express uniform, joined them, her blue eyes attentive and curious.

Once they were gathered in a quieter section of the restaurant, Detective Scott began the conversation. "Thank you for your cooperation, Jared and Lucy. We're investigating the murder of Joy Pritchard, and we believe that she may have had some connection with a man named Peter. Do either of you know anything about him?"

CHAPTER SIXTEEN

Jared glanced at Lucy, who then spoke up, "Peter... Peter Collins, you mean? He's been coming here for a while."

Detective Beaumont inquired further, "Can you tell us more about Peter Collins? How often did he visit, and what was his relationship with Joy like?"

Jared answered, "Peter's a regular customer. He usually comes in for lunch on weekdays. Joy was one of our servers who often waited on his table. They seemed to get along well, and Peter always left a good tip."

Lucy chimed in, "Yes, Peter and Joy chatted quite a bit. He was friendly, and Joy was her usual cheerful self around him."

Detective Scott asked, "Did either of you notice anything odd or suspicious about Peter's interactions with Joy?"

Jared considered the question before responding, "No, not at all. They just seemed like friendly acquaintances."

Lucy added, "Joy never mentioned any problems or concerns regarding Peter. She seemed comfortable serving him."

The detectives continued to gather information from Jared and Lucy, learning that Peter Collins was indeed a regular customer at Pizza Express. He had a friendly rapport with Joy, but nothing unusual or concerning had been observed during their interactions.

As the interviews concluded, Detective Beaumont thanked Jared and Lucy for their cooperation and took note of Peter Collins as a potential person of interest. Unfortunately, Jared and Lucy couldn't provide Peter's address, but promised to alert the DI personally the next time he came to the restaurant.

Chapter Seventeen

Detective Inspector George Beaumont, recognising the urgency of the investigation into the murder of Joy Pritchard, decided to set up a press conference at Elland Road. The purpose of the press conference was to allow Joy's grieving family, her husband Shane, and their two young children, Seth and Gwen, to appeal to the public for any information that could assist in solving the case. It was an effort to generate public awareness and encourage potential witnesses to come forward with valuable information.

The DI had also invited Penny Haigh's parents to appeal for information, but they'd declined, telling George they were too upset to do anything.

George understood and ensured the FLO was still creating a respectful and supportive environment for the grieving family during this challenging time.

"Are you ready?" George asked Shane.

The grieving man was dressed in a dark suit and held a framed photograph of Joy in his hands. His presence conveyed the weight of the family's loss. "Not really, mate, no."

"You doing this could break the case," George explained. "I really appreciate you all doing this."

"OK, mate, whatever you think."

CHAPTER SEVENTEEN

The press had gathered in the room beyond, nosy vultures, setting up their cameras and microphones.

Detective Inspector Beaumont and Detective Chief Inspector Atkinson stood alongside Shane Pritchard, whose eyes were red from grief, offering their support. Nearby, a child psychologist was on standby to assist Seth and Gwen should they become overwhelmed.

As the press conference began, Shane Pritchard, accompanied by his children, stepped up to the podium. His voice quivered with emotion as he spoke about his late wife, Joy, and their desperate need for answers in her tragic murder. He shared anecdotes about Joy, her love for their children, and the void her absence had left in their lives.

Seth, dressed in a neat shirt and tie, with his tiny hand clutching his father's, and Gwen, wearing a light-coloured dress and closed-toe shoes and holding a stuffed toy for a sense of security, stood by Shane's side as he made a heartfelt plea to the public. Shane Pritchard's appeal to the public was heartfelt and emotional. His words emphasised the devastating impact of Joy's loss on their family.

Seth and Gwen, though too young to speak in detail, stood as a symbol of the family's pain and suffering. Their presence resonated with the public, evoking empathy and compassion.

Detective Beaumont reiterated the importance of the appeal, urging anyone with information related to Joy's murder to come forward. He assured the public that their information would be treated with utmost sensitivity and confidentiality and that no matter how insignificant it might seem, to come forward and assist in the investigation.

That was when chaos ensued, and Seth Pritchard broke away from his father's hand. "I miss my mummy!" he screamed.

"A bad man took her away, and this man," he said, pointing at George, "is going to catch him. So please, help him!"

The psychologist got involved then and pulled the family away from the press conference, meaning Detective Inspector George Beaumont, having already facilitated a press conference for Joy Pritchard's case, now found himself addressing the media once more, this time to appeal for information about the murder of Penny Haigh. He approached the podium with a sense of determination, flanked by DS Luke Mason and DS Yolanda Williams, DC Tashan Blackburn and DC Jay Scott, who showed a united front and a commitment to solving the case.

Standing confidently at the podium, Detective Beaumont was dressed formally in his suit. He exuded an air of authority and seriousness as he prepared to address the media and the public.

Detective Beaumont's appeal was clear and purposeful. He began by acknowledging the tragic loss of Penny Haigh and the pain it had caused her loved ones. He then delved into the details of the investigation, highlighting the significance of a man named Peter, who was believed to be a close acquaintance of Penny. He then stressed the importance of any information related to Peter and his connection to Penny, ensuring he got his point across that even seemingly insignificant details could be crucial to the investigation. Again, he assured potential witnesses that their information would be treated with the utmost confidentiality and that the police were committed to providing support and protection for those who came forward.

Then a man with salt and pepper hair that was receding asked the question he'd been expecting. "Is there a link between the murders of Joy Pritchard and Penny Haigh with what is going on in Bradford at the minute?"

"No, there is not," said George, and he ended the questions so he could return to the solace of the Incident Room.

Ultimately, the press conference was a poignant and emotional moment, capturing the attention of both the media and the public. The event was broadcast live on television and streamed online, ensuring widespread coverage. It served as a reminder of the human toll that crime takes and the importance of community cooperation in solving such cases.

And it helped the public, too, because it showed that Detective Inspector George Beaumont remained committed to pursuing every lead, and the press conference was just one step in the ongoing effort to bring justice for Joy Pritchard and Penny Haigh and closure for their grieving families.

Chapter Eighteen

Detective Inspector George Beaumont sat in Incident Room Five at Elland Road Police Station, his gaze fixed on the CCTV footage displayed on the large monitor. The grainy video showed Joy Pritchard stepping out of her blue Vauxhall Mokka, which was parked on the bend of Thwaite Lane, where the Renault was parked the previous day.

The Renault had been a dead-end, an older couple walking their dog who had seen nothing and heard nothing.

Joy's movements appeared hurried and tense as she scanned her surroundings before approaching the graffiti-covered bridge.

George knew he needed to act quickly. The circumstances surrounding Joy Pritchard's death were unsettling, and he couldn't afford to waste any time. He reached for his phone and dialled the number for Lindsey Yardley.

"Lindsey, it's DI Beaumont." He explained about the abandoned Mokka on Thwaite Lane. "I need you to attend the scene immediately. We've got a potential lead on Joy Pritchard's case," he said with urgency in his voice.

While waiting for the CSI unit to arrive and get to work, George made a swift decision. He knew that being on the scene himself might provide valuable insights and allow him

CHAPTER EIGHTEEN

to gather critical information. He grabbed his coat, slipped his phone into his pocket, and headed out of the Incident Room.

Moments later, George Beaumont was behind the wheel of his Mercedes, navigating the streets of Leeds. The sky was overcast, casting a gloomy atmosphere over the city. As he approached Thwaite Lane, he couldn't help but feel a sense of unease. Something was not right about this case, and he was determined to get to the bottom of it.

With each passing minute, the mystery surrounding Joy Pritchard's murder deepened. DI Beaumont knew he was racing against the clock to find answers and bring those responsible to justice.

* * *

As Detective Inspector George Beaumont arrived at the scene on Thwaite Lane, he was greeted by the Crime Scene Manager, Lindsey Yardley. Lindsey, a confident and experienced blonde woman, was known for her meticulous approach to crime scene management.

"Lindsey," George nodded in acknowledgement as he stepped out of his Mercedes. "Thanks for coming out here so quickly. We've got a potential lead with Joy Pritchard's case, and I want to make sure we don't miss anything."

Lindsey Yardley gave a nod in return, her professional demeanour unwavering. "Of course, George. I'm here to assist in any way I can. Let's get to work."

Together, they approached Joy Pritchard's blue Vauxhall Mokka parked on the bend of Thwaite Lane. The vehicle was a key piece of evidence, and Lindsey wasted no time in instructing her team to start processing it for any potential clues.

As they meticulously examined the car and the surrounding area, George and Lindsey remained focused on their task. The graffiti-covered bridge ahead cast an eerie shadow, and the atmosphere was tense with the uncertainty of what they might uncover.

George knew that having someone as competent and dedicated as Lindsey Yardley managing the crime scene was essential. Her attention to detail and expertise would be crucial in piecing together the puzzle of Joy Pritchard's disappearance. Together, they were determined to bring the truth to light and ensure justice was served.

While Lindsey and her team meticulously combed through Joy Pritchard's blue Mokka, searching for any clues or evidence to shed light on her disappearance, George kept looking at his watch. He was supposed to be at Mia's already, having planned an overnight stay for Jack last week.

As the time wore on, and CSI carefully examined the vehicle, Lindsey soon made a critical discovery that would prove crucial to the case.

Hidden beneath the driver's seat, Lindsey found a small, crumpled piece of paper. It appeared to be a handwritten note, partially torn and stained with what looked like coffee. She carefully extracted the note with gloved hands, unfolded it, and placed it into an Exhibit bag.

She passed it to George, who read it. "Meet me at the bridge tonight. Bring the money. Peter."

This message sent a shiver down George's spine. It was a potentially crucial lead in the case. The note hinted at a clandestine meeting at the graffiti-covered bridge. This was also the second handwritten note they had. He needed to

CHAPTER EIGHTEEN

get it back to the lab ASAP so the graphologist could inspect it, as with this new piece of evidence in hand, they now had a direction to follow. The mysterious note suggested a possible connection between Joy Pritchard's murder and an undisclosed meeting, possibly involving money and an unknown individual referred to as Peter.

"Could it be the same Peter who Penny was seeing?" George said aloud.

If so, they needed to find him ASAP.

* * *

As George arrived at Mia Alexander's house to pick up their son, Jack, the tension in the air was palpable. The history between them was marred by betrayal and heartbreak, and today, was no exception. George had moved on with his life, engaged to Isabella Wood, and they had a beautiful baby daughter named Olivia Beaumont. However, the wounds from Mia's past actions were still fresh.

Mia's betrayal had been a devastating blow to George, as she had cheated on him with the serial killer the press had named the Miss Murderer, shattering their engagement and trust. Now, standing in the doorway of Mia's home—no, his home—he couldn't help but feel a surge of anger and resentment.

Their argument erupted almost instantly, their voices rising as accusations and pent-up emotions spilt into the open.

"You didn't call to say you were picking Jack up, George," Mia said, "So you can't have him tonight."

George's voice was laced with bitterness as he confronted Mia. "You're going to stop me from seeing my son?"

Mia folded her arms defensively as George's bitter words

hit home. Then suddenly, her eyes softened, and she stepped closer to George. "I'm not trying to stop you from seeing our son, George. I just need a little more notice. It's unfair for you to show up unannounced and expect everything to be OK. Surely you understand that?"

She attempted to place her hand on his arm, but George recoiled as if her hand was a snake.

George furiously shook his head and clenched his fists, struggling to contain his anger. "You've always got an excuse, Mia. You know I have a right to see my son, whether I call ahead or not." He ground his teeth. "You've known about this since last week."

Mia's face flushed with frustration. "Of course, you have a right, but you also have a responsibility to let me know when you're coming. Jack has a schedule, and you can't just disrupt it whenever you please."

"How am I disrupting it if you knew about it since last week?"

"Because you always let Jack down whenever you have a big case!" she screamed. "I know all about the murders. I just assumed, OK!"

Their argument had become a familiar dance of blame and resentment, with Jack again caught in the middle. Their voices escalated, echoing through the hallway and drawing the attention of young Jack, who had been playing quietly in the living room. He peeked around the corner, his small face etched with confusion and concern.

George's frustration turned into desperation. "Mia, for Christ's sake, can't we just put our differences aside for Jack's sake? He deserves to have both parents in his life, without all this drama."

CHAPTER EIGHTEEN

Mia's resolve wavered for a moment as she looked at their son. Her voice softened slightly, but the hurt lingered. "I want what's best for Jack George, but you need to respect our routines. We can't keep living like this."

The argument hung in the air, heavy and unresolved. Jack watched his parents, his innocent heart heavy with the weight of their conflict. It was a stark reminder that, despite their shared history and love for their son, the wounds of betrayal and mistrust continued to drive a wedge between them, making it difficult to find common ground.

"Are you sure you want what's best for Jack and not what's best for you?" George asked.

"What the hell do you mean?"

"You know exactly what I mean, Mia!" He bit the inside of his cheek. "If all of this is your way of trying to manipulate the situation to get us back together, then—"

"Don't flatter yourself, George; I've moved on, and so have you," she said, her tone laced with venom. "How dare you accuse me of trying to manipulate anyone after you didn't tell me the truth about you and Isabella!"

"Just remember it was you who destroyed our family, Mia. For God's sake, you cheated on me with a serial killer."

"I know I made a terrible mistake, George, but I've paid for it by losing you. I've been through therapy, and I'm trying to be a better person for Jack." She paused. "I'm struggling so much." She shook her head. "You never understand!" Then suddenly, her face etched with regret, and she fired back, "Don't forget that you put mine and our son's life in danger when you let that blonde bimbo invade your life!"

She was referring to the serial killer the press had dubbed the Blonde Delilah, who had threatened Mia and Jack's lives.

George's frustration boiled over. "Therapy won't erase the issues you continue to cause, Mia!" He paused. "If you're struggling so much, maybe I should have Jack for a bit. He can be with me and his sister for a bit whilst you get the help you need."

On the verge of tears, Mia said, "You can't keep Jack away from his mother, George. I love him, and he deserves to have both of us in his life."

"I agree, but if you're struggling, then—"

"No, he stays with me!"

The argument raged on, a whirlwind of hurtful words, regrets, and unresolved emotions. Jack, caught in the middle of this emotional storm, watched with wide eyes, his innocent heart torn between his parents.

As the argument ended, and George left the East Ardsley house without Jack, it was clear that the wounds from their past ran deep, and finding a resolution would not be easy. It was a painful reminder that the scars of betrayal were not quickly healed, and the road to reconciliation would be long and arduous.

Chapter Nineteen

George returned home to Morley, parking the Merc on the drive.

With a sleeping Olivia Beaumont in her arms, Isabella Wood glanced up as George let himself in. "You looked extremely hot on TV tonight, babe," she said with a wink.

"Thanks," he said, mirroring her wink. "Sorry I'm late, gorgeous; it's been one of those nights."

"Where's Jack?" she asked.

"Mia wouldn't let me have him," George explained.

Isabella looked at George with a mixture of concern and disappointment. She carefully laid Olivia down in her cot before walking over to him. "I can't believe she did that to you again," she said, putting her arms around his neck and pulling him in tight. "George, this has to stop, you know. You have a right to see your son; she can't keep using him against you like this."

George sighed, running a hand through his blond hair. "I know, Isabella, but it's just so difficult dealing with her sometimes. Every time I try to reason with her, it becomes a huge argument."

Isabella pulled away and began kissing him lightly on the lips. She then placed her hands on his cheeks and kissed his forehead. "I get it; it's not easy, but we have a family now, George, and Jack is a part of that. We can't let Mia's actions disrupt our lives like this. We need to find a way to handle this situation better."

George nodded, appreciating Isabella's support. "You're right, as always. Thank you." He paused. "Do you think I should talk to a solicitor tomorrow?"

"I don't know, George, that's up to you."

"I think we need a more formal arrangement for Jack's sake and ours."

Isabella gave him a reassuring smile. "We'll figure this out, George. We're in this together, and we'll make sure that Jack gets the love and stability he deserves."

* * *

Later—after eating their Chinese because neither could be bothered to cook—the pair discussed how they could effectively sort out the issue with Mia, Izzy said, "How come you were home so late, anyway?"

"We have a suspect."

Izzy's eyes brightened. "And?"

"We've arrested him, but Jay's not convinced because he hardly seems capable," George explained. "He denied the murder and said it had nothing to do with him. We do know he'd been into victim two's house because I got confirmation on the way home from Mia's that his prints were on the spare set of keys they kept outside."

"Guess you'll at least have him for unlawful entry, eh?" she said.

"That's what I said to Jay, but he kinda shrugged it off."

"He's young and ambitious, babe," she said. "He'll want to be a DS soon, and this is probably his way of making that happen."

"Yeah, you're probably right, gorgeous," he admitted. "I think if we find something else to connect him with the two victims, then it's him, whether he denies it or not." He shrugged. "The team's working on it, but we all need a break at some point."

She grinned. "Yep, or you'll burn yourselves out."

Chapter Twenty

George looked up from his toast and coffee as Isabella entered the kitchen, heading straight for the kettle. He was in pain, the injuries from the accident plaguing him. But he didn't want to take his painkillers because they dulled his mind.

The Chinese from last night was repeating on him, which didn't help.

Isabella broke the morning silence. "What are your plans for today, gorgeous?" Isabella said.

"First, I'm heading back to Joy Pritchard's house. I want to interview her husband again now that he's had some time to process the murder. He might provide valuable insights into Rathmell's obsession with Joy. And I want to ask him about Peter."

George headed to Richmond Hill, and whilst on his way, he called Luke to update him on his location. The DI then knocked on the Pritchard's front door, and Cathy, the FLO, answered. Cathy, dressed casually in jeans and a T-shirt, had a dual role—to support the family and discreetly monitor any suspicious activities or information.

"Good morning, sir," Cathy greeted him.

George asked, "How's everything going in there?"

"As well as can be expected. The kids seem to be coping

but spending most of their time in their room on tablets or watching TV."

"And Shane?" George inquired.

"He mostly sits in the living room, unsure of what to do with himself. There's not much he can do regarding funeral arrangements since we don't know when Joy's body will be released. He's not talking much, although I've tried to engage him in conversation."

The situation was challenging to navigate. Cathy was there to assist with the investigation but couldn't push too hard, given the family's grief.

"Has he mentioned anything that might aid the investigation?" George asked.

"Not so far. I've asked Shane several times if he could think of anyone who might have wanted to harm Joy, but he always says no. According to him, everyone loved her."

George nodded. That's what Shane had told him. "What about his extended family? Has he contacted any of them?"

"No, he's adamant he wants to be alone with the children."

"Has he shared any general thoughts about Joy, their relationship, or how she interacted with the kids?"

It felt like grasping at straws. George doubted he could either if Cathy couldn't get him to open up.

"Not really. He's been in a daze. When he's not preparing meals for the children, he's just sitting there, lost in thought. Taking care of them is what's keeping him going. I've offered to help, but he insists on doing everything himself."

"OK. I'm going to have a chat with him."

Together, they entered the living room, and Shane Pritchard looked up.

"Would you like me to make you some tea or coffee?" Cathy

offered.

"Coffee would be great," George replied, hoping the caffeine would alleviate his headache. The DI then turned her attention to Shane. "How are you holding up, mate?"

"How do you think?" he responded, the pain evident in his eyes. "I still can't believe it. I keep hoping Joy will walk through the front door as if nothing happened. But I know she won't, not after seeing her at the morgue." He leaned forward, burying his head in his hands and emitting a low groan.

George felt a pang of sympathy. The DI wanted to console him and assure him that things would get better, but he knew it most likely wouldn't get better. That, and Shane could still be a suspect in Joy's murder.

"What about the kids? How are they dealing with all of this?"

"Dunno; they're spending a lot of time in their rooms, glued to their technology. Normally, we limit their screen time, but this is far from normal, so I'm letting them stay on for as long as they want. What else can they do?" He shrugged. "I don't want them to go back to school until after the funeral. But I don't know when that will be," he replied, his jaw tightening. "Do you?"

George shook his head. "Unfortunately, mate, the timing is out of our control. You have to wait until the coroner releases Joy's body before the funeral arrangements can go ahead."

"I understand," Shane said, letting out a heavy sigh.

"During our investigation, we came across a man named Jordan Rathmell. He was a frequent customer at Pizza Express. Did she ever mention him to you?"

Shane slowly shook his head. "She rarely talked about her work. It wasn't 'er career, just a way to earn some extra money that fit in with me, the kids, and her studies," he explained,

CHAPTER TWENTY

furrowing his brow. He paused for a long time, then said, "Actually, she did mention one guy who she thought had a crush on her. Is that who you're referring to? The one who sent her some flowers."

George knew from the interview with Jordan that he'd sent her flowers but was shocked she'd shared that fact with her husband. The shock must have been evident on George's face because Shane added, "We had that kind of relationship, Detective—no secrets. She said he was harmless. And a great tipper."

"And you were fine with that?" George questioned, his surprise evident. Most men he knew wouldn't take such news so lightly. What did it imply? Were they short of money? Did he need to delve deeper into their bank accounts?

"I didn't like it." He shrugged. "Who would? But the fact that she told me meant it didn't mean anything."

"I'm sorry to inform you that we have reason to believe he was stalking Joy. He knows where you live." George left him to connect the dots.

"You think it's him?" His trembling hand moved to his chest.

"We're still investigating, but he certainly had more than a passing interest in her. Did Joy ever mention anything missing recently?" George broached the sensitive topic.

"What do you mean?" Shane inquired.

"Did she ever report any missing items, perhaps underwear, especially from the washing line?"

"Not that I know of. She rarely hung laundry out; she preferred to use the dryer," he replied, not offering the information George hoped for. If Rathmell hadn't taken the underwear from the laundry line, there was only one other way he could have acquired it. "It pissed me off that she used the dryer, like, but she didn't want the neighbours to see her underwear."

"Does anyone else have keys to your house? Or had you or Joy lost your keys recently?"

"What? Why?" Then, as if realising what the DI meant, Shane tensed, his entire body going rigid. "You think he entered our house?" He stared at George, his eyes wide. "Did he have Joy's underwear? Is that what you're saying?"

George took out his phone and pulled up a photo of two pairs of white lacy underwear found in Rathmell's bedroom. He then sat down beside Shane on the sofa.

"Please take a look at this photo. Do you recognise these?" George held his phone out, and Shane stared at it.

Shane's face drained of colour as he exclaimed, "Oh. My. God. Those are Joy's. See the little J's on there? I got them custom-made for her for our wedding. Her something new. She wanted two pairs so she could wear them on our wedding night, too." He blushed, but his face soon turned an angry red. "That means he's been here. I'll kill the bastard if I see him," his eyes flashing with anger.

"We don't know for certain that he came into your home uninvited," George said, trying to calm him.

"Joy would have mentioned if he'd turned up. As far as I know, she had no idea he knew where we lived. Joy was home during the day, so if he came in, he must have waited for her to go out. And then I'd have been in the with the kids, so I'm not sure how." And then it clicked what George had meant. "Wait, uninvited. What the fuck are you suggesting?"

"I'm not suggesting anything," George said, holding up his hands. Shane's explanation seemed plausible. But how had

Rathmell gained entry into their house? "Assuming he did come in while everyone was out, how would he have gained entry?" George inquired. "Would it be even possible?"

"Yes, it's possible," he replied, leaning forward and clutching his head in both hands. "Ever since the time Joy locked herself and the children out, we've kept a set of door keys hidden in the front garden. He must have known. But how, though?"

"Maybe she mentioned it in the pub, or he'd been watching her. Maybe she'd forgotten her keys one day and had to use the spares?"

"I guess so," he said, resigned to the possibility.

"Let's go and check to see if the key is still there," George suggested.

Shane got up, and the DI followed him out of the front door and into the garden. He stopped beside a row of gnomes.

"It's here," he said as he lifted the one that was nearest the door, furthest away from the living room window, but there was nothing there. "It's gone. He must have taken it."

"Check under the other gnomes," the DI urged.

"It won't be under any of them. We chose the first one because we got married on the first of the month."

"Let's just check," George insisted, bending down and lifting the gnomes. To both their surprise, the DI found the keys under the sixth gnome. "As I said."

"We didn't put them there," Shane noted, his voice trembling. "She wouldn't put it there."

"You're sure of that?" George asked, and Shane nodded. So, George pulled out an evidence bag and put on some gloves. "I'll take the keys and get them dusted for prints." Then they returned inside, where Shane appeared numb, coming to terms with the realisation that someone had been inside their home.

"Are you sure Joy wasn't concerned by Rathmell's behaviour when she was at work?" George inquired.

"No," Shane replied. "She was used to customers liking her. It helped with tips."

"Were you struggling for money?" George asked.

"Who isn't these days?" Shane said.

George nodded. According to Tashan, statements were on their way. "Do you know a man named Peter?"

"Peter, what?"

"We don't have a surname."

Shane narrowed his eyes and thought for a moment. "Her ex was called Peter."

Interesting. "Peter, what?"

"Drury."

George sent a quick email to the shared inbox, wanting somebody to look into Peter Drury.

"Did she always tell you what happened at work?"

Shane recoiled, confused by the change in questioning. "Yes, of course," Shane answered. "I trusted her. She said her boss watched out for all of the staff, so I knew nothing was going to happen... except it did," he said, collapsing inwardly and emitting a deep groan. "How am I meant to carry on without her?"

Cathy, the FLO, entered the room carrying a tray with three mugs of coffee.

"I've been explaining to Shane that we're aware of someone following Joy and knowing where they lived. We'll be investigating further and will keep him up to speed."

After finishing his coffee, George walked to the door, with Cathy following.

CHAPTER TWENTY

"We've arrested the one who was stalking Joy, but I don't want Shane to know until we've confirmed our suspect's guilt. But it's looking most likely," George explained.

"I won't mention anything," Cathy assured him. "Did he kill Penny Haigh too?"

"He's saying no, but we're pushing," said George. "Stay with Shane. He's in a bad way and appears as if he's about to break. Try to convince him to call some family."

"Yes, sir."

"If you can't, find out why. Is he running from something? Or someone? We haven't yet got her laptop back from forensics. There might be something on there that could point to any family issues. And he keeps mentioning money. Maybe someone's out to get them."

* * *

George drove back to the station, his mind preoccupied with thoughts of Shane Pritchard and his grieving family. On his way to the incident room, he noticed DCI Atkinson heading in his direction and groaned inwardly. "Sir," he acknowledged with a nod.

"I understand you've been to see the victim's husband and mentioned the stalker who's now in custody," Atkinson said.

"Yes, sir. We've arrested someone, and I've requested to keep him in custody for ninety-six hours to give us time to line up our evidence."

"I'll expedite the request to ensure it goes through quickly. Excellent work. It's about time we solved a murder promptly instead of having it linger, potentially leading to more," he said, wearing a self-satisfied smile.

"Well, sir, while it appears likely that our suspect is responsible, we must determine the motive and why he committed the murder in that specific manner. His guilt is not yet confirmed." He paused, and the DCI frowned. "We also still don't know how he connects to Penny Haigh's murder."

"You know how these stalkers can be. Maybe he asked her to leave her husband, and she turned him down flat, embarrassing him in front of others at the restaurant," Atkinson theorised. "And as for your link, maybe we have two killers on the loose, as much as I'd hate that." He, too, paused. "Yes, I think that'll be the case. It's obvious Jordan Rathmell heard about Penny's murder last night and decided to be a copycat to try to get away with it."

George was not convinced. The victims had been laid out the same. And then there was the handwritten note to consider. The graphologist was currently studying evidence they'd obtained from Jordan Rathmell, which would likely make or break their case. "We'll investigate all angles," George replied, clenching his fists at his sides.

DCI Atkinson nodded and walked away.

Chapter Twenty-one

George placed his jacket on the back of the chair in his office and was about to turn on his laptop when Jay burst through the door and approached him.

"Everything OK?" he inquired.

"We've discovered another body, boss," Jay replied.

"What?" He swallowed hard. "In Stourton?" George couldn't believe it. Not another one. It was now undeniable they were dealing with a serial killer.

"No, boss, in Woodhouse."

His heart sank. It was precisely what he didn't need that morning. Then something else occurred to him. Shite. "We've still got Rathmell in custody. You know what that means, don't you?"

The DC looked smug but immediately tried to hide it.

"It means you were right, DC Scott," George said.

"Should I arrange to have him released?" the DC asked.

"Not until he's charged with illegally entering the Pritchard household and stealing Joy's underwear."

"I'll do that personally, boss."

"Thanks. Also, inform SOCO and the pathologist of this latest murder."

"Do you want me there as well, boss?"

"No. You charge Rathmell; I'll take Tashan with me."

The young lad looked disappointed. "Oh, OK, boss," he said, turning and heading back to the incident room.

George headed after him and pulled Tashan to one side, explaining that he wanted the young DC to accompany him to the scene.

* * *

Upon arriving at the scene, George ensured proper security procedures were in place before proceeding up Rosebank Road. He'd parked his car at the outer cordon, and the uniform there had advised the entire Rosebank Park had been cordoned off, with fifty uniforms guarding the perimeter.

The stone circle in Rosebank Park was visible from the road, visible from the flats opposite that lined Rosebank Road.

"The killer sure had some ball," PS Greenwood said. "He must have killed her somewhere else and left her here."

"What makes you say that?" asked George.

"It's far too exposed." He pointed towards the flats that overlooked the park. "Students live in those and are up at all hours."

"You got your officers knocking on doors?"

"Of course, sir," he said. "We'll hopefully have something for you."

"Thanks."

George suited up in a Tyvek suit, blue shoe covers, mask and gloves, and Tashan matched him before they headed towards the clearing where the body was.

Dr Christian Ross was already there, as was Lindsey's team, who were taking photos and examining the body. When he

CHAPTER TWENTY-ONE

glanced up, George nodded a greeting.

"Just stay where you are for a minute, son," the pathologist called out.

They halted a few feet from the body. The victim was a young and voluptuous naked woman with pale skin and dark hair, but her neck and chest were caked in dried blood this time.

"That's different," George muttered, casting a concerned look at Tashan, who turned away, his face pale. No matter how many gruesome crime scenes DC Blackburn encountered, the sight always affected him, which was why he usually brought Jay with him. In contrast, George had developed a coping mechanism that allowed him to distance himself from, in most cases, what he was witnessing.

"It's quite different, aye," Christian remarked. "Same victim selection, however."

George nodded. It appeared their killer had a fetish for twenty-year-old white women with black hair.

"She was stabbed on the altar," Christian explained. "Look." He pointed towards a puddle of blood that had started to congeal on the ground.

"Killer didn't collect blood or clean up the scene this time, did he?" asked George. "Could he have been interrupted?"

"She was strangled, like the others, and I would assume the stab was caused peri-mortem, like victim two."

"Joy," George said. "Her name was Joy."

Christian nodded. "I say this because the bruises on her neck suggest she was strangled with one hand, with the thumb to the left."

"Left-handed?"

Christian nodded again. "The angle of the wound will probably be similar to Joy's, too," he explained.

George asked, "The killer crossed his arms?"

"Correct."

They were already looking at left-handed killers with an MO of strangulation or stabbing on HOLMES. They had an extensive list to look through, but now they knew they were looking for a killer who preferred white women with black hair; they could narrow down their search. Luke was back at the station, so George texted him, asking him to look.

"Until I get her back, I can't say for sure that she was dragged along the ground like Joy was," Christian explained, "but on closer inspection, it appears her mouth was taped." He pointed. "You can see the residue. I'll collect that at the morgue and send it off for testing."

George asked, "Was there a note?"

"I didn't find one."

It was clear that the killer was toying with them.

"Anything else?"

"Yes, and I don't quite know how to interpret it," the pathologist said.

"What do you mean?"

"The blood around the wound is smudged."

George frowned. "Smudged?"

Christian said, "As if her neck came into contact with something." He paused. "It reminds me of smudged lipstick, and so I honestly think the killer had, at one point, placed his lips on her neck."

George raised his brows with shock. "He was sucking her blood from the wound? Is that what you're getting at?"

Christian hesitated for a moment, carefully considering George's question. "It's possible," he finally replied, his voice sombre. "I can't say for sure at this point, but the way the

CHAPTER TWENTY-ONE

blood is smudged suggests some intimate contact between the killer and the victim's neck."

George's mind raced as he absorbed this chilling revelation. If the killer had indeed indulged in such a gruesome act, it added a horrifying layer to an already disturbing case. It painted a picture of a sadistic, possibly deranged individual who took pleasure in not only ending lives but also in desecrating their victims in a dreadful manner.

He knew this detail could potentially be a game-changer in their hunt for the killer. The idea that the murderer might have left behind such a personal and grotesque signature hinted at a level of arrogance or compulsion that could ultimately lead to their downfall.

Christian continued, "I've preserved the area carefully. Once I collect the residue and test it, we might be able to identify any DNA or other trace evidence that could link it to our killer."

"Time of death?" George inquired.

"Based on the body temperature, the death occurred between midnight and six this morning."

In his peripheral vision, George saw the SOC coordinator, Lindsey Yardley, approach.

"I've found some identification for you, DI Beaumont," she explained. George raised his brows. "Her clothes and bag were discarded in the woods." She held out a plastic Exhibit bag. "I've photographed everything, so you can take this."

George smoothed out the plastic bag to find a student ID card bearing the victim's name. Despite the blood on her face, the pictures matched.

"Tashan, call Luke and ask him to find next of kin and personal details for Laura Bennett, a student at Leeds Beckett University."

"Yes, sir," Tashan replied, stepping away from the body as he pulled his phone from his pocket.

"Cheers, Lindsey. Did you find anything else?"

"We'll take everything to the Calder Park lab to see if they can find anything, but no murder weapon or anything." She grimaced. "Sorry."

"Speaking of the murder weapon, did your contact figure anything out?"

"Scissors," Christian said.

"Scissors?"

"Yep, a pair of scissors with a sword-shaped blade has the unique feature of being shaped like a sword. This design enables power to be delivered at the tip. My contact tells me the scissors were recently sharpened, which I can confirm via the finding of metal filings inside the neck wounds of Penny and Joy."

"Could a pair of scissors really cause that?" George asked.

"Oh yes," he said. "The shear of the sword has a ridge that runs all through the length of the blade, which was how he identified it. That, and the fact the blade is shorter than other scissor blades."

"Thanks, Dr Ross," George nodded, his determination deepening. "Keep me updated on any findings. We need to catch this monster before more lives are destroyed."

George approached Tashan, who was on the phone.

"I've got Laura's details," he reported after finishing his conversation with Luke. "She's from Wakefield but lives in one of those flats over there," he said, pointing at the red-bricked block, "and was a second-year student at LBU."

"Anything else?" he asked Tashan.

"I've got the address for her parents in Wakefield."

CHAPTER TWENTY-ONE

"We'll drive out there now to inform them."

As he left the scene, George's thoughts were consumed by the gruesome details of the case. The hunt for a left-handed killer with a penchant for targeting specific women had just taken an even darker turn, and he knew that time was running out to stop this sadistic predator from claiming more victims.

* * *

The drive took them approximately twenty-five minutes, and upon arriving at the sandwich shop, George was relieved to see no customers inside.

They entered to find a woman in her fifties with blonde hair pulled back into a ponytail beneath a baseball cap bearing the name of the sandwich shop.

"Good afternoon," she said, greeting them with a smile. "We're about to close up, but I'm happy to take your order."

"We'd like to speak with Mrs Bennett," George said.

The smile that had once reached her eyes dropped ever so slightly. "That's me."

"I'm Detective Inspector Beaumont West Yorkshire Police Homicide and Major Enquiry Team and this is Detective Constable Blackburn." Both detectives extended their warrant cards for the woman to inspect. "Is your husband here as well?"

"Yes, he's in the back cooking."

"We'd like to talk to both of you in private. Is it possible to close the shop for an hour?"

"Why? What's happened?" Mrs Bennett asked.

"It's better if I explain everything to you both together."

As if sensing the worst, the woman clutched the edge of the

counter. "Please just tell me what's going on."

"Tashan, please turn the sign to 'closed' and shut the door for me," George instructed.

"Yes, sir."

"Is there a private area in the back where we can speak?" George asked, the lines around his mouth tightening as usual.

The woman nodded, and they followed her through a door.

"Jono, the police are here," Mrs Bennett called to her husband.

He stopped what he was doing and washed his hands. Whilst he dried them, he asked, "What's up?"

"Is there a place where we can sit down?" George asked.

"We have an office and some chairs," Mrs Bennett said.

George nodded, then gestured in a way that suggested, 'After you.'

They were led into a small room with an ancient computer in the corner. Paperwork covered the table, which Jono removed whilst his wife placed four chairs.

They all sat down, George and Tashan's elbows touching. It was all very snug, and George realised that Laura was a real mix of both her mother and father.

Where Mrs Bennett had blonde hair, her husband had a shock of black hair.

"Want a brew?" Jono asked, nodding to the kettle.

"No thanks, we really need to discuss your daughter, Laura." Jono frowned. "What about her?"

"Is she OK?" Mr Bennett's complexion turned ashen.

"We found a female body in Woodhouse and believe it to be Laura. We found her student photo ID at the scene."

"No fucking way!" Jono said, leaping from his chair. "It's a mistake."

"I'm afraid it's not, Mr Bennett."

"W—what happened?" Mrs Bennett's voice barely registered.

"We're treating her death as suspicious. I can't provide any details until we receive the pathologist's report. I'm very sorry for your loss," George offered his condolences, though, as usual, the words felt inadequate.

"Is this connected to the other two murders?" Mr Bennett inquired. "I've heard about the two deaths in Leeds."

"Yes, it is," George confirmed.

Jono blinked tears from his eyes. "How did she die?"

"We're awaiting the pathologist's findings. Once we know, you'll know. We'll need someone to positively identify Laura." George cleared his throat. "In the meantime, we will provide you with a Family Liaison Officer."

"I can do that. When?" said Mrs Bennett, her eyes full of shock, the whisper almost inaudible.

"We'll both do it," Jono said, placing his hand on his wife's. "When?"

"Whenever you feel able to."

"Tonight?" Jono asked.

George took a deep breath. "Yes." He pulled out a card. "Call this number, and a car will be arranged to escort you."

"Is there someone who can be with you until the Family Liaison arrives?" George asked.

"No, but thank you," Mr Bennett responded, struggling to keep his composure. "We're fine on our own, really."

Tashan asked, "Would you be OK answering a few questions before we leave?"

"OK," he agreed with a sharp nod.

The young DC asked, "Can you confirm Laura's address for

us?"

Mrs Bennett provided the address, which matched what Luke had given them earlier. "Why would somebody do this to our baby?"

"Hayley," Jono said, "there are some sick people in the world, love, that's why." He turned to George with pleading eyes.

George had seen those kinds of eyes before. I'll do my best to find this bastard, he promised. But he had to be professional. "I'm sorry that I can't provide more answers now. When was the last time you spoke to Laura?"

"A couple of days ago," Hayley Bennett replied.

"Did she mention anything unusual or strange? Was anybody following her?" Tashan asked.

"Nope, nothing." He shrugged. "She was excited about Halloween and was going to help us out at the shop. That's it." His words hung heavy in the air. They'd now not be able to rely on their daughter for shifts.

"Can you give us a list of Laura's friends or flatmates so we can contact them?" asked Tashan.

"We'll do that," Jono said.

"You misunderstand our intentions, Mr Bennett," George said. "We want to interview them."

"Oh. Right." He turned to his wife. "Hayley, any idea?"

"There're eight of them on that floor. There's a Jade, a Holly, an Abbie, an Elizabeth and a Jane. I'm not sure about the other two, sorry."

"That's OK, we'll speak with the owner of the flat," George said. "Thanks anyway." He stood up, realising they couldn't glean much from the parents. "Just out of interest, where were you both last night and this morning between ten and eight?"

Jono stood up and said, "We didn't do anything, Detective."

"I know, but I have to ask."

Hayley said, "We were here."

George looked at Hayley. "Both of you?"

"We got fish and chips from opposite the road and watched TV. That new Celebrity SAS we recorded."

"Tony'll tell you," Jono said.

"Thank you," George said.

Leaving the shop, George turned to Tashan. "We need to return to the Incident Room immediately."

Chapter Twenty-two

When George and Tashan arrived at the Incident Room, DCI Atkinson stood by the board, engrossed in conversation with Luke.

He walked over to them and stared at the board, which showed nothing but names and photos. Three murders in three days. Another serial killer.

"I need to borrow DS Mason," Alistair said.

"OK, sir, may I ask why?"

"His expertise is needed on the copycat case, George," the DCI explained. "DSU Smith was asked to head up a task force to deal with the Ripper copycat." He clapped Luke on the shoulder. "He specifically asked for DS Mason to be part of that team."

"I'm happy for DS Mason, but it means I'm going to struggle—"

"I've already resolved your issue," he explained. "Candy Nichols will temporarily join your team. You'll give her on-the-job training, so keep her with you during the case, OK?"

"Yes, sir."

The DCI left, and George embraced his old mentor. "I'm gonna miss you, mate."

"Me too, son."

CHAPTER TWENTY-TWO

"Good luck, yeah?"

"From what I've heard, I'm gonna need it. The bastard has killed a second sex worker, incapacitating her with a ball pein hammer and finishing her off with a sharpened Phillips-head screwdriver."

George raised his brows. "Jesus Christ!"

"He tried a third last night, about eleven-ish, but he was disturbed by someone."

"Where was this?"

"Bingley," said Luke as the DCI popped his head into the Incident Room.

"Come on, DS Mason, we need to get to Bradford ASAP."

"We, sir?" asked George.

"That's correct, Beaumont," Alistair explained. "My father was involved in the original Yorkshire Ripper case and even wrote a book on it. He passed away last year, but I grew up on the Ripper. They want my knowledge, and I said you'd be fine here for a day or two."

"Thank you for the confidence, sir."

"Don't let me down, Beaumont."

* * *

"OK, everybody, I believe by now it's common knowledge that we have a Ripper copycat in Bradford," George explained. The atmosphere in the Incident Room became suffocating, and the temperature dropped. The room suddenly felt oppressive, as if the walls were closing in on him. "We're to continue our investigation, but DS Mason has temporarily left the team to help the DSU and DCI—" A knock on the Incident Room door caused George to stop. "Ah, speaking of which, I'd like to introduce you to Constable Candy Nichols," the DI explained as a young woman with red hair entered the room.

The young woman, Constable Candy Nichols, stepped into the Incident Room calmly and confidently. Her red hair framed her face like a fiery halo, and her emerald eyes scanned the room, assessing her new colleagues.

George noticed Jay couldn't quite meet her eye. He'd been such an idiot during their brief relationship, but George did sympathise with him. After all, he had been drugged by the serial killer the press had dubbed the Book Club Killer.

George continued, introducing her formally, "Constable Nichols will be joining our team temporarily. She comes highly recommended from the DCI and, whilst fresh out of uniform, brings fresh eyes to the case."

Candy nodded in acknowledgement, her expression revealing a mixture of determination and curiosity. "Thank you, sir. I'm eager to contribute and help bring this bastard to justice."

The detectives in the room exchanged grins, their excitement palpable. George knew Candy would bring renewed energy to a team working tirelessly.

"Let's crack on then, shall we?" asked George and the team nodded. He pointed at the Big Board. "This is Laura Bennett, twenty, from Wakefield, and the case is getting weirder by the minute," the DI explained. "Whilst his victim selection is the same, her neck and chest were caked in dried blood this time."

"Same MO though, boss?" asked Jay.

"She was strangled like Penny and Joy, yes, and then stabbed peri-mortem on the altar like Joy Pritchard," George explained.

Candy Nichols listened attentively, taking notes. She seemed determined to prove herself, which George appreciated.

CHAPTER TWENTY-TWO

"There was much more gore than the previous two scenes," the DI continued.

"I struggled to look at the body; it was that bad," admitted Tashan.

"Was there a note?" Jay asked.

"No, not this time," George said. "Well, not one that anybody has found yet, anyway."

"So, the killer didn't collect the blood this time?" asked Jay, and George shrugged. "Maybe he got disturbed and had to leave? I've looked on Google Maps, and it's pretty open."

"I agree, but as I said before, the case got weirder."

The young DC frowned. "How?"

"The blood around the wound was smudged."

DS Williams frowned. "Smudged?"

George said, "Like her neck came into contact with something." He paused. "It reminded Dr Ross of smudged lipstick, and so he suggested the killer had, at one point, placed his lips on her neck."

Yolanda raised her brows with shock. "No!"

Nodding, George said, "Yes."

"Can somebody give me a clue," said Jay.

The DI looked at his young DC. "The killer, it appears, had sucked some blood from the victim's neck."

George saw Jay visibly shiver. The room had become pressingly silent.

"So, we're chasing a vampire?" Jay eventually managed. He shook his head. "Why do all the weirdos come out around Halloween?"

"I don't know who or what we're chasing," said George, "but I'm hoping we can get some DNA from the body."

Jay looked up and grinned at his boss. "I didn't even think

of that, boss! What a result!"

"What an idiot!" said Yolanda.

"I thought the same, DS Williams," said George. "My bet is he isn't on the system, so it may not matter if we have his DNA or not. But we could always get lucky."

"Here's hoping, boss," said Jay.

"Have you had anything from Christian yet?" asked Yolanda.

"We're awaiting confirmation from him as to what killed her, but it appears she was taped by the mouth to stop any sound and was dragged to the altar. And then, like Joy Pritchard, she was strangled and stabbed. He's usually pretty good at letting me know if anything's different."

"Did Lindsey's SOC team find anything?" asked Yolanda. She'd stood up and was ready to head to her room to get started on CCTV.

"We're waiting to hear back. I'll give CSI a nudge later."

"Is it worth having a police guard in place at the scene?" Tashan asked. "I'm only asking because he killed two in Stourton, so it would make sense to kill two in Woodhouse."

George nodded. "I'll give PS Greenwood a call, but I doubt the killer will be back in Meanwood," he explained. "It's too open." He frowned. "I'm surprised he managed to do what he did without being disturbed."

"So, what do we do next, boss?" asked Jay.

"I want you looking into previous cases involving blood, vampirism, and paganism, Jay," George said. "And whilst you're at it, look for any more potential stone circles or altars in Leeds where our killer could strike again."

"On it, boss."

The DI Turned to his other male DC. "Tashan, I want you to look into victim selection," he explained. "We know our killer has a type, women who are young with black hair and white skin. Start in Leeds and look at unsolved murders, then stretch it to Yorkshire, and then the north."

"The usual, sir?"

George nodded. "I also want you to keep looking into these Peters. We need to find them."

George looked at Yolanda. "I want you on CCTV as usual, DS Williams." George cleared his throat. The sleeping medication he was on made his throat dry. "There are a lot of buildings around the perimeter of Rosebank Park, and PS Greenwood and his uniforms are scouting the area. I'm convinced we will have our killer on tape, but I suspect he will have worn a mask like before."

"Yes, sir."

"Because of the copycat, CID is stretched, but we may be able to get some DCs from other HMETs on our floor." He looked at his team. "If you need any support, ask, and I'll do my best."

"What are you doing, sir?"

"Candy and I are going to the different Leeds universities because it appears all three victims were students." A loud tone came from his pocket. He paused and pulled out his phone. After reading the message, he said, "Scratch that. Candy and I are going to the morgue as Dr Ross has something for us."

* * *

With Constable Nichols in tow, George hurried down the corridor towards the lab where he was due to meet Dr Ross. On the journey to the hospital, the DI hoped the pathologist would have something for him because PS Greenwood had informed George of the disappointing door-to-door enquiries and the lack of CCTV.

The pair entered to find Christian, wearing a white coat, standing in the centre of the lab.

"Now then, Dr Ross," he said.

Christian turned around.

"Hello, son," Christian said, smiling broadly as usual. "And who is this delightful young lady?"

"Constable Candy Nichols," George explained. "Meet Dr Ross."

The constable and the pathologist shook hands, and then George watched as Christian studied Candy. Eventually, Dr Ross said, "Ah yes, your reputation precedes you, young lady."

"All good, I hope?" she asked, her cheeks tinged red.

"Of course, of course. I've heard only the best of things."

"You seem pretty happy, doctor," Candy said.

George was about to comment, but Dr Ross got there first. "Because I have something exciting for you both." He threw a thumb over his shoulder towards Laura Bennett's body.

George advanced, fixing his gaze upon the lifeless figure sprawled across the table. The Y-shaped incision, a signature of Christian's meticulous work, adorned the body while dried blood clung to every corner of the victim's stomach, head, face, feet, and hands.

"She's in a dreadful state," Dr Ross observed, his head shaking with dismay. George held out hope that Christian would restore some dignity to her before her parents arrived for the formal identification.

Christian's voice held a sombre note. "I've never encountered anything quite like this."

George furrowed his brow. "What do you mean? Surely, with your extensive experience in conducting post-mortems, there can't be much you haven't witnessed."

Christian nodded gravely. "As we discussed at the crime scene, it appears the perpetrator may have drunk the victim's blood."

George's nod was grave in return. He still couldn't quite believe it. "Did you find any foreign DNA?"

"I did indeed, son," Dr Ross said. "Do you need the DCI's approval on this?"

"I'm in charge, Dr Ross," George explained.

Candy watched as the DI ticked the box for a 24-hour turnaround and watched him sign again at the Premium Charge Acknowledgement box.

"Any other evidence?" he asked.

"Some nylon fragments."

"From the ropes?" asked George, and Christian nodded. "Were the same ropes used to restrain her as the other victims?"

"It's highly probable. As I said, I've sent the rope fragments for testing, so we should have confirmation soon."

"Did the assailant tie her up before anything else?"

"Yes. And he taped Laura's mouth shut, if you recall."

George nodded. "What about the time of death? Do you have something more specific?" George asked.

"Between four and five this morning," the pathologist said. "It's very dark in the mornings now."

"Anything else?"

"No, but I've heard back from toxicology regarding our first victim."

George raised his brows. "And?"

"It's clear."

"Shite."

"Shite, indeed, son."

George rubbed his head.

"You OK, son?" the pathologist asked. "You feeling healthy?"

"I've felt worse," the DI said. "Work's just a bit manic with this whole copycat investigation intruding on ours," he explained. "We've got three bizarre deaths."

"They're escalating, sir," said Candy.

"What?"

"The killer, they're escalating each time," she explained. "Penny was strangled to death first, then stabbed, and then her blood collected." Candy paused. "From the evidence, Joy was strangled to death whilst she was stabbed, and then her blood was collected." She ran her tongue across her teeth. "And finally, Laura, like Joy, was strangled to death whilst she was stabbed, but instead of the killer collecting her blood, they drank it from her neck." She shrugged. "That's a clear escalation to me, sir."

George nodded. "But why? What does all that mean? What's his endgame?"

"That's for you to work out, son," Christian said, "and I know you'll figure it out soon."

Chapter Twenty-three

Detective Inspector George Beaumont and Constable Candy Nichols made their way to Naansense, the bustling Indian restaurant in Woodhouse. It was a crisp autumn evening, and the aroma of spices and curries hung in the air, mingling with the laughter and chatter of university students who frequented the place. As they entered the restaurant, the colourful decorations and soft Indian music transported them to a different world.

They approached the host at the front of the restaurant, who greeted them with a warm smile. "Table for two?"

George flashed his warrant card. "I'm Detective Inspector Beaumont, and this is Constable Nichols. We're here to speak with the manager regarding one of your employees, Laura Bennett."

The host nodded and motioned for them to follow him. He weaved through the labyrinthine layout of tables and booths, filled with patrons savouring their meals until they reached the restaurant's office, George and Candy following her. He knocked gently on the door before opening it to reveal a middle-aged man seated behind a cluttered desk, engrossed in paperwork.

"Sir," the host said, "the police are here to speak with you about Laura Bennett."

The man looked up, his face a mixture of curiosity and concern. "Of course, please, have a seat," he said, gesturing to two chairs in front of his desk.

George and Candy took their seats, and he introduced himself as Arjun Singh, the restaurant owner. He was a stout man with a thick moustache, his attire reflecting his profession's demands, with an apron still tied around his waist.

"What can you tell us about Laura Bennett, Mr. Singh?" George inquired, getting straight to the point.

Mr. Singh leaned back in his chair, folding his hands on his desk. "Laura has been a reliable employee for the year she's worked here. She's punctual, hard-working, and pleasant with the customers. I've never had any complaints about her."

George nodded, and Candy made notes.

"May I ask what this is all about?" Arjun asked.

George decided to break the grim news to Mr Singh. He leaned forward slightly and spoke with a sympathetic tone, "I'm afraid we have some unfortunate news, Mr Singh. Laura Bennett has passed away."

The colour drained from Mr Singh's face, and he gasped in shock. "What? How? What happened?"

George decided to provide only the necessary details for now. "We're investigating the circumstances of her death. It's suspicious, and we are trying to piece together her activities leading up to it."

Candy added, "That's why we're here, Mr Singh, to gather any information you may have about Laura's recent days or if she had any issues you were aware of."

Mr Singh seemed shaken by the news but composed himself as best he could. "I had no idea anything was wrong. Laura never mentioned any trouble to me. She was always focused on her job."

George nodded understandingly. "We understand, Mr Singh. We'll need access to her employment records, schedules, and any contact information you have for her. We're trying to build a timeline of her activities leading up to her death."

Mr Singh quickly retrieved a folder from a nearby shelf and handed it to Detective Inspector Beaumont. "Here are her records, including her work schedule for the past few weeks and her contact information. Please find out who did this to her and bring them to justice."

Candy assured him, "That's our goal, sir. We will do our best to solve this case. In the meantime, if you recall anything unusual or hear anything related to Laura that might be helpful, please don't hesitate to contact us."

The owner nodded and offered a solemn, "Of course. Anything to help."

"I'll need to speak to your staff."

Arjun stood up and headed to the door. "Certainly. I'll send Raj in first, our head waiter. He was Laura's mentor when she first started with us."

George and Candy made themselves as comfortable as possible in the tiny office.

Raj Patel, with his welcoming smile, greeted them warmly. "Good afternoon. How can I assist you today?"

Detective Beaumont replied, "Thank you, Raj. We appreciate your cooperation. We have some questions about Laura Bennett, your colleague. We understand that you've been working closely with her."

Raj's expression turned sombre as he nodded. "Yes, I mentored Laura for a little while. She's a bright young woman."

Candy Nichols continued, "Can you tell us about your interactions with Laura? Did you notice anything unusual about her behaviour in the days leading up to her disappearance?"

Raj furrowed his brow in thought. "Well, Laura's a sweet girl, always eager to learn. We spent a lot of time together during her early days here, and I mentored her as best I could. But lately, she seems a bit distant. She hasn't been as talkative as usual, either."

Detective Beaumont pressed further, "Did she ever mention any personal problems or concerns to you? Anything that might have been bothering her outside of work?"

Raj hesitated momentarily before replying, "Not directly, but she once mentioned something about financial troubles. It was just a passing comment, so I didn't pry. I thought maybe she was just stressed about money like many of us are. And she's a student, so it comes with the territory, right?"

Candy leaned forward, her tone empathetic. "Raj, do you recall if Laura had any conflicts or disagreements with anyone at work or if she had any run-ins with difficult customers?"

Raj shook his head, his face still etched with concern. "No, not that I'm aware of. Laura's good with people. She got along well with everyone."

George then changed the line of questioning, "Raj, can you think of anyone who might have had a grudge against Laura or any reason to harm her?"

Raj appeared genuinely baffled by the notion. "No, not at all. Laura's liked by everyone, and she never had any enemies here, as far as I know."

Constable Nichols took a different approach. "Did Laura have any habits or routines outside of work that you were aware of? Maybe places she frequented or people she spent time with?"

Raj thought for a moment before responding. "Sorry, we weren't that close."

George nodded. "Thank you for sharing and speaking to us, Raj. Please don't hesitate to contact us if you remember anything else or hear anything related to Laura's case."

Raj nodded, his concern evident. "I will, officers. I hope you can find out what happened to her. She deserved better."

They interviewed Mina Khan, a talented chef in the restaurant's kitchen known for creating some of Naansense's most popular dishes. Mina didn't have much to do with Laura other than while delivering orders from the kitchen to the tables.

Next, they spoke with the host, Ajay Desai, a man with a keen memory for faces and names, which certainly would help him ensure the restaurant runs smoothly during busy hours, but nothing to help with the investigation into Laura's death. All Ajay could tell them was that he only spoke to Laura about work-related business, such as coordinating seating arrangements and raising any complaints.

Eventually, they got to speak to the manager, Aarav Gupta, Mr Singh's right-hand man who oversees the day-to-day operations, handles customer complaints, and manages the staff schedule. According to Mr Singh, Aarav is known for being strict but fair, and Laura would have had regular interactions with Aarav, especially regarding her work schedule and any workplace issues.

Unfortunately, he, too, didn't have much to do with Laura outside of work, suggesting she spent much more time with her university friends than her work colleagues.

The two detectives were about to leave when a young woman,

clearly out of breath from running, knocked on the open door.

"I'm Antigone Holland; I work as a dishwasher and kitchen assistant."

Detective Beaumont began the conversation, "Thank you for taking the time to speak with us, Antigone. We have some questions about Laura."

Antigone nodded, her expression serious. "Of course. I'll help in any way I can."

Candy asked, "Did you work closely with Laura? Did you notice anything unusual about her in the days leading up to her disappearance?"

Antigone's eyes flickered as she recalled. "Laura and I didn't interact much directly, but I noticed something different about her lately. She seemed quieter, more preoccupied, you know? Like her mind was somewhere else."

George probed further, "Did she ever mention any personal problems or concerns to you?"

Antigone hesitated before answering, "Not really, but once I overheard her talking to Raj about money problems. She said something about debts and how it was stressing her out. She's a student though, like me, so I didn't think owt of it."

Candy followed up, "Did you ever witness any conflicts or disagreements between Laura and anyone at work, or did she have any confrontations with difficult customers?"

Antigone shook his head. "No, I never saw her argue with anyone. But then again, I'm usually stuck 'round the back, you know?"

George shifted his focus, "Antigone, can you think of anyone who might have had a reason to harm Laura? Anyone who had a grudge against her?"

Antigone's brows furrowed as she pondered the question.

"Nah, she was a lovely lass."

Candy decided to explore Laura's activities outside of work. "Did Laura have any routines or habits outside of work that you were aware of? Perhaps places she visited regularly or people she spent time with?"

Antigone hesitated momentarily before replying, "Her friends used to come in a lot because of the discount perks," she explained. "But as I said, I'm 'round back most of the time."

Detective Beaumont noted this detail, knowing they had to visit Laura's friends, Holly, Abbie, Elizabeth, Jade and Jane, to interview them. "Thank you for talking with us, Antigone." He stood up, and Candy followed suit. He handed Antigone a business card and said, "Please don't hesitate to contact us if you think of anything else."

After collecting the necessary information, George and Candy left the office. They stepped back into the vibrant restaurant, where patrons continued to enjoy their meals, seemingly unaware of the tragedy that had befallen one of their servers.

As they made their way out and got into George's Merc, Detective Constable Jason Scott, the young detective who had initially discovered Laura Bennett's connection to Naansense, called.

"Boss, I've managed to get in touch with Laura's university friends," he explained.

"Set up an interview with them, please, Jay," George said. "You're on speaker, by the way."

"Hi, Candy," Jay said. Then, as if realising his boss was waiting, he said, "They're waiting for you now at the flats. All five of them." Jay paused. "I've got something else."

"Go on then, lad, spit it out!"

"I've been doing some background checks on Laura Bennett. It turns out she had some rather significant debts."

George raised an eyebrow. "Debts? Student loans?"

"No, that's separate," Jason explained. "I couldn't find exact numbers, but she had a history of missed payments on loans and credit cards. It's possible she was struggling financially."

Candy chimed in, "That might explain why she was working at Naansense. She could have been trying to make ends meet."

George nodded thoughtfully. "It's a lead, at least. We should dig deeper into her financial situation and see if it could have had any connection to her death. Get her statements and go through them. If you need any help, ask DS Fry."

With the newfound information, they headed to the block of student flats on Rosebank Road to further investigate Laura Bennett, hoping to uncover any clues that might lead them closer to solving the mystery of her untimely demise.

Chapter Twenty-four

After concluding their interviews at Naansense, Detective Inspector George Beaumont and Constable Candy Nichols made their way to the student flats on Rosebank Road in Woodhouse, the next logical step in their investigation into the tragic death of Laura Bennett. They were eager to speak with Laura's friends - Holly, Abbie, Elizabeth, Jade, and Jane - hoping to uncover more information about Laura's life outside of work.

The student flats were nestled in a lively part of town, with the chatter of university students and the occasional sound of music filling the air. George got in the lift whilst Candy climbed the stairs to the specified flat and knocked on the door. Moments later, it swung open to reveal a group of young women, all with concerned expressions upon seeing the police warrant cards.

Detective Beaumont introduced themselves, "Good afternoon, ladies. I'm Detective Inspector Beaumont, and this is Constable Nichols. We want to speak with you about Laura Bennett."

Holly, who appeared to be the most composed among them, nodded. "DC Scott said you were coming. Please come in."

They entered the cosy and well-lived-in student apartment,

reflecting its occupants' vibrant and youthful energy. The living area was an open and inviting space, seamlessly connecting the living room, dining area, and kitchen. It was not ideal for interviewing people because the open layout encouraged social interaction among the room-mates and allowed for the free flow of conversation.

After refusing drinks and sitting on the plush sofa, Candy started the conversation, "We understand that Laura was friends with all of you. We're trying to gather as much information as possible about her recent activities and relationships. Can you tell us about her?"

Abbie, who was sitting in one of the two armchairs adorned with colourful throw pillows and cosy blankets, spoke up. "Laura was a great friend. She was always there for us when we needed her. We've known her since the beginning of our time at the university."

In the other armchair, Elizabeth added, "She was responsible and hard-working, but she also knew how to have fun. We often went out together and enjoyed each other's company." She reached across to the cluttered coffee table in the centre, the long sleeves of her top glancing against a glass of water, it nearly falling over a laptop that was leaning dangerously close to the edge. "Ah, shit, nearly," she said, embarrassed.

George smiled and took in the room. The walls were decorated with various posters, photographs, and artwork.

Jade said, "She was also the one who introduced us to Naansense. We loved going there for dinner. Laura always made it a memorable and cheap experience."

Bookshelves and shelving units lined the other walls of the flat, displaying an array of textbooks, novels, and DVDs. There was a mix of films, from soppy romances to gory horrors.

CHAPTER TWENTY-FOUR

Jane, who had been quiet until now, finally spoke, "But lately, she seemed different. She was more withdrawn, and we could tell something was bothering her." She burst into tears.

George noted this observation. "Can you tell us more about that? Did Laura mention anything specific that was troubling her?" The atmosphere in the student flats on Rosebank Road had turned sombre as they continued questioning. Once full of youthful energy, Holly, Abbie, Elizabeth, Jade, and Jane were now visibly shaken by the loss of their dear friend.

Holly wiped away a stray tear, her voice quivering with emotion as she said, "Laura mentioned financial troubles a few times. She said she had debts and was struggling to make ends meet."

Abbie, her eyes red, nodded. "Yes, and she was also worried about her job. She felt like she was falling behind on her responsibilities at the restaurant." The tears started again, forcing Abbie to wipe away tears with the back of her hand.

Elizabeth sniffled softly and said, "We tried to offer support, but she was the type to keep her problems to herself. She didn't want to bother us."

Constable Nichols continued, "Did Laura have any routines or habits outside of work that you were aware of? Places she visited regularly or people she spent time with?"

"She started seeing somebody new," Jade replied, clutching a tissue, trying to compose herself.

Jane, who was staring down at her hands, her eyes glistening with tears, said, "Jade is right, but Laura was secretive about it. She didn't tell us much."

Detective Inspector George Beaumont, recognizing the importance of uncovering more details about Laura Bennett's financial troubles and her new boyfriend, decided to probe further. The group of friends were becoming increasingly visibly upset by Laura's death as George questioned them. George spoke with a gentle but inquisitive tone.

"It was mentioned earlier that Laura was facing some financial difficulties," George said, directing his question to Holly, who seemed to be the most composed among them. "Can any of you provide more information about her financial situation? Did she mention specific debts or financial challenges?"

Holly nodded, her eyes still filled with tears. "Yes, Laura did mention financial troubles. She had loans and credit card debt that she was struggling to manage. It was causing her a lot of stress."

Abbie expanded on Holly's answer. "She was always worried about money but didn't want to burden us with the details. We tried to help her where possible, but she was quite private about it. I don't think her parents even knew."

George nodded in understanding before turning to the subject of Laura's new boyfriend. "It was also mentioned that Laura was seeing someone new recently. Can any of you provide more information about this person? Did she ever introduce him to you or share details about their relationship?"

Elizabeth hesitated before responding, "Laura was quite secretive about her new boyfriend. She didn't give us a lot of information. We didn't even know his name."

Jade added, "We asked her about him a few times, but she just brushed it off, saying it was still early in the relationship. She didn't want to jinx it."

Detective Beaumont continued to probe, "Did any of you ever meet this new boyfriend, even briefly?"

The room fell silent momentarily, and then Jane spoke up, her voice low and hesitant. "I think I might have seen him once,

CHAPTER TWENTY-FOUR

but it was from a distance. Laura was talking to a guy outside a café, and they seemed to be having an intense conversation."

George took note of this information. "What did he look like?"

Detective Inspector George Beaumont, keen on gathering as much information as possible, turned back to Jane, who had mentioned seeing Laura with the man outside the café. He asked, "Jane, can you describe what the man looked like? Any distinctive features or clothing?"

Jane hesitated for a moment, trying to recall the details. She then replied with a shudder, "He… he looked a bit like Peter Sutcliffe, you know, the Yorkshire Ripper? It was unsettling, to be honest."

George's eyebrows raised in surprise at the unexpected and chilling reference. "Could you elaborate on that, Jane? What specific features or characteristics made you think of Peter Sutcliffe?"

Jane recounted, "It was mostly the facial hair. He had a full beard and moustache, just like Sutcliffe had in those old photos I've seen. And his hair was dishevelled. It was just a glance, but it sent shivers down my spine."

George frowned. "But why specifically Sutcliffe?"

"I study psychology, and we've recently started a module on serial killers. Sutcliffe was very active in this area, as I'm sure you know, so the lecturer likes to use him as an example," Jane explained.

George hated that the sick bastard known as the Yorkshire Ripper was being used as a study example, but he was a deeply scarred man. His delusional system embraced the idea that God had given him a mission to rid the world of prostitutes.

The DI exchanged a meaningful glance with Candy. The

resemblance to a notorious serial killer was certainly a striking detail. Could he be their ritual killer and the Copycat Ripper?

Surely not.

George then asked, "Did you overhear any part of their conversation or get a sense of their relationship?"

Jane shook her head, her expression troubled. "No, I couldn't hear anything from where I was. They seemed engrossed in their conversation, and I didn't want to eavesdrop. She wanted privacy, so I gave her it."

George nodded in understanding. "Thank you, Jane. This information is helpful. Please don't hesitate to reach out if you remember anything else or think of anything related to this man."

Jane and the other friends nodded solemnly, their concern for their late friend evident in their eyes. As Detective Inspector George Beaumont and Constable Candy Nichols left the student flat, they acquired a potentially significant lead that must be carefully investigated. The reference to Peter Sutcliffe's appearance in connection with Laura's new boyfriend added an intriguing and ominous layer to the mystery surrounding her death.

George thanked them for their cooperation and gave them a business card. "If any of you remember anything else or if you hear of anything related to Laura's case, please don't hesitate to contact us."

Holly nodded solemnly. "We miss her already. Please find the bastard that did this!"

As George and Candy left the student flats on Rosebank Road, they felt they were getting closer to unravelling the mystery surrounding Laura Bennett's death, especially when George received a phone call.

CHAPTER TWENTY-FOUR

"Boss, you're never gonna believe this," Jay said.

"Never gonna believe what?"

"You need to get back to the station ASAP; somebody here wants to speak to you."

Chapter Twenty-five

DI George Beaumont stared at the man sitting across from him in the dimly lit interrogation room. A uniform had already taken a statement from Peter Hardgrave, and George had spent an hour or so re-reading it, letting the young man sweat.

With his dishevelled appearance and haunted eyes, Pete looked like he had been through hell. George knew he had to tread carefully with this case. It had already garnered significant media attention, and the pressure to solve it was mounting.

"Let me make sure I understand this, Pete," George began, leaning forward across the table. "You're telling me that you didn't kill Penny Haigh, but you know who did, and you didn't come forward earlier because you were scared of this masked killer?"

Pete nodded, his hands trembling. "That's right, Detective. I didn't kill Penny. I loved her. But that masked man… he's dangerous."

DI Beaumont leaned back in his chair, studying Pete's face. The man's fear was palpable, but the detective couldn't ignore the inconsistency in his story. "Pete, you said this happened at the Stourton Stone Circle. Can you describe the masked man for us? Anything that might help us identify him?"

CHAPTER TWENTY-FIVE

Pete took a deep breath, attempting to compose himself. "He wore a black hooded sweatshirt and a mask covering his entire face. I couldn't see his features. But he had this soft Yorkshire accent. I swear, it was chilling, hearing him talk like that."

The detective jotted down the information in his notepad. "And you say he attacked you and Penny. What happened next?"

Pete's voice quivered as he recounted the horrifying encounter. "I tried to reason with him, to get him to leave us alone. But he didn't listen. He knocked me down, and then he... he took Penny."

As he spoke, Beaumont could see the pain and guilt in Pete's eyes. "And he threatened to harm you with scissors if Penny screamed or fought back?"

Pete nodded, tears welling up in his eyes. "Yes, Detective. He said he'd kill me if she made a sound. I had no choice. I ran as fast as I could, hoping to find help."

George sighed and indicated for Candy to close her notepad. He needed to corroborate Pete's story, but the man's fear seemed genuine. And only the killer or somebody involved in the murders would know about the scissors. "Who did you go to for help?"

"What?"

"You said you ran as fast as possible, hoping to find help. Who was that?"

Pete said nothing.

"As far as I'm concerned, you were the last one to see Penny Haigh alive, and as such, you're my prime suspect until we rule you out. Do you understand?"

Pete nodded, his shoulders slumped in resignation. "I know,

Detective. But I didn't do it. I loved Penny, and I'd never hurt her."

The tension in the air was palpable, and the detective knew this was a pivotal moment in the investigation. He leaned forward, his gaze fixed on Pete. "Pete," DI Beaumont began, his voice steady and authoritative, "I need you to walk me through the events of that night at the Stourton Stone Circle in as much detail as you can. Start from the beginning."

Pete took a deep breath, his hands trembling slightly. He stared at the cold, metallic table, his mind racing to relive that horrifying night. "It all started because I wanted to play a prank on Penny," he began, his voice quivering. "We had arranged to meet at the stone circle because we knew it would be quiet and we could just have a laugh."

George nodded, encouraging Pete to continue.

The DI took a mental note of Pete's account of their playful banter. "And then, what happened when you got closer to the stone circle?" he asked.

"That's when the killer arrived," Pete said, his expression darkening. "I stepped in front of Penny protectively and demanded to know who he was and what he wanted."

George leaned in, his eyes fixed on Pete. "Tell me, Pete, what did the masked man look like? Can you describe him?"

Pete shook his head, his frustration evident. "I wish I could, Detective, but he was wearing a hooded sweatshirt, all in black, and a mask that covered his entire face. I couldn't see a thing. But he had this soft Yorkshire accent, and that's what I remember the most. It sent shivers down my spine."

Beaumont jotted down the information in his notepad. "A male with a Yorkshire accent," he mused. "There are over two million men who have Yorkshire accents, and then there are those who can put them on." George sighed. "Describe the mask for me."

"Erm, the mask was made of a matte-black material, obscuring the wearer's entire face. It was snugly fitted, as if it had been custom-made, leaving no gaps or loose edges and impossible to see the person's skin or any facial features beneath it," Pete explained. "But the most unsettling feature of the mask was the absence of a mouth hole. And instead of traditional circle eyeholes, there were two perfectly symmetrical, narrow slits that allowed the wearer to see out. These slits were just wide enough to reveal the faint glint of the wearer's eyes but nothing more. So don't ask me what colour they were because I don't have a clue."

George shook his head. This guy was such an exhibitionist, the DI thought.

"The darkness behind those slits gave the impression of empty, soulless voids as if he had no eyes, but that wasn't the worst part."

Absorbed in his story, Candy had leaned forward. "What was the worst part?"

"Where the mouth should have been, there was just a smudge of red that reminded me of a predator after it had fed on its prey," Pete explained. "And it was weird because there were no openings for breathing, which added to the mask's eerie and suffocating appearance." Pete paused. "If you ask me, it was as if the wearer had chosen to erase all traces of humanity from their face."

"Would you be able to describe all of that to a sketch artist so we could put posters out?" George asked. He turned to Candy. "They might be selling in certain shops if it wasn't custom-made, which could give us a lead."

Candy nodded and pulled out her phone. She would take the initiative and text, Jay, asking him to contact a sketch artist so they could get on with that ASAP.

George turned back to Peter. "So what happened next?"

Pete took a deep breath to steady himself. "I tried to reason with him, to get him to leave us alone," he explained. "I told him it was just a prank gone wrong. But he didn't listen. He knocked me down, and then he…"

Pete's voice trailed off, and George leaned in further. "What did he do, Pete?"

"He took Penny," Pete said, his voice barely above a whisper. "He grabbed her and covered her mouth with a gloved hand. He said, 'Don't fight, my love. Don't scream. If you do, he dies.'"

As he recounted the terrifying moment, George could see the pain and fear in Pete's eyes. "And then?" he prodded gently.

"The man pulled out a pair of scissors," Pete continued, his voice trembling with raw emotion. "He pointed them at me, and that's when I ran. I just ran as fast as I could, hoping to find help."

George leaned back in his chair, taking in the harrowing tale. Pete's account was consistent with his initial statement, and the fear in his eyes appeared genuine. Still, the DI knew he had to be thorough in his investigation.

"Pete," he said carefully, "I want to reiterate that you are our prime suspect. We need to rule you out as the killer. Do you have anything else to add to your story? Any other details that might help us?"

Pete looked up, his eyes pleading. "Detective, I didn't kill Penny. I loved her. I would never hurt her. I just want to find the person who did this."

George nodded, his expression unwavering. "We'll do everything we can to find the person responsible, Pete. But we need to be sure, and that means investigating every angle of this case."

With that, George read out the caution and then motioned for an officer to escort Pete back to a holding cell. The detective had a lot of work to do. He needed to check the CCTV cameras near the Stourton Stone Circle again and gather any evidence that might support Pete's story.

Chapter Twenty-six

George sat on his comfortable sofa in his Morley house, his eyes fixed on the television screen, Olivia snoozing in his arms. The room was dimly lit, with the only source of illumination coming from the soft glow of the TV. Beside him, his fiancée, Isabella Wood, sat with a concerned expression, her fingers nervously twisting a lock of her brunette hair.

On the screen, Detective Superintendent Jim Smith and Detective Chief Inspector Alistair Atkinson, two of George's colleagues from the West Yorkshire Police, were fielding questions from the press at the Bradford District Headquarters, Trafalgar House. They were discussing the unsettling case that had gripped the region—the Copycat Ripper.

The Copycat Ripper had struck fear into the hearts of the local community, leaving two women dead in Manningham and another in an induced coma in Bingley. The heinous crimes bore a chilling resemblance to the notorious Yorkshire Ripper murders of the past, and the media frenzy surrounding the case had reached a fever pitch.

As George watched, Jim Smith, a seasoned investigator with a sharp mind and a stern demeanour, addressed the gathered reporters. "We are fully committed to bringing this perpetrator to justice. Rest assured, we are leaving no stone

CHAPTER TWENTY-SIX

unturned in our efforts to apprehend the Copycat Ripper and ensure the safety of our community."

Alistair Atkinson, the younger of the two detectives, added, "We have a dedicated team working round the clock to gather evidence and follow leads. We urge the public to remain vigilant and report any suspicious activity. We also appeal to anyone with information about the case to come forward."

Isabella turned to George, her eyes reflecting the unease she felt. "I can't believe someone would want to copy such awful crimes."

George nodded, his jaw clenched. "It's a nightmare, Isabella. But Smith'll catch this sick bastard and put an end to it."

Their attention returned to the television as a reporter asked, "Can you shed any light on the possible motives of the Copycat Ripper?"

Jim Smith replied, "At this stage, we're open-minded. We're exploring all possibilities, including whether the perpetrator is driven by a fascination with the original Yorkshire Ripper case or if there are other motives at play."

"Detective Superintendent Smith," a male journalist said, "can you elaborate on the similarities between the Copycat Ripper case and the Yorkshire Ripper case? Are you considering any connections?"

"We are certainly aware of the historical context here. The Yorkshire Ripper case was a gruesome chapter in our region's history, and we understand the concerns this new case has raised." Smith hesitated. "However, at this point, we can't confirm any direct connections between the two cases. We are keeping an open mind and exploring all possibilities."

"Why lie, DSU Smith?" asked another journalist. "We know a ball pein hammer and a Phillips-head screwdriver were used in their murders. If that's not a similarity or connection to Sutcliffe, then what is?"

George could see that his boss was rattled.

"Well, that's precisely why we've called him a copycat," said Smith. "Next question."

A woman in her late thirties wearing a neatly tailored blazer and a pressed blouse stood up. Even through the TV, George could see she carried herself confidently, exuding an air of authority. "In reference to the previous question, can you tell us if the victimology in the Copycat Ripper case matches that of the Yorkshire Ripper?"

With a look from his boss, DCI Alistair Atkinson stepped forward and spoke into the microphone. "We are working with profiler Mark Finch, who is helping us to carefully examine the victim profiles, and while there are some similarities, there are also differences. The Yorkshire Ripper primarily targeted sex workers, and while the Copycat Ripper's two victims were sex workers, the most recent target was not. As such, it's too early to draw any definitive conclusions." He paused. "As I said, we're consulting with experts and profiling specialists to better understand the offender's motives."

"Is there any indication that the Copycat Ripper may be someone with knowledge of the Yorkshire Ripper case? Are you looking into that angle?"

Jim Smith, again, nodded at the DCI to answer this. "Excellent question," Alistair said. "To answer your question, yes, we are considering all possibilities, including whether the Copycat Ripper might have a fascination with the Yorkshire Ripper case. It's a disturbing thought, and we are actively investigating any leads related to individuals who might have a deep knowledge of the Yorkshire Ripper's crimes. We

CHAPTER TWENTY-SIX

encourage anyone with information to come forward."

The journalist, a man in his early fifties, dressed in a sharp, dark-coloured suit with receding salt-and-pepper hair, didn't sit down. Instead, he asked, "Does that mean you're a suspect then?"

That got a few laughs from the other journalists, but in a blink-and-you'd-miss-it-moment, Alistair ground his teeth and clenched his fists. "I am part of this investigation because of my deep knowledge of the Yorkshire Ripper's crimes."

George recognised the journalist, known among his colleagues for his dogged determination to dig deep into stories—an absolute pain in the arse to detectives and their work.

The journalist said, "Because of your late father's knowledge."

"Correct." Atkinson forced a smile. "Next question.

Another man stood up, about a decade younger than the previous journalist. His outfit consisted of a dark suit, a crisp white shirt, and a simple tie. The man looked switched on and professional. He adjusted the thin-framed glasses on his face and then asked, "Detective Smith, in the Yorkshire Ripper case, there were concerns about the police's handling of the investigation, particularly the prolonged time it took to apprehend Peter Sutcliffe. Can you assure the public that lessons have been learned and the Copycat Ripper case will be handled differently?"

Smith nodded. "We understand those concerns, and it's essential to acknowledge past mistakes. The West Yorkshire Police have evolved significantly since the Yorkshire Ripper case, and we now have more advanced investigative techniques and technology at our disposal. Rest assured, we are working tirelessly to resolve this case swiftly and effectively. We have a dedicated team of experienced officers committed to bringing the Copycat Ripper to justice."

The press conference continued with similar questions and responses, with the detectives providing as much information as possible without compromising the investigation. Jim Smith and Alistair Atkinson were careful not to draw direct parallels between the Copycat Ripper and the Yorkshire Ripper, recognising that the cases had their unique elements. They emphasised the importance of public cooperation and their commitment to solving the case while maintaining transparency with the media and the concerned community.

As the press conference concluded, George felt a sense of dread gnawing at him. He had been a detective for over a decade and had faced his fair share of gruesome cases, but this one was particularly chilling.

Chapter Twenty-seven

That morning, George arrived at the station to some good news. The two detectives that the other HMETs had loaned George, DC Holly Hambleton and DC Reza Malik, had looked through the footage Yolanda had managed to source from a security camera attached to the graffiti-covered container near the Stourton Stone Circle overnight.

Finding the footage had been an incredible result in the first instance, but the two Detective Constables had worked extremely hard overnight to secure a positive outcome for them.

In the video, George and his team watched the moment when Pete and Penny arrived, Pete arriving after Penny, sneaking up on her so he could pretend to rob her. It was clear from their body language and interactions that they were not engaged in any hostile or aggressive behaviour toward each other. They both appeared relaxed and even shared a laugh.

As the video continued, the investigators watched in horror as the masked assailant, dressed in black with a hood and a mask concealing their face, suddenly emerged from the shadows. The attacker approached Pete and Penny, but it was evident that Pete did not instigate the violence. He had tried to protect Penny, not harm her.

The masked assailant's actions were chilling and aggressive, confirming Pete's account of the events. They saw the attacker knocking Pete to the ground and forcibly taking Penny. Her terrified expression was evident as the attacker covered her mouth, preventing her from screaming.

The most critical moment was when the attacker brandished a pair of scissors, pointed them at Pete, and threatened him—this moment on the CCTV footage matched Pete's description of the attack perfectly. It was clear that Pete had been a victim, not a perpetrator.

DI George Beaumont knew that they had found the evidence they needed to clear Pete from their investigation, as the CCTV footage unequivocally showed that Pete had not been the aggressor and that the masked assailant was the one responsible for the violence that night.

With this newfound evidence, Pete's innocence was established, and the investigation shifted entirely toward identifying and apprehending the masked assailant who had taken Penny Haigh.

And with a simple tick of a box resulting in a premium charge, that's precisely what happened next.

George and the team had identified their serial killer.

Chapter Twenty-eight

Detective Inspector George Beaumont stood in the cramped, fluorescent-lit lab, waiting for Dr Ross to arrive, who had promised something that could potentially change the course of his investigation. The sterile scent of chemicals hung heavy in the air, and the rhythmic hum of machines seemed like a constant reminder of the urgency of their work.

Pathologist Christian Ross arrived, a man whose expertise had often proved invaluable in solving complex cases, breaking the tense silence. "Morning, son," Ross said in his usual calm and measured tone, "I've got the results of that DNA sample."

George leaned against the wall, his heart pounding with anticipation. "Tell me some good news, please."

Christian grinned. He wore a shirt and tie under his crisp, white lab coat. His salt-and-pepper hair was neatly combed and well-maintained, indicating his increasing age.

"Does it match anyone on the database?" George asked.

The pathologist paused for a moment before responding. "Yes, George, it does. The DNA belongs to a thirty-three-year-old man named Frederick Harman from Leeds. He was on the database because he was charged with voluntary manslaughter."

Frederick Harman. The name didn't ring any immediate

bells in George's mind. "Thanks, Christian. I owe you one."

"I only ask that you bring cakes next time."

Leaving the lab, George made his way to Elland Road, calling DCI Atkinson on the way.

"What is it, George? I'm a bit busy," Alistair said.

"We've found him, sir. Frederick Harman, thirty-three, from Leeds," George said. "I want a BOLO."

A BOLO or a be on the lookout, is used when a suspect is circulated on the Police National Computer (PNC) as wanted.

The DCI said, "Done. I'll get on it now."

"Thank you, sir." George rang off and then called the station. DS Yolanda Williams answered, who put him on loudspeaker.

George said, "I've just spoken with Dr Ross. The DNA matches a Frederick Harman from Leeds, charged with manslaughter. Tashan, I need you to dig up everything you can on Frederick Harman—his background, criminal record, associates, everything. Also see what links he has to the three victims. We have their phones and laptops, right?"

"On it, sir," Tashan acknowledged, and George heard the door open and shut, assuming the young DC had quickly left the room to begin his research.

George spoke to Yolanda next. "Yolanda, contact the Crown Court and find out about Frederick Harman's sentence."

"Will do, sir."

George cleared his throat. "Candy, I want you to search the PNC and see who oversaw Frederick Harman's case. It might be the detective is still around, and if so, I could do with talking to them."

"Will do, sir."

"What about me, boss?"

"Jay, start calling the universities in Yorkshire. Tell them

CHAPTER TWENTY-EIGHT

we're looking for a student named Frederick Harman. Start with Leeds and then expand the search radius. All three victims were students."

George could hear scratching, assuming it was Jay with a pen and paper, writing down his instructions.

George ended the call and continued towards Elland Road, where he slung the car into a space and jogged up to the Homicide and Major Enquiry Team floor, then straight into the Incident Room, where his dedicated team of detectives awaited. The room was buzzing with activity as Detective Sergeant Yolanda Williams, Detective Constable Jay Scott, Detective Constable Tashan Blackburn, and Constable Candy Nichols went about their respective tasks.

"An update, please, everyone," George said.

"Sir, Frederick Harman wasn't sentenced to prison," Yolanda explained. "He was given a Section 37 hospital order with Section 41 restrictions. I'm looking into that more, sir, and will let you know when I've found something."

George's mind raced, trying to process this unexpected turn of events. Section 37 meant that Frederick had been detained in a psychiatric hospital instead of serving a prison sentence. Section 41 restrictions were even more ominous, implying that Frederick Harman was considered a significant risk. "Thank you. Does anybody else have anything for me?"

"Still looking into Frederick, sir," said Tashan. "Nothing on the victims' phones or laptops indicate they were in contact with Frederick, however."

"And I'm still trying to contact the universities." Jay shrugged. "They're not making it easy."

George nodded. In fairness to his team, he hadn't given them that long. The drive from the hospital back to the station had been relatively quick due to the early hour.

"Candy?"

"It was Detective Chief Superintendent Mohammed Sadiq, sir," Candy reported, her voice steady. "He was the Senior Investigating Officer for the Harman case, though only a Detective Chief Inspector at the time."

"Good work, Candy," Beaumont said, a glimmer of hope in his eyes. "Now, I need you to do something else for me. Call DCS Sadiq's office and leave a message. Tell his secretary we must urgently speak with him about the Harman case. Let's see if he remembers something that can help us."

Candy nodded and placed the call, leaving a concise but urgent message with Sadiq's secretary. She hung up the phone and turned back to the laptop.

The team dispersed to their tasks; George grabbed Candy's attention. "Candy, you're with me. We're off to Hunslet to interview Penny Haigh's parents first. Let's see if they know anything about this Frederick Harman."

Beaumont and Nichols headed downstairs and got into the DI's Merc. He'd just pulled out of the station when his phone rang, the ringing from the speaker almost deafening them. "DI Beaumont."

"Please hold for Detective Chief Superintendent Sadiq," a pleasant and polite female voice said.

"Now then, George," a deep, authoritative voice greeted him. "I got your message regarding the Harman case."

"Thank you for getting in touch so quickly, sir," George said, his heart racing with anticipation.

"It's been a while, how are you?"

"Fit and confident as always, sir, thank you." He paused momentarily. "What can you tell me about Frederick Harman."

CHAPTER TWENTY-EIGHT

"Straight to the point as always, eh?"

"I'm on my way to visit the victims' parents; I intend to ask them if they knew Frederick. Constable Candy Nichols is also here with me, and you're on speaker, sir. Anything you can tell us will be helpful."

Sadiq's voice remained measured and composed. "I remember the Harman case well. It was one of the most perplexing cases I ever worked on. His face has haunted my dreams for years."

George listened intently, eager to hear more.

Sadiq continued, "Harman was a troubled young man. I did some digging into his past, and it wasn't pretty. He was born and raised in Bradford before being moved to Hunslet because of his father's job or something. By age five, he exhibited evidence of all three parts of the Macdonald triad, a theory suggesting the development of violent psychopathy."

Beaumont's eyes widened. "The Macdonald triad?" That was a chilling revelation.

"Yes, George. The Macdonald triad consisted of three behavioural traits often associated with violent criminals, particularly serial killers. These traits are cruelty to animals, fire-setting, and persistent bed-wetting beyond a certain age."

Candy shuddered at the thought of young Frederick exhibiting such disturbing behaviour.

Sadiq continued, "In Frederick's case, there were reports of him torturing neighbourhood pets, starting fires, and bed-wetting well into his adolescence. He became a heavy drug user as he grew older, which only exacerbated his behavioural issues."

George nodded, the pieces of the puzzle slowly falling into

place. "Thank you, sir. This is invaluable information and opens up new avenues for our investigation. Is there anything else you can tell us?"

"I'll have a think, Beaumont, and have a look at the case files to see if I've missed anything." The DCS paused. "I know he got off lightly for what he did and ended up being sectioned rather than imprisoned. That was a disappointment for us all."

"Who did he murder, sir? The files I have access to are redacted."

"They're redacted for a reason," was all the DCS said.

* * *

When George and Candy arrived at the Haigh residence, they were greeted by Susan and Roger Haigh, Penny's grieving parents. The Haighs looked weary, their faces etched with pain.

After again offering condolences, George gave them an update on the case, omitting the new information about Frederick Harman, only asking them if they knew him. Both Susan and Roger exchanged puzzled glances before shaking their heads.

It appeared Frederick Harman was a stranger to them.

The detectives thanked the Haighs and headed to Richmond Hill to interview Joy Pritchard's husband, Shane. Family Liaison Officer Cathy Hoskins answered the door, her expression worried. She explained that Shane was struggling, both emotionally and physically, and that he was refusing to see a doctor.

Shane was a broken man, his eyes hollow with grief. He

CHAPTER TWENTY-EIGHT

spoke softly, barely looking at the detectives. After providing an update on the case, George gently inquired about Frederick Harman. Just like Penny's parents, Shane claimed he had never heard of such a person.

The morning pressed on, and George and Candy continued their journey, making a final stop in Woodhouse to interview Laura's friends—Elizabeth, Jane, Holly, Jade, and Abbie. They all were still very shaken by Laura's disappearance and were eager to help with the investigation.

George asked each of them in turn about Frederick Harman. The answers were consistent, all resounding nos, until Jane spoke up. Her words sent a shiver down George's spine. "The man Laura was in the café with, the one who looked like Peter Sutcliffe, she called him Freddie."

George and Candy concluded the interview by obtaining the address of the café, which was situated on the corner of Woodhouse Lane and Blenheim Walk.

Before George could fully digest this information, his phone rang. It was Tashan who had been researching into Frederick's background. "Sir, Frederick's father, Benjamin Harman, lives on Woodsley Road in Woodhouse. That's just around the corner from you."

"Have you found Frederick yet?" George asked.

"No, sir. We've given all the airports and seaports Frederick's description so he can't leave the country. And the BOLO is now in effect," Tashan explained.

"Should we go check Frederick's father out?" Candy asked. "They should find Frederick soon, but his father may give us something to go by."

George agreed, and they rushed to the address, with George's phone ringing again. "Sir, I've emailed over some transcripts from Frederick's time in the hospital. They're sending me more, but I thought you'd want to hear about Frederick's childhood before speaking with his father."

George thanked Yolanda and parked the Mercedes by the curb. The DI then decided to take a quick look at the emails Yolanda had sent him while waiting in the car.

As he read through the reports, a mixture of disgust and terror overcame him. The details in those documents painted a disturbing picture, one that would challenge everything they thought they knew about their investigation. George knew that whatever came next would be a descent into a darkness they could never have imagined.

Chapter Twenty-nine

"To tell you the truth, Frederick was a disappointment from the moment he entered the world," Mr Harman explained. George frowned, and Benjamin Harman smirked. "Is there a problem with my honesty, Detective?"

The DI narrowed his brows further, saying nothing.

Candy squirmed in her seat. The tension was palpable.

"I suppose you're not used to honesty in the police force, are you? It must be refreshing for you."

"We just want to know everything you can tell us about your son," George explained. "Including his current location."

"I haven't seen or heard from him in years." Benjamin shrugged. "As I said, he was a disappointment to me. His mother, however, had a crushing, oppressive interest in the kid." He shrugged again as if trying to alleviate any embarrassment. "It's probably why you're interested in him, right?"

"You tell me," said George.

A light grin tickled Benjamin's cheeks, but the smile never met his eyes. "I'll be honest, the boy suffered from my constant criticism, but if anyone's to blame for his transgressions, then it's his mother. She never allowed the boy any time to himself, and so he spent every waking moment in his bloody mother's company, subject to the whims of her varying moods. Sometimes, that meant he would be allowed unlimited ice cream for dinner; sometimes, that meant helping her throw out all the food I'd bought at the weekend because she believed I had somehow poisoned them." Benjamin ran a hand through his dark, greasy locks and grinned again. "I was busy with work and regretted not spending more time with Frederick."

"Whys that?" George asked.

Benjamin cackled. "Well, with nobody else to turn to, Freddie became the container for his mother's many troubles. She poured all her madness and hatred into him and eventually twisted him against me and the world."

"Tell us more about Joanne," George said.

"A ridiculous woman who convinced Freddie that he was sick. He's the perfect self-fulfilling prophecy." Benjamin shook his head and looked down at the floor. "She'd wake him up in the dead of night, fussing endlessly over him, keeping him awake with her fancies." He shrugged. "I'd always hoped I could level the boy out, hoping he would learn from me and turn out like a normal person if I just put the work in."

Benjamin reminded George of his own father, a bully of a man who would use his fists to demand discipline and obedience. They had the same aura about them. But George hadn't turned into a serial killer like Frederick had, which made the DI wonder more about Freddie's upbringing.

"All I wanted was a son that could bear the Harman name without bringing shame to it, and as such, I applied the necessary discipline to ensure it." Benjamin shrugged again. "Or so I thought."

George ground his teeth. His own father had been precisely the same, applying pressure to George in order for him to submit. But George and Frederick were different people, complete opposites, and the DI knew from the psychiatry reports that the pressure Benjamin had applied to the developmentally stunted Freddie, who was constantly suffering the ill effects of two—albeit contrasting—overbearing parents, did nothing to help Freddie's mental state. It was no wonder Freddie had been quiet and insular, even for a child with no friends. George asked, "What do you mean?"

"Well, Joanne fell pregnant again, and I'd just started a new job. We'd discussed divorce extensively when Freddie was young, but somehow, our marriage had survived Freddie's early years. The pregnancy meant we needed to move house. The one-bed flat was crowded enough with the three of us and would have been a nightmare with four of us, so with the money I was making from the new job and a possible fresh start for our family, we moved out of Bradford and into Leeds. The house in Hunslet was beautiful, with a large garden, and I hoped that by getting Freddie outside, playing away from his mother's watchful eye, my boy might have finally gotten a grip on reality."

George knew that the house was in the centre of suburbia, with easy access to the river where Benjamin had planned on taking his son for long walks at the weekends to keep him out of his mother's reach. Or that's what the psychiatry report had told him. That, and throughout the early years of Freddie's life, he'd suffered in silence as both of his stressed parents lashed out at him.

It all sounded so familiar to George, moving from one place to another in the hope that everything would suddenly be OK. His own mother had suffered with her mental health, but not to the same extent that Joanne Harman had, and George immediately felt grateful. Looking into the demise of Frederick Harman had made George realise how lucky he was to have a mother who at least attempted to put him first, even if she didn't leave his father when George had asked her.

"But what I hoped would be tranquillity turned into a storm. Jo had spent years complaining about the flat in Bradford, moaning about the humdrum life that I had apparently condemned her to. But for Joanne, the change was even more terrifying. I'd destroyed her routine, apparently. I'd taken her flat away from her, her neighbours, her city, and the place she was born. And when her parents passed, she blamed me."

A single tear fell from Benjamin Harman's eye, and George frowned. The DI pondered the reason for the tear and was about to ask Ben the question when the tall, thin man continued.

"Joanne became so ill, tearing at her stomach daily with her nails, screaming at the swollen mass to stop stretching and distorting as our daughter rapidly grew inside her. She accused me of cheating on her, of not being attracted to her any more, and even of planning to leave her to look after two children on her own when she struggled to cope with just one." He wiped away another tear. "I told her I loved her, loved our family, loved her swollen stomach, but I was accused of lying to her. And that's when she snapped."

Benjamin sipped his tea and forced himself to take deep, calming breaths. His leg was bouncing up and down, and his hands were shaking. George said nothing, and Candy followed suit.

Eventually, Benjamin said, "Aren't you going to ask why she snapped, detectives?"

George kept his eyes on the man but still said nothing.

CHAPTER TWENTY-NINE

Ben cocked his brow. "Fair enough, but I'll tell you anyway. Her paranoias played out in the form of abuse. She lashed out, not only at me, as usual, but also at Freddie, screaming at my boy for the slightest of sins, then damning me for how I disciplined my boy in her next breath."

"How did Freddie react to the move?" asked Candy.

Both detectives already knew from the psychiatry report that any loud noise made Freddie flinch, and the sound of his parents arguing regularly forced him to curl up into the foetal position.

"Frederick became erratic," Ben explained. "He started randomly screaming and shouting, often for no apparent reason. And instead of spending his time in the garden, he stayed in his bedroom, hiding under the duvet or pretending to be asleep."

Ben breathed out a sigh. "And then Elsie was born." He smiled as more tears fell from his eyes. "She was so beautiful, like a little cherub, and I saw the opportunity to raise her properly without being infected by Jo's madness. She was the apple of my eye, and, like I should have done when Frederick was born, I put in place a strict set of rules about Elsie's care—rules that Jo was surprisingly willing to follow.

"Whatever our troubles, I still very much cared for Joanne, and by staying with her, I proved I was putting effort into our marriage. And so, Jo started to commit wholeheartedly to our marriage, too. I saw it as an opportunity for her to cast aside the shadow of her anxieties and become the woman she had always wanted to be."

The woman you'd always wanted her to be, thought George. He'd bitten the inside of his cheek and was struggling to remove the metallic, bitter taste that lingered.

"I'll admit that Jo tricked me, especially at first," Benjamin admitted. "She kept the new house pristine and even smiled when she met me at the door when I returned from work. She put in the work that she had been neglecting all the years we'd been living in the tiny flat to make things better for all of us. And because, when Elsie arrived, Joanne fussed over her day and night, Frederick was left to his own devices and even started taking longer walks by the river and wandering around the woods by Thwaite Mills.

"By this point, Frederick was well embedded in school where, from what I remember, he was well thought of by his teachers, no doubt due to the extremely pliant, people-pleasing attitude I'd instilled into him, and was average when compared against his peers." Benjamin paused, wondering what to share next. "The teachers throughout primary school only had one issue with Frederick, and that was how he didn't seem to know how to respond to praise. Eventually, we agreed to keep the praise to a minimum to avoid embarrassment for them and us."

"You mentioned he was of average intelligence," Candy said, and Benjamin nodded. "How was he with his peers?"

"He made many... friends," Benjamin eventually managed, "but didn't seem to socialise with any of them outside of school. Many children from his primary school lived in the same estate, but for some reason, he never sought them out to join in with their games, instead heading out on his own on his expeditions into the woods."

"Did school change him?" asked Candy.

"Yes and no," admitted Benjamin. "He stopped pissing the bed, which helped at home because then his mother wasn't as stressed." He paused. "I feel as if the school gave him structure, something we couldn't really give him due to my job, his mother's spiralling mental health, and his younger sister. I also think the fact that Joanne was obsessed with Elsie also helped Frederick, and I remember wishing at the time it would allow him to grow as a person into the man that he would someday become."

"A serial killer?" asked George, bluntly.

Benjamin immediately stood up and pointed at the door. "You know that's not what I meant." He took a deep breath. "If you're going to antagonise me, then leave!" And when George and Candy made no move, Benjamin screamed, "Now!"

"I apologise," said George, after taking another sip of tea, "but your son is a serial killer. That's a fact."

Benjamin scowled as he said, "And what, you think we did this?"

"I've looked into police reports from the time you and your family lived in Hunslet, Mr Harman," George explained, "and it appears that with no real explanation for it, cats started to disappear."

"Cats?" Ben looked between the two detectives, a bemused look on his face. "What the hell do cats have to do with this?"

Chapter Thirty

George stood up slowly, pulled a sheet of folded-up paper from his inside jacket pocket, and ambled towards Benjamin. "Sit down and read this."

Benjamin furrowed his brows but stood his ground. For a man twenty years George's senior, Benjamin was in shape, whilst George was not. In the past, he would have stood his ground, too, and would even have taunted the older man, but this time, he stepped back and raised his brow. "Read it, Mr Harman." George then retreated and sat back down next to his colleague.

Benjamin Harman waited for George to sit before he, too, sat down. He pulled out his reading glasses and began to read the document the DI had provided, shaking his head as he did so, a smirk on his face.

"Wild dogs blamed for missing cats in Hunslet. Could the Stourton cat killer be an escaped zoo animal? Has there been a genuine panther sighted in Leeds? Lotherton Hall stag murdered by black smudge, says tourist." He looked up at George. "What the hell are all of these?"

"Headlines and articles from the two years you spent in Hunslet, Mr Harman," George explained. "Freddie ignored all those warnings, according to notes taken by his therapist, because he was the cat killer. He was the escaped zoo animal."

"That's bullshit, detective," said Ben. "Frederick had a habit of taking the credit for things he didn't do to make him look good."

"So why would you let him wander the woods?" asked Candy. "I know for a fact that if my mum and dad thought there was a predator on the loose, they would have stopped me from going out of the house. So why wasn't Freddie stopped?"

"I've no idea," said Ben. "It could be his mother's hands were full. She was looking after a young girl and desperately trying to maintain her façade of normalcy. Joanne could only do so much."

"Sounds like an excuse to me," said George.

"Take it however you want, detective," said Ben. "You have no evidence."

"Yet we do," said George, "we have Freddie's therapy reports where he admitted to killing the cats. And when he was about ten, he told his therapist his mother had caught him carrying a dead cat into his garden, which she placed in a shoe box and buried at the bottom of the garden."

"That's completely untrue, detective," said Benjamin. "Joanne would have told me, and I have no knowledge about that particular event." The man shrugged. "Frederick must have made it up."

"Well, it's not as if we can just ask Joanne, is it?"

Benjamin's face darkened. "No, it's not."

"Do you want to know what I think?" asked George.

"Not particularly," replied Ben.

"I think your wife was suffering with her mental health so much she pushed any worries out of her mind, her brain understanding she would not be able to cope with the implications of Freddie's actions. Instead of considering her son a monster, she assumed some mistake had happened. Which is why she didn't bother to tell you about it."

According to the therapist, the lack of censure from Freddie's parents was assumed to mean approval, and as such, he began bringing his prey back to his back garden so he could toy with them in comfort. Freddie knew his mother was keeping an eye on him. He'd see her in the kitchen window staring at him, so sadistically, he decided to follow his mother's example and bury each of his murdered playthings at the bottom of the garden when he was finished with them. That acceptance from his mother, who appeared to be OK with what Freddie was doing as long as everything was properly covered up afterwards, only made Freddie want to kill more.

And ironically, it was the perfect metaphor for England in the nineties: as long as everything looked good and things were covered up well, the rotting stuff beneath the surface could easily be ignored.

Whilst furiously shaking his head, Ben said, "You're a bastard, you know that."

"I'm just being honest with you, Mr Harman," said George. "And I'd like you to give us the same respect."

"You think I'm lying to you?"

George shook his head. "No, I think you're being dishonest because of your bias towards Freddie." George smiled. "You're his father, so I don't blame you."

Benjamin took a deep breath. "When did this cat burying occur?"

George pulled out his PNB and checked the date he'd written down.

"It's starting to make sense," Benjamin eventually said.

CHAPTER THIRTY

"What is?"

"It's no secret Jo clung so desperately to her sanity, detectives, and clearly the weight of this secret bout of murder seemed to be too much for her to bear." He paused and scratched his beard. "I say this because the date you've given me is my birthday, and I remember the argument we had that night and the resulting change in my wife from then onwards."

Neither detective said anything, inviting Benjamin to continue. Candy was tapping notes on her tablet whilst George didn't take his eyes off the serial killer's father.

"Her old habits began to creep back in—as did her suspicions about me. I appeared happy, and she wasn't making me happy, so somebody else must have been. When I denied it, she accused me of loathing her. When I asked her where she got that idea from, she explained she was stuck in the house with the children while I got to escape every single day to work. And, when not working, I would go and get my dick wet, as she used to call it." He shook his head once more. "She'd accuse me of going to Miggy Woods in the car and parking up in the car park late at night for a quick shag. Like now, Miggy lasses didn't have a particularly good reputation back then, especially not down in Hunslet."

You're digressing, Mr Harman," said George.

"Ah, yes, I am." He scratched his beard again. "Joanne accused me of poisoning her with my seed and wondered which bimbos I was poisoning on a daily basis. She blamed me for Frederick, telling me his evil must have come from me." Ben shrugged. "I didn't think the lad was evil, but thinking about it now, with more context, she was referring to the cats, right?"

Neither detective said anything. They had Benjamin talking now, and hopefully, he wouldn't stop until they had something worthwhile.

"Anyway, Jo changed. She got more aggressive. She'd rant and rave. She'd kick off if you didn't do what she wanted immediately when she asked you to do it. It got so bad that as soon as I left for work, she'd put Elsie in the pram and leave to spy on me." As if the conversation was boring him, the tall man yawned. "It didn't take long for my boss to take notice of the deranged woman lurking outside the office, and he soon demanded that I sort her out."

"And did you?" asked George.

Benjamin narrowed his eyes. When he did that, he looked like the pictures George had seen of Freddie. "Did I what?"

"Sort her out?"

He started nodding his head profusely. "Yes, yes, I bloody well did." He shrugged. "Things were different twenty or so years ago, you know that," he said, pointing at George. "She needed sorting, so I sorted her, though probably not in the way you'd expect."

"So you didn't hit her?"

"Of course I did. It was hard not to. Whenever she got violent, I had to be more violent; otherwise, the late-night arguments would never stop." Benjamin took in a deep breath. "Anyway, I finally turned to medicine for help, despite mental illness being pretty shameful in the nineties."

Ben scratched his beard again, and George wondered whether it was a nervous tick of his. "Mental health still has stigma now, but back in the nineties, the stigma was huge," Ben explained. "But despite that, we sought psychiatric help. Naturally, she was resistant at first, but after lying to her and tricking her into seeing somebody, she finally relented. Well, I say relented; her first meeting basically consisted of her lying incessantly to them, accusing me of being an abusive husband, a cruel man who had driven her to despair rather than Jo acknowledging any part of her own responsibility."

George said nothing. They had all read those initial reports, and looking at how Benjamin carried himself, George wasn't sure Joanne had been lying. "Have you read any of the reports?"

"Only the first one," he explained. "They didn't let me read any others despite asking."

It made sense. The staff at the centre had seen how Benjamin treated Joanne and was starting to believe her stories when she began spinning tales about how terrible and evil Freddie was. As such, Joanne was exposed as a liar because there was no way that the poor little boy the psychiatrists had seen flinching away from his mother in fear could possibly have done any of the terrible things he was being accused of.

When George had read that conclusion, it had angered him to no end. If only they'd believed her instead of Benjamin, then Freddie may have been saved.

"I remember driving her to Wakefield and Bradford to see different therapists because that original round of talking therapy had worsened Jo's behaviour. That, and the therapist there had forewarned his colleagues in Leeds. It was a complete shitshow."

George had managed to get a copy of that report forewarning his colleagues, and it didn't make good reading. Joanne's behaviour was described as extravagant, and she was accused of inflicting her paranoia and delusions on her family rather than internalising them.

"Whilst Frederick's mother was going through all of this, I noticed my son had started spending more and more time outdoors now, which I took as a good sign that he was growing up."

What Benjamin clearly didn't know was that more cats were going missing, more and more each month and that dogs had started to go missing, too. The police reports George had unearthed made it clear they were no longer looking at wild animals but at something more sinister. But it was the nineties, and they didn't have the human resources to look into it as deeply as they should have.

DI Beaumont thought back to the reports he'd read and remembered how, out in the woods, Freddie had learned how to hunt with his bare hands, catching rabbits and birds. The report had chilled George to the bone, especially when Freddie described, in gory detail, how he once climbed a tree and snatched a chick from a nest before pulling out his pocket knife and dismembering the poor chick. But believe it or not, it wasn't the dismembering that had chilled George; it was the fact that Freddie had not intended to deliberately kill any of the animals he caught; they just happened to die before he was finished with them.

The therapist asked Freddie why he tortured the animals to death, but Freddie denied torturing them. He said he was exploring how they were put together like a student at school scouring a biology textbook—that both disgusted and chilled George.

George said to Benjamin, "So Freddie didn't notice his mother was going through therapy or anything? It didn't worry him. Or change him?"

Benjamin thought momentarily, then said, "As I said, he barely noticed because he was always out. And when he was at school, he went with the flow and pleased other people. That's

CHAPTER THIRTY

what Frederick was like, a real people pleaser."

It made sense what Benjamin was telling him, George thought. Freddie had no control over anything at home and school, so he did what he could to appease everyone. But out in the woods, however, he had the opportunity to live as himself and finally be in control of everything around him as if he were a god. Sat on the sofa, staring into the dark eyes of Benjamin Harman, George thought back to the report sitting on his desk in his office back at Elland Road station. He hadn't managed to read it thoroughly, but in a passage halfway through, Freddie described the warmth he felt and the beginnings of sexual excitement only a ten-year-old could describe as he sank his fingers deep into the warm flesh of a cat he'd trapped and stabbed. Recalling that made George shudder, and he continued to shudder as he recalled Freddie stating the animals he captured lived or died at his whim or were sliced open or crushed to death at his whim.

Frederick Harman was in charge when he was in the woods.

And that terrified George.

Chapter Thirty-one

"Earlier, you said that when Freddie was at school, he went with the flow and pleased other people," said George.

"Correct, I did say that," said Benjamin.

"So, there were no concerns?"

"I didn't say that, did I?"

George said nothing. He hated it when people played with information. There was no reason why Benjamin would keep anything from them. They weren't offering him anything. They had nothing Ben needed. Yet he was still trying to use his information like a currency.

Eventually, when the silence became too loud, Benjamin explained, "At school, teachers began to notice Freddie's shyness because it was becoming more pronounced. My boy only spoke when spoken to, as I taught him, and I don't mind admitting it pissed me off when they complained about it." He paused and scratched his beard again. It was dark and greasy, with some hairs longer than others, spiky and protruding out like the bristles of a brush. "I suppose they mentioned something about him not listening during lessons and how he daydreamed a lot. I told them he was bored, and they needed to change the lessons up because he clearly wasn't being stimulated by school."

CHAPTER THIRTY-ONE

"Anything else?"

"I vaguely remember something about him hanging out with the high school kids after school. The school thought he was smoking, but I could never smell tobacco on him. It leaves a certain scent, and I must admit I hate the smell. I'd have known if he were smoking, and he wasn't."

Candy asked, "So, what was he doing with the older kids?"

"No clue."

George knew. It was all there in the psych reports. Freddie had an addiction to fire. The smoking kids kept him around because he'd always have matches and lighters on him, which he played with whilst they smoked. When asked how he managed to get a hold of the lighters and matches, he told the therapist he would steal them from Morrisons.

"If he didn't smell of tobacco, then why did the teachers accuse Freddie of smoking?" George asked.

"Because he was playing with a book of matches if I remember right."

George nodded. It was clear from the reports that as soon as Freddie realised how easy the matches were to steal compared to the lighters, he began hoarding them and hid them under his mattress where his mother wouldn't find them. Freddie also admitted to having another stash out in the woods near the watermill, where he would build little fires and incorporate them into his sadistic play.

"Did he ever light fires at home?" asked George.

"I can't remember if he did." Ben shrugged. "But home was becoming more and more chaotic. I was working more hours, and his mother's mask of sanity was slipping once more. I guess that's why I didn't want to be home. I couldn't be arsed with the arguments. That, and my boss was a prick. The time I spent dropping Joanne and Elsie off at home after her stalking sessions had to be worked off at twice the hours; otherwise, I'd have had no job. No job meant no food, no nappies, no house, no talking therapy, no nothing."

George could see the man's knuckles turning more and more white as he spoke about his wife.

"When I told Joanne to stop stalking me at work, she instead began conversing openly with our neighbours about her horrible life and how I badly abused her. Her accusations that I had a violent nature caused trouble because I was beginning to rebuild my reputation at work. My wife's rumours of her terrible home life came to light, bringing judgment from all corners and embarrassment to the local company I worked for. It cost me the job that we had relocated to Leeds for and put a barrier in the way of my career that, if I'm honest, I still haven't recovered from. Don't get me wrong, I've never struggled to find a job, but the only work I could get was unskilled labour that paid only a fraction of the amount I had brought home before."

George could see the man looked agitated. They'd need to bring the interview to a close soon, but they were receiving essential intelligence from the man. Their entire job consisted of them treading a thin moral line.

"And that meant one of two things had to happen. One, my wife had to cut back, or two, we had to start spending our savings." Benjamin nodded at George. "Heard you've just had a baby, so you'll know exactly which option my wife decided on."

What a prick, George thought. If necessary, Isabella would cut back, just as he would. But it appeared Joanna and Benjamin Harman were his and Isabella's complete opposites.

CHAPTER THIRTY-ONE

"You burned through your savings?"

"Correct, which meant more erratic behaviour from Joanne. It was like a vicious cycle. The worse Jo became, the harder it was to drag us back from the precipice. And yet, to most people, I was a bastard or a wife-beater. In truth, I simply worked my fucking arse off to provide for my family."

Around the time Benjamin had regularly changed jobs, the police had been to the Harman house no less than fifteen times in the space of two months, and the records were rather detailed. On ten out of those fifteen occasions, there was evidence that Benjamin had beaten Joanne, but they couldn't do anything because Joanne didn't want to press charges.

But clearly, from what Benjamin was saying, those regular police visits set the rumour mill chugging again.

"How did all of this affect Freddie?" George asked.

"I'm not sure it did, to tell you the truth," Ben said. "Outside school hours, Frederick stayed in the woods or lingered in the garden."

George knew otherwise. It was exceptionally well documented just how much the arguments and his father's constant changing of jobs had affected Frederick Harman. The boy had no peace and quiet at home, so he spent more and more time in the woods, mutilating more and more animals and setting fires to whatever he could. But it appeared nothing Freddie did would help him shake loose the stress and anxiety he thrust upon him at home.

Freddie wasn't angry with his parents for being like they were. According to the therapist, rage wasn't something Freddie had ever really expressed as a child. Even when he was ripping apart living animals with his bare hands, he wasn't doing it because he was angry at them; he did it because it was necessary. It was all about being in control. As such, it did nothing to dampen the well-stoked flames that his mother and father had instilled into him. But the constant barking of a particular dog nearly did.

"Are you suggesting you don't remember this?" asked Candy. She got up and held out a blue paper folder. Benjamin swiped it from the young lass and rifled through it, finding only one piece of paper that appeared to be a photocopy of a news article.

"Johnathan Duke, editor of that paper, was very kind and found the original print so we could copy it and use it to jog your memory," said George.

Benjamin nodded. "I suppose I forgot about this on purpose. Perhaps my brain did it to protect me?"

George said nothing.

The news article showed a picture of a blackened dog kennel at the bottom of a garden.

"Fuck," was all Benjamin said.

Freddie needed the barking to stop, so he made it stop the best way he could by tying up the dog in the wooden kennel and setting it alight.

Then he sat and watched, observing the blaze as it grew into something resembling a bonfire. The sound of the dog barking was mixed with the crackling of flames. Those two noises mixed to form a symphony that blocked out his mother's screaming and his father's shouting.

In that moment, Freddie had described the feeling as bliss.

That was until the dog's owner, their neighbour, realised something was awry and emerged in a panic, shouting his head off before finally dousing the flames with a host attached to his outside tap. When the neighbour looked around, he saw

Freddie standing by the fence, watching the fire with a massive grin on his face.

"If there's one thing that can be said for my Frederick, is that he's not a liar," Benjamin said once he'd finished reading the article. "I do remember this. I remember fighting with Mark, our neighbour, giving him a black eye and a fat lip because he accused my son of causing the fire."

"Freddie did cause the fire."

"I know, but Mark accused Freddie of killing the pup, too."

George narrowed his brows. "He did kill the dog."

"Not intentionally," said Benjamin, pointing. He started shaking his head erratically. "He was messing with matches, and when one lit, he panicked and tossed it over the fence." Ben jabbed at the page. "Look, it's here in black and white. You've seen this, right?"

George nodded.

"It was an unfortunate accident. Yes, it could have been avoided, but it was an accident, plain and simple."

"Except we know now it wasn't an accident," said George. "With his conversations with a therapist after what happened with Joanne, Freddie admitted to tying the dog up inside and purposely causing the fire."

Benjamin said nothing and picked at his fingernails.

There wasn't much that could be said, not really. But George wanted to pick up on something he felt was inaccurate. He met eyes with Mr Harman and said, "You mentioned fighting with Mark, the neighbour, giving him a black eye and a fat lip."

Benjamin nodded.

"Freddie's version of events is entirely different to yours."

"Well, of course, it is," Ben said, shaking his head.

"He states the neighbour dragged him by the arm to your

front door and, for the first time that Freddie could remember, it was you who rushed to open the door. And instead of asking what was wrong and being protective over your son whom somebody outside the family was manhandling, you got angry and shouted at him, asking what he'd done wrong."

Benjamin opened his mouth to defend his actions, but George got there first. "Instead of protecting your son and standing up for him, you slapped him across the cheek with the back of your hand, causing him to fall to the floor. You then got into a fight with Mark, your neighbour, because he disagreed with the way you'd assaulted your son."

Benjamin scoffed. "Assaulted. Fuck off. I've never assaulted anybody in my life!"

"Every time Freddie picked himself up again and tried to tell his side of the story, you gave him another slap. If that's not assault, I don't know what is!"

A snarl erupted across Benjamin's face. "You said it yourself, didn't you? He burnt that kennel down with the dog inside it on purpose. Frederick is a monster, an uncontrollable monster! I slapped him because he was telling lies. And I knew he was telling lies because I watched him do it from upstairs!" Benjamin began panting, struggling with each breath as he sucked air in and puffed it out. "Imagine seeing your son do that. Kill something innocent in such a sick, twisted way. I'd heard rumours about the cats and how they'd been buried at the bottom of the garden, but I didn't believe anybody until that day!"

"And that's when you began treating him differently."

"Well, wouldn't you? The sick little bastard terrified me!"

"That's not all though, is it?" asked George.

"What do you mean?"

"You had to pay Mark to keep quiet, didn't you?"

Benjamin closed his eyes and nodded. "The cash amount obliterated our already minute savings balance."

"And you took that out on your son, didn't you?"

Benjamin continued to nod his head.

Benjamin was correct in his evaluation of his son. He didn't lie. Every word recorded by the therapists and the psychiatrists was true.

And that meant, as soon as the neighbour had left and Benjamin Harman had shut the door, Ben turned his full, unbridled fury onto his son. Instead of the backhanded slaps, this time, Benjamin used his fists, and Freddie's world exploded into darkness and pain. And the blows continued to rain down on the boy for much longer than any sane man would have continued for. In fact, from the description Freddie gave, the blows inflicted upon him by his father were long past the point of corporal punishment and more akin to attempted murder.

George shuddered when he remembered what Freddie described next. Because, in between the bouts of darkness and pain, all Freddie could see was his father's twisted snarl and lifeless eyes. All Freddie could hear was the list of ways that he had ruined everything Benjamin had built and how he had destroyed the family. That he was a monster, that he was evil.

Yet to Freddie, the twisted snarl and lifeless eyes that generally belonged to a monster belonged to his father, who was beating his son bloody.

Chapter Thirty-two

DI George Beaumont sat in his cluttered office reading psychiatry reports, the dim overhead lights casting long shadows across the stacks of case files and the ageing, worn-out furniture. The faint hum of activity outside his door was a constant reminder of the ceaseless rhythm of police work in the bustling city of Leeds. They were hunting Frederick Harman, but he was nowhere to be found.

From reading more of the reports Yolanda had sourced, it appeared the Harman family finances were already at breaking point even before Frederick burnt down the kennel. The complaint to Benjamin's boss put in by their neighbour, Mark, and the compensation Ben had provided, depleted what little was left of their savings. In truth, the family had been living beyond their means ever since moving to Hunslet, and now the time for pretence was over.

So, another fresh start was enforced upon the Harman family. They held an open house and sold all their furniture and extravagance that Joanne had continually purchased because where they were going, there wouldn't be room for it.

The house they moved into on Woodsley Road in Woodhouse was as tiny as the one where Frederick had spent most of his younger years. It had one bedroom and only offered a few modern comforts. But Frederick was eleven at that point, a tall, gangly boy who had to share the bedroom with his little sister.

As someone who craved solitude and silence, he hated the noises she made, hated the smell that came from her, hated that they shared the same oxygen. He'd stay awake at night, listening to her breathe, desperately wanting her to stop so he could get some sleep. He often wondered how much peace there would be if he simply took his pillow and suffocated the little witch.

But he kept his desires in check and did his best to ignore the fact that he and his family were smudged together like sardines in a tin.

And he missed the woods in Stourton. He'd spent so much of his youth exploring himself in those woods, and now they were denied to him. He could walk, of course, or get the bus, but he had no money and, in truth, no sense of direction. The places he found were often found by accident during his exploration of the world.

The loss of the woods was a turning point in Frederick's life. It meant he lost the outlets he used to manage his internal conflicts. There was nowhere nearby that he could stalk and kill animals in peace. There was nowhere that he could build his fires without being noticed. Like the Harman family and the new house, Woodsley Road and the surrounding houses were packed in tight like sardines. That meant he had no way to regulate his rapidly fluctuating moods and the masking he was doing at home to always try and act perfect.

The summer holidays meant they could change Frederick's high school to Lawnswood School without it affecting him, or so his parents thought. The separation from the peers he'd been used to since his youth and the resulting new, colossal environment filled with differing subjects, new teachers and children meant extra pressure was put on Frederick. During school, Freddie, as he was now known, kept his mask up, managing successfully to build relationships with new friends and teachers, but that meant the cover came down at home, and without the woods to go to, he daydreamed endlessly about ending his devil of a sister's life. He'd wake up from dreams where he'd strangled his sister, his hands clenched together tightly, only to find his pants wet from where he'd had a wet dream. Wet dreams were normal for high school-aged boys, of course, but Freddie only seemed to have them after dreaming of murdering his little sister.

His teachers considered him well-behaved, with above-average intelligence, and his peers liked him. However, because he kept to himself, he had an air of mystery that appeared particularly attractive to the girls he encountered. If it weren't for his reluctance, he could have had any girl he wanted, even any of those older than him. It appeared just as his family had always projected normalcy towards the rest of society, Freddie managed to do the same.

* * *

DI George Beaumont had barely settled back into his cluttered office when his phone rang again. The familiar voice of DCS Mohammed Sadiq filled the room.

"Beaumont, I've got more information for you regarding the Harman case," Sadiq announced without preamble.

George leaned forward, his curiosity piqued. "OK, sir. What have you found?"

CHAPTER THIRTY-TWO

Sadiq proceeded to share another intriguing lead. "I did some digging into Frederick Harman's past, as I said. I remember now there was a next-door neighbour of the Harmans named Elliot Dreggs. He worked at Frederick's high school, Lawnswood."

Beaumont's interest deepened. "Elliot Dreggs, you say? What was his connection to Frederick?"

Sadiq explained, "Elliot Dreggs was more than just a neighbour; he was a close family friend and had a significant presence in Frederick's life. He had a special interest in Frederick. Some reports even suggest he acted as a mentor of sorts."

Beaumont furrowed his brow. "A mentor? That's unusual, especially considering Frederick's troubled history."

Sadiq nodded. "Indeed, it struck me as odd as well. There were rumours and whispers about their relationship, though nothing substantial. But given Frederick's behavioural issues and Dreggs' involvement in his life, it might be worth looking into."

Beaumont made a mental note of the new lead. "Thank you, sir. This could be a significant piece of the puzzle. We'll thoroughly investigate Elliot Dreggs and his connection to Frederick Harman."

As he hung up the phone, Beaumont couldn't shake the feeling that they were on the brink of a breakthrough. The involvement of Elliot Dreggs, a mentor figure in Frederick's life, added a layer of complexity to the case that demanded exploration.

He gathered his team, including Constable Candy, and briefed them on the latest developments.

DI George Beaumont knew that unravelling the mystery

of Elliot Dreggs and his connection to Frederick Harman required a deeper dive into Dreggs' role at Lawnswood School. Armed with this new information, he contacted the Head of Lawnswood, Evelyn Price, to learn more about the caretaker and this possible relationship with Freddie.

Beaumont dialled the number for Lawnswood School, his heart pounding with anticipation. After a few rings, a voice on the other end answered, "Lawnswood School, how may I help you?"

"Good morning, this is DI Beaumont of the West Yorkshire Police," he replied, his tone professional yet inquisitive. "I'd like to speak with Headteacher Mrs Evelyn Price, please. It's regarding a matter of some importance."

There was a brief pause before the receptionist replied, "One moment, please."

Beaumont waited, tapping his fingers impatiently on the desk. Soon, Mrs Price's voice came on the line.

"Mrs Price, this is DI George Beaumont. I'm investigating a case involving a former caretaker at your school named Elliot Dreggs. I'd like to ask you a few questions about him if you have a moment."

Mrs Price's voice held a hint of curiosity. "Of course, DI Beaumont. I remember Elliot Dreggs. He was indeed our caretaker for several years when I wasn't the head. What would you like to know?"

Beaumont got straight to the point. "Can you tell me more about Dreggs' role at Lawnswood? Was he involved with any students or have any unusual interactions that you're aware of?"

Mrs Price hesitated momentarily before responding, "Mr Dreggs was responsible for the maintenance and upkeep of the school premises. He wasn't involved in teaching or directly responsible for students. Regarding unusual interactions, there were a few instances where he seemed overly attentive to certain students, but when we conducted our enquiries, nothing came of anything."

Beaumont's interest deepened. "Were you teaching when a lad named Frederick Harman was there?"

"I was."

"Did Mr Dreggs have anything to do with him?"

"Mr Harman was one of those overly attentive students, yes."

"Can you provide more details about his interactions with Frederick Harman?"

Mrs Price recalled, "There were reports from staff and students alike that Mr Dreggs would often seek out Frederick during his time at Lawnswood. He would strike up conversations, sometimes offering advice or guidance. It raised some eyebrows, as it wasn't typical behaviour for a caretaker."

Beaumont made a mental note of this information. "Thank you, Mrs Price. Can you think of anything else?"

"Only that I heard what happened to Frederick and the trial that never happened." She paused. "He was a very disturbed individual."

Beaumont thanked Mrs Price for her cooperation and ended the call, his mind racing with new leads and questions. The connection between Elliot Dreggs and Frederick Harman was becoming more evident, and it seemed that Dreggs' role as a caretaker held more significance than anyone had initially realised.

As such, after he shared the information with his team, they decided to visit him in person. After all, they were no closer to finding Freddie, and Dreggs may have the lead they desperately needed.

Chapter Thirty-three

"This is the place, boss," DC Jason Scott said, pointing at the house next to the convenience store on Woodsley Road.

George pulled the Merc up by the kerb, and both got out. George took a moment to stretch, and Jay took the area in. It was a typical Leeds back-to-back terraced street not that dissimilar to Headingley, where he'd grown up, which made sense considering they were a stone's throw away from each other. But Jay had witnessed areas like this in different parts of Leeds during his policing career.

"Do the honours, Jay," George said, pointing to the house beyond a broken gate. Behind the gate post was a minute garden lined with broken flagstones and a mass of bottles and cans, clearly from customers of the off-license next door.

Jay nodded and entered the garden before taking the four steps and pounding on the door.

The downstairs windows revealed stained net curtains behind steel bars, but it was too dark to see within. Upstairs, the windows were open, causing the brown curtains to lap against the windows. Not a single light was on, and despite the loud knock, there was no movement.

Jay peered through the letterbox, seeing open doors, stairs covered in a threadbare grey carpet, and a pile of unopened mail on the floor. Jay banged on the door again, this time using his police knock, the sound echoing through the rooms of the house.

"The place looks deserted. Guess he isn't home," Jay said, stepping back to look through the letterbox again. "I thought he was expecting us?"

"He is. Did you take down his number?"

"Aye, boss, give me a minute."

George tapped his foot, considering their next move before realising they had none. Not without a warrant. And anyway, Elliot had important information for them. He nodded at Jay to knock on the door again, which the young DC did.

Then, a head appeared from one of the upstairs windows, protruding between the brown curtains. "What the fuck are you playing at? Some of us work nights!" a voice screamed.

"Police," said George. "We were under the impression you were expecting us."

"Oh shit, give me a minute."

In the end, they had to give him five minutes, though to George, it felt like an hour.

"Where is Frederick Harman?" George asked.

"I'm sorry I have no idea," Dreggs said.

"Tell us about him," the DI ordered.

"From what I remember," Elliot said after the detectives declined an offer of drinks and sat on the sofa, "Freddie was quite a popular lad. But he was never home, you see. Always out. But not causing any ruckus from what I remember."

George nodded. He'd read the reports that Lawnswood School had provided, and they very much said he was a popular, bright boy.

"But I suppose that changed a little once their parents

decided to separate and get divorced."

Towards the end of year seven, Freddie's home life imploded as his parents, who had spent their entire adult lives hating each other, decided to separate with the intention of divorce. Where before, the most significant thing preventing the separation was their attempt to conform to societal norms; their destitution meant that they could no longer continue their pretence.

"It was Joanne who left Benjamin if I remember right," Elliot said. "I had a girlfriend at the time, and I'm sure Joanne told her leaving a bankrupt husband was a hell of a lot easier than leaving one who was providing well for the family. And it made sense, I suppose, because she really fucking hated that man, believe me."

"What do you mean?" asked Jay.

"Well, think about it. She could stay with him and stay poor, raising her two kids alone, even with a husband around. Or she could leave and find somebody else to help raise her children." He shrugged. "Benjamin was a fucking waste of space, anyway."

Despite already knowing the answer, George asked, "How did you get to know the family so well?"

"I was the caretaker at Lawnswood School as well as their neighbour," Elliot explained. His jaundiced face instantly turned red, but he continued his explanation before George could inquire as to why. "Anyway, back to Freddie. One day, Freddie was attending his lessons as usual, then was suddenly gone the following day. His teachers were baffled, and his friends were concerned for him." Then Elliot frowned at George. "You should already know this, but the truth of where Freddie had gone to was revealed only after a home visit by you lot, the police."

"Humour me," the DI said.

"Well, for the first time in their lives, Freddie and Elsie were completely free from the controlling presence of their dad when they moved to live with their grandmother in Miggy."

"Middleton?" Jay asked.

"Aye, that's right. Dolphin Road. I remember because of the weird name."

"Did you lose contact with them?" asked George.

"No, because as it turned out, Joanna was pretty mental. You see, we thought Benjamin was the problem, and he was, but without Benjamin around, there was nobody to counter the madness ticking around her brain."

"Struggling with your mental health doesn't mean you're mad," said George.

"You're right, forgive me, but I'm old fashioned," said Elliot. "She did struggle with her mental health, but she was mad, trust me."

"Explain."

"Oh, I will." He took a sip of his drink. "Joanne thought leaving Benjamin and living with her mother would improve everything. But without Benjamin's strict structure, she began worrying about Freddie's health, and her anxieties became hard to ignore."

"How do you know all this?" asked Jay.

Elliot turned red. "Well, I was seeing Joanna for a bit. It's why I know so much about them."

That was something George didn't already know. "You were in a relationship?"

"Oh, aye. I helped her with Freddie and Elsie, especially when she was at her lowest."

CHAPTER THIRTY-THREE

George knew what Elliot meant by this. Elsie was more grounded than Freddie, so their mother's anxieties and health worries didn't affect her. But from the notes taken by Freddie's therapist, at night, he admitted he would lie awake and attempt to feel for any symptoms that his mother had insisted he was exhibiting throughout the day. She claimed that he had two instances of bony protrusions, like devil's horns atop his skull, which he would then spend hours prodding and poking until it hurt, but not finding anything.

But that wasn't all. Freddies's concerns about poisoning were more problematic than those peculiarities. For years, his mother had accused his father of using household chemicals to poison her and Freddie. Now that the couple were no longer together and the symptoms of poisoning had stopped, she managed to convince everyone of her theory.

But Freddie didn't feel as if he were getting better. He'd run around the house manically, getting his heart to beat faster and faster, before plugging his ears with his fingers so he could listen to the pounding. That should have been evidence of him being alive, but to Freddie, he was sure he could hear his heart missing beats and became paranoid there was an issue with his heart. So, he naturally put two and two together, making five, and convinced himself that his father was poisoning him, intending to kill him.

"What happened to the relationship?" asked George.

"Jo and Benjamin started texting and calling each other more regularly." Elliot frowned. "She never admitted it to me, but I know for a fact she was seeing Benjamin behind my back."

"Right."

"And eventually she left me and got back with him, somehow

convinced that their relationship had resolved all of its issues and that they would return to the dream they had shared when they were first married." Elliott shook his head. "Fucking ridiculous if you ask me."

"Why ridiculous?" prompted George.

"Because it was impossible for either of them to alter who they were, what they wanted in life, or, in the end, their relationship with each other. If you think about it, it makes sense. They hated each other, and the damage had already been done. But she wouldn't listen to me, no matter how much I pleaded with her."

Jay asked, "So, you continued to live next door to them, despite everything?"

"Well, yeah, of course." Elliott turned red again. "I secretly hoped she'd leave him again, kick him out of that house so we could be together."

George knew the parents had gotten back together and knew it had been a peculiar time for Freddie. On the one hand, he was back at Lawnswood, around his friends and teachers, and back to his usual school routine; he was once again living with his father, a man who, it appeared, showed his love through his fists.

One benefit of returning home was the change in his mother's strange behaviour. Not once did she mention the horns growing on his head whilst his father was around.

"How was Freddie when his parents got back together?" asked George.

"Not that good, to tell you the truth. Some of his teachers knew I was his neighbour, and a couple even knew I'd been in a relationship with his mum. They'd come to me and check up on his welfare as they'd observed that he was less involved

CHAPTER THIRTY-THREE

and eager, as though he was no longer concerned with his qualifications."

"Did they have a theory as to why?" George asked.

"Of course. They put it down to his chaotic home life affecting his schooling. But the boy wasn't himself. Teachers would challenge him during lessons for his opinion, and he'd tell the teachers what they wanted to hear rather than give his view. That, or he'd become obstructive."

"Obstructive, how?" asked the DI.

"Well, he'd take the piss or answer in a silly way. And unfortunately, as that became his natural response, he was labelled as something of a rebel. It was great for his reputation, the clown of the class, if you know what I mean, but it did him no favours with the adults at the school."

"How so?" asked George.

"Well, the teachers started to take it out on him," said Elliot. "Freddie was sent home with complaints, and the following day, he would return to school wounded and hurt and no more willing to follow the rules than he had been the day before. Every beating seemed to harden him even more if anything. It just seemed to solidify his determination in a way that other boys would break." He scratched once again the bald spot atop his head. "You've got to remember I was here when Benjamin beat Freddie." He pointed at the joining wall. "The walls are thin."

Jay asked, "So you're saying he changed his behaviour once his parents got back together?"

"Yeah, both in and out of school," Elliot explained. "Don't get me wrong, Freddie was always out of the house, but now he had a lot of mates due to being the class clown, and so he spent a lot of time mingling with different groups of kids." Elliot shrugged. "I don't know about you, detectives, but when I was at school, I had a group of friends I stuck with. Freddie was the complete opposite. He'd have different groups of kids knocking at the door every day of the week."

"Why is that an issue?" asked George.

"I mean, I'm no expert, clearly, but if you ask me, and you have, it wasn't doing his reputation any good."

"I don't understand," said the DI.

"Because of his increased popularity, Freddie soon started meeting up with girls who were… how do I put it, more fun and less respectable than the ones he usually hung about with. And you know what boys are like at that age; I mean, we've all been there, haven't we?"

Elliot chuckled, but neither detective said anything. They already knew Freddie Harman was a hit with the ladies. They just wanted to know why and how that affected him.

"Is there anything else you can tell us?" asked George.

Elliot scratched the bald spot atop his head whilst he thought. He clicked his tongue against his teeth. "I once caught him in my house, looking through my alcohol cupboard, and when I asked him what the hell he was doing, he gave me some sob story about wanting to fit in with his friends and how they'd dared him to steal. My door had always been open to the boy. I'll admit, I had a soft spot for him." He pointed at George. "In a fatherly way, of course. Nothing sinister. I refused his request, of course, and later found out he'd stolen from the shop next door. It's been there donkey's years, though with different branding. The owner came to me with the CCTV footage, not wanting to speak with Benjamin due to his reputation, hoping I could do something."

Jay asked, "And did you?"

"Did I what?"

The DC frowned. "Do something?"

Elliot shook his head. "It wasn't my place. The kid was in year eleven at that point. But I know what his dad didn't do."

The DI narrowed his brows.

Elliot explained, "I wasn't the only one Freddie stole from. The boy entered the house three doors up, the house of an elderly man at the time who stupidly didn't lock his front door. The man's son caught Freddie and got the police involved immediately."

George nodded. He knew what Elliot was going to say because he had the police report on his desk back at Elland Road.

"Poor kid wasn't even protected by his dad, either." Elliot shook his head. "That fucking father of his didn't attempt to defend his son, but luckily Freddie only got a warning and a slap on the wrist. It improved his reputation at school with his peers, but the teachers became even more wary of him."

George stood up, his question rhetorical. "Is there anything else?"

"Sorry, detectives, they moved to Miggy a couple of months later, and I guess I wasn't thought of ever again."

"And you don't know where Freddie is now?"

Elliot shook his head. "Sorry, I've not heard from him in years."

George said, "Before we go, we have one more question for you."

"Shoot."

"You mentioned earlier that your door had always been open to Freddie, and you had a soft spot for him."

He frowned. "And?"

"I spoke with Lawnswood School before coming here, and they investigated your relationship with Freddie."

"So what."

"There was nothing more?"

Elliot stood up with fire in his eyes. "Absolutely fucking not!"

Chapter Thirty-four

Back at the station, and despite the October chill, George's hair was stuck to his scalp, dampness lined the neck of his shirt, and his trousers were stuck to his legs. The weight he'd piled on since his accident was steadily shifting, albeit slowly, but he found wherever he went, he sweated profusely.

And he was stressed, too. Stressed that they couldn't find Frederick Harman, worrying sick that he might kill again.

DS Tashan Blackburn sat in the shared office, staring intently at his screen as usual. George went over to him. "Hello, sir."

"Alright, Tashan?"

"Yes, sir." Tashan took a sip of his tea. "Get much from Elliot Dreggs?"

"We already know most of it already, but he was apparently in a relationship with Joanne Harman."

"Cheating?"

"No, whilst they were separated and living in Middleton with her mother."

"Interesting."

"He didn't appear biased, but I'm taking everything he said with a pinch of salt."

"That's the best way, sir." Tashan stood up and handed

George a blue folder. "More transcripts, this time from Bridge House near town. They took him on when the family moved from Woodhouse to Middleton. They're very basic, so I'd read them alongside his section 37/41 therapy transcripts."

"Cheers, Tashan," George said, immediately heading to his office to read.

From the report, it appeared that Freddie entered into a series of brief relationships that all went in the same direction. The problem was, despite being young, he wanted to enter into a committed relationship, and the girls he was seeing didn't. So respectfully and never taking advantage of them, he'd move on.

DC Blackburn had already scoured the police reports to see if any complaints had been filed, but there was nothing, suggesting what he told his therapist was the truth.

As George continued reading, he found that only two girls he went out with liked him enough in year eleven to allow him to have sex with them. But despite them telling him they were ready and even buying condoms from the pharmacist, Freddie didn't appear bothered whenever it came to doing the act, often making excuses and rescheduling.

The DI wondered why that was, but he didn't have to wait too long to find out. Right before his GCSE exams, a third girl, Klara Clarke, from year twelve in the sixth form, seduced him. She, too, lived in Middleton, and her parents were working late, so Freddie decided it was time to lose his virginity.

Everything was going well for Freddie, too well at first, as he became erect at seeing a naked woman—other than the times he'd spied on his mother in the bath—for the first time. And whilst he could initiate sex, he could not keep his erection long enough to finish.

CHAPTER THIRTY-FOUR

From the section 37/41 reports, George read that Freddie blamed Klara. Broke up with her immediately. His sole objective in the relationships had been sex, as had hers, but clearly, something was wrong with her and not him. He was sure he'd told her she wasn't beautiful enough or had been with too many boys, so she wasn't tight enough.

In truth, Freddie was the one with the problem, but he had no idea why he could not maintain an erection. It had never caused him any trouble in the past. In fact, he admitted he was so hard it hurt every time he had an animal pinned out in the woods and was cutting into its flesh, repeatedly orgasming. So why couldn't he do the same when inside a woman? According to the therapist, he obsessed over it all day and all night. He became adamant he was flawed in some way. Then, he became paranoid that his father was poisoning him again. Because despite everything going on and his obvious flaw, he desperately needed sex, yet there was nothing he could do about it.

Immediately, Freddie became obsessed with Middleton Woods, but they weren't the same as the woods in Stourton. They were too busy. Miggy itself was too busy. He couldn't steal cats and dogs like he used to because it appeared everyone was watching him.

So, he decided he needed to devise another means to release the tension without such rites. So, he turned to drink again. And when that didn't stop him from obsessing over sex, he began experimenting with drugs.

Because he'd kept in touch with his friends from Lawnswood and his new friends at his high school in Beeston, he had easy access to marijuana and quickly developed into a strong user. As he became increasingly engrossed in these new addictions, his previously immaculately maintained look disappeared. He found addicts who were experimenting with LSD through his present pals, and it was through them that he was able to have access to that substance. Among all his drug habits, using LSD was the most beneficial to him in the short run, but it also had adverse long-term effects on his health.

Naturally, he'd not admitted any animal killing or drug use to his therapist at Bridge House, only admitting to this once in the hospital. However, the therapist at Bridge Street had shared her concerns over his appearance and tardiness.

To his hospital psychiatrist, Freddie admitted he believed that using LSD allowed him to go deeper into his thoughts and face some of his inner demons. His anxieties about his health and erectile dysfunction would have dominated him, and his mental state would have been much worse without the almost psychedelic excursions he experienced with LSD. However, the drugs also permanently severed his connection to reality.

Even at his most stable moments, his grasp on reality was shaky, and the cannabis and LSD seemed to compound that effect. And George knew that despite his physical and behavioural changes, his mother refused to acknowledge these changes. He was just being a typical teenager who'd just left school. Why should that worry her?

DS Tashan Blackburn had even printed out a police report from the system from when Freddie was picked up by the police, who took him into custody for possession of marijuana in proportions that made them believe they'd busted a dealer. Unfortunately for them, that was just the amount that Freddie consistently took. They'd arrested a user rather than a dealer.

Still, the CPS instructed them to take Freddie to the Youth Court, a type of magistrates' court that deals with young people, because he'd already received a warning and a slap on the wrist for theft the previous year.

They had a wealth of information about the court case on their systems but didn't initially have a first-person point of view. Now they did.

Not only did they have the transcripts from Bridge House, but they also had further transcripts from Millpond Hospital in Meanwood, where Freddie had been sectioned. It was a wealth of information.

DI Beaumont reread them, looking for nuances that may help him find the bastard, but all he really found out was that the last of Freddie's confidence in his father was shattered in court. It appeared to George that Freddie had been expecting Benjamin to defend him but had forgotten the humiliation he had endured the previous time.

This time, instead of beating him black and blue in front of their neighbour, Benjamin decided not to support his son by refusing to pay for a solicitor. In Freddie's eyes, the one provided to him was on the police's side and was biased, which was why he lost his case and was sentenced to community service.

Benjamin then made it a point to regularly search Freddie's room for any drugs or alcohol, which meant he could only access what he needed when he was not home. But his weekends were spent cleaning up rubbish, mopping up sick from nightclubbers in the city centre, and removing graffiti.

All he had now were his nights, as he was required at college during the day. That was despite receiving a lot of Ds, Es and Fs in his GCSEs. He was lucky the college had allowed him to enter, usually requiring a minimum of five grade Cs, which Freddie was nowhere near getting. Luckily for Freddie, one of his previous teachers had managed to influence the head of his college course, explaining Freddie had the potential and that they owed it to him.

Joanne Harman was ecstatic that Freddie had continued his studies, having convinced herself her son was brilliant. Benjamin Harman didn't feel the same. He put pressure on Freddie to leave college and get a job. Now that he was a man, he better shape up, act like one, and start providing for himself so he could leave their home as soon as possible.

Freddie sided with his mum, believing that the future where he was portrayed as a genius with limitless potential was the more desirable of the two. Not to mention the potential independence that attending college would provide him instead of forcing himself to adhere to the rigid schedule of a job he detested, like his father, who always complained about the nine-to-five slog.

The issue with college was that his peers were always having house parties. One such Saturday night, Freddie had become so drunk that he'd voluntarily shared his erectile dysfunction with a school friend, a virgin who had pestered Freddie for details of his sexual escapades, wanting to get a kick out of Freddie's frequent encounters with women. It was understandable then that the lad was not prepared for Freddie's honesty, even ending the conversation and leaving Freddie on his own as Freddie went into great detail about how the dysfunction was destroying his life.

The next morning, Freddie woke up and threatened the lad after realising what he'd done and just how much of himself he'd shared. Under no circumstances was he to discuss what Freddie had shared with him, or else.

For Freddie, it was lucky he had brought his penknife with

CHAPTER THIRTY-FOUR

him; otherwise, the lad may not have listened.

Not only that, but Freddie had wanted to emulate Peter Sutcliffe during that heated moment, even telling his psychiatrist about the time Sutcliffe was 18 and on holiday with a male friend in the Lake District. Apparently, as Sutcliffe and his mate were getting ready for bed, his friend made a joke about sex and Sutcliffe's inability to perform, sending Peter mad with anger, resulting in Sutcliffe using a knife to slash at his friend's private parts. Whilst slashing, Sutcliffe had said, "I'm going to cut your dick off, you bastard!" which Freddie thought was one of the greatest quotes ever. Apparently, Sutcliffe's friend had to go to the hospital for stitches.

One such benefit of being in college was the health services they provided, and he was quickly referred to a psychiatrist who specialised in treating teenage issues in order to talk about his erectile dysfunction. He talked extensively about his sexual shortcomings, being careful not to mention that he liked to murder animals and set fires because he had learned his lesson about those topics well enough to keep those details private. However, even in the absence of that crucial piece of information, the psychiatrist quickly pointed out that, in cases where there was no apparent physical cause, repressed anger was frequently the root cause of male impotence. The psychiatrist, noting several red flags that led her to believe that Harman was suffering from a more severe mental disorder, suggested he see a therapist instead because the medicine she could prescribe wouldn't work on its own.

During his first therapy session at the college, Freddie arrived and smelled so strongly of cannabis as he walked into the room. The stories he told his therapist blended fact and fiction, reality and fantasy in a way that was inconsistent with a stable world-view. Rather than being a result of the boy's stress, this blurring could indicate a problem with Freddie's ability to perceive the world as it was. She helped him with some anger management techniques and taught him a few basic coping mechanisms, hoping he would continue to return to therapy voluntarily. She also advised that the specific type of erectile dysfunction that Freddie was experiencing was frequently brought on by thoughts of resentment and loathing for women, typically resulting from issues with their mother. Therefore, she suggested that Freddie make an effort with Joanne in an attempt to heal their connection. Even though it was not what Freddie wanted to hear, he heeded the advice but left without looking back.

Freddie did nothing to try to repair his relationship with his mother. If she were the cause of his shame, then why should he? He thought about how she'd brought him up, touching the sides of his skull as he did so, feeling for the horns his mother had seen up there.

But he found nothing.

His own growing hypochondria had not waned over the years but had now reached a stage where he was trying to self-monitor his own heartbeat, plugging his ears, and touching his chest in public whenever he thought something wasn't quite right. He almost entirely did this in public in order to avoid his father's fury so he wouldn't show the same signs as his mother, though this did not mean he did not live in continual worry for his life and health. In fact, he'd call the college health centre with almost daily inane questions, even though he had learnt to keep his signals to himself.

"Boss," a voice said, which caused George to immediately look up.

CHAPTER THIRTY-FOUR

"DC Scott?"

"Sorry for interrupting, boss, but DSU Smith and DCI Atkinson are looking for you."

Chapter Thirty-five

Detective Superintendent Jim Smith and Detective Chief Inspector Alistair Atkinson sat in Smith's dimly lit office, shrouded in an atmosphere of tension and anticipation. Their minds were consumed by the relentless pursuit of a brutal killer who had haunted the streets of Bradford for far too long. As they contemplated their next move, a soft knock echoed through the room, and without waiting for a response, George, the seasoned detective, entered.

George, a man of few words but many actions, sat before the two senior officers, his eyes sharp and alert. He leaned forward, his expression a mix of curiosity and determination, and asked the question that hung in the air, "How can I help?"

Smith leaned back in his leather chair, a hint of weariness in his eyes, and began to unravel their suspicions. "Beaumont, we know you've been tracking Frederick Harman for quite some time now, and we might have stumbled upon a connection that could finally put an end to this nightmare. We think there's a link between Harman and the Ripper copycat in Bradford."

George raised an eyebrow, intrigue evident in his features. "Why do you think that?"

Alistair chimed in his tone grave. "Our lead comes from the

survivor in Bingley, Lauren Robinson. She managed to provide a description of her attacker to a sketch artist who created an e-fit." He handed George a photograph. "Take a look at this."

George examined the image and couldn't help but be taken aback. It was eerie how closely it resembled Peter Sutcliffe, the infamous Yorkshire Ripper. But the e-fit also bore an uncanny resemblance to Frederick Harman, especially with the nose and the wiry black hair. "The images we have of Frederick all have him as clean-shaven. Does that mean he's grown a beard?"

"Prick thinks he's Sutcliffe," DSU Smith muttered, echoing George's unspoken thoughts. "And yes, men can grow beards, George."

George's mind raced as he processed the information. "So, what do you need from me?"

Smith leaned forward, a glint of determination in his eyes. "Last night, a young woman, white skin, black hair— Frederick's typical victim selection—was brutally attacked in Bradford. She was a prostitute, and the weapon used was a hammer. It fits the ripper's MO. If it is Harman, then we need your expertise." He paused. "Mark Finch will also be involved."

George nodded solemnly, the weight of the situation settling on his shoulders. "OK, sir. I'll meet you at the scene."

* * *

On the way to Manningham in Bradford, they took a squad car so that Jay could drive and George could continue to read.

A week after Freddie turned seventeen, his parents decided they would separate and get divorced this time. Unlike before, when they'd flown apart in a rage, things were different. They agreed to a mutual understanding to part ways rather than continue to bother each other's every waking hour. They gave their children the choice to live with either of them as they wished, and Benjamin would continue to provide Joanna a percentage of his salary for her maintenance. Without a second thought for their mother, Elsie chose their father, whilst Freddie struggled with the choice. So, he did what he usually did; he placated both, living with his mother but seeing his father daily.

The fact that he and his mother continued to live on Dolphin Road, and his father and sister only moved to a house on Newhall Garth meant his journey to spend time with his father every day was short and easy.

To Freddie, his parents showed genuine gratitude to him for his efforts during that period, realising that his sensitivity was not a sign of weakness but rather of generosity. Over the years, his father attempted to remove the boy's tenderness when he should have cherished it the most. According to the hospital psychiatry reports, Freddie found he spent more time with his father during that period than ever before, even having pleasant, father-son conversations that Benjamin had never really had with his own father.

George wondered whether this change forced Benjamin to face the painful reality that he had mistreated his son severely over the years and that despite everything, Freddie had still shown kindness to his father and tormentor by turning the other cheek.

The DI thought not. Benjamin Harman was a prick, just like his own father.

CHAPTER THIRTY-FIVE

* * *

The night had draped Manningham in an inky shroud, and the full moon cast an eerie glow on the quiet streets. Detective Constable Jay Scott parked the Merc discreetly from the crime scene and they sat in solemn silence for a moment, their faces masked by a mix of anticipation and dread.

The location they were about to enter was notorious, even among seasoned officers. Manningham, a district in Bradford, had seen its fair share of violence and despair over the years, but tonight, it held an ominous weight. The chilling details they'd received from Smith and Atkinson had sent a chill down their spines, and they knew they were stepping into the heart of darkness.

The victim's name was Jacqueline Bell, a woman who had once known dreams and aspirations but had been swallowed by the unforgiving underbelly of the city. George thought back to the photos where Bell's lifeless body lay sprawled on the cobblestone pavement, illuminated by the cold, unfeeling glare of the streetlights. Her once-black hair now glistened with the grotesque evidence of her final moments.

George and Jay stepped out of the car and approached the scene cautiously, mindful of every step they took. The air was thick with tension and an unshakable sense of foreboding. Uniformed officers bustled about, keeping curious onlookers at bay. That morning, the flashing blue and red lights would have painted the surroundings with an eerie, surreal quality.

The victim had become another statistic in the city's grim tapestry of crime.

George and Jay approached Lindsey Yardley and her team, who were meticulously examining the scene. Their faces were grim as they observed the gruesome tableau before them. The details were unsettlingly familiar—a prostitute, attacked with a hammer and left for dead in Bradford.

* * *

On the way back to Elland Road, George pulled up the email on his phone, zooming into the transcribed text so he could read the transcripts DC Tashan Blackburn had managed to procure from Joanna Harman's therapist.

Joanne appeared to struggle during the second separation, feeling betrayed by Freddie due to him sneaking off to spend time with his father—a man who already had Elsie to keep him company. Despite her feelings, she could not criticise him for it, for she always knew her precious son was far too generous for his own good, just like her. For you see, she told the therapist she had always tried her hardest to be kind to her son in order to make up for his terrible father, but now that they were by themselves, she admitted she had nothing left to give. During the marriage, the only thing that worked in her favour was that she was a better mum than the man who was physically abusing her child.

But instead of accepting Freddie's generosity, she admitted to reacting violently, using him as her emotional punching bag because she knew he would accept it, just as he had all his life. And it made her realise that despite suffering from mental illness, she was every bit the tyrant Freddie's father had ever been, though her demeanour had been sufficiently subdued for Benjamin to be aware of what was happening.

Joanne watched as her son disintegrated in front of her eyes. It made her believe that when parents mistreat their children, the children cease loving themselves, not the parents. So, no wonder Freddie was the way he was. Everything was Benjamin's fault, for it was he who had brought about all this chaos.

She also became angry with Benjamin and Freddie for stopping loving himself. But it all blended, according to the therapist, so instead of trying to be kind and helpful to Freddie, every day they spent together increased Freddie's level of hypochondria. And it was worse when he returned from his father's because Joanne was paranoid that the boy was only feeling ill in her presence and not his, which caused even more anger to flare.

George closed down the email and sighed.

"Everything OK, boss?"

"Yeah, and it's now all making sense," replied George.

"What is, boss?"

"The reasons Benjamin Harman cited as the grounds of divorce," said George.

"The unreasonable behaviour?"

George nodded. "Benjamin commented that whilst he had the mental strength to endure Joanne's unreasonable behaviour and the emotional intelligence to recognise what Joanne was doing to him, his son, Freddie, had no such defences." He paused. "I'm guessing Benjamin could see how Joanne was torturing the boy and correctly guessed that it was similar to how she had troubled him during their years of marriage."

But it was even worse than that, and George knew it. At that point, Benjamin Harman had been put into a situation that could have been interpreted as animosity towards his spouse. He said to Jay, "Having realised his mistakes and attempting to mend his relationship with his son, I'm guessing Ben found himself in the situation where he had to choose between allowing Joanne to continue abusing the boy or speaking out against the acts of cruelty, even at the risk of jeopardising the bond he had been trying so hard to forge with Freddie."

"Which was why he took the same action he had taken during their marriage?" asked Jay, and George nodded.

"That's right, Jay, the prick remained silent and did nothing."

Chapter Thirty-six

Frederick Harman reclined in his worn-out armchair, his eyes fixed on the flickering television screen. His tiny, cluttered flat in Bradford felt even smaller as the press conference unfolded before him. The room was dimly lit, the only source of illumination being the muted glow of the television. The air hung heavy with tension.

Detective Inspector George Beaumont, his nemesis, stood tall and blond at the podium, a sea of flashing cameras capturing his every move. Frederick's lips curled into a sardonic grin as he watched George, the man who had been pursuing him relentlessly.

George's voice resonated through the small room, amplified by the microphone before him. "Ladies and gentlemen of the press," he began, his tone oozing confidence. "We have a suspect in the recent string of ritual killings that have plagued Leeds." The anticipation in the room was palpable.

Cameras clicked incessantly, capturing every word and gesture. The room buzzed with an electric energy fuelled by the unfolding drama. In Freddie's opinion, George was a man who loved the spotlight, and today was no different.

The detective reached into a folder and produced a photograph. Frederick's heart skipped a beat as he recognised himself in the image. But there was a cruel twist; the picture was of a much younger Frederick, a version of himself from years ago. He couldn't help but chuckle at the irony. Where now he was sporting a full, black beard, the image that stared back at Freddie from the TV screen was clean-shaven.

"They say a picture is worth a thousand words," George said with a wry smile. "But sometimes, even a thousand words can't capture the true essence of a man." He gestured toward the image on the screen. "This is Frederick Harman, our prime suspect. He may look like a normal man, but I assure you he's a monster!"

Frederick's laughter echoed in the tiny flat. They were relying on an outdated photograph. He had changed so much since then; the world had changed him.

George's stern expression belied the tension in the room as he continued, "I must emphasise that Frederick Harman is an extremely dangerous individual. We know he is responsible for the heinous murders of Penny Haigh, Joy Pritchard, and Laura Bennett, and we have reason to believe he may be planning more."

Frederick's laughter subsided as he listened intently. The cat-and-mouse game had reached a critical point. It was clear the DI respected Freddie, knowing he was dangerous but also knowing he was brilliant.

That's all Freddie wanted.

George leaned in toward the microphone, his voice low and ominous. "I implore the public: if you encounter this man, do not approach him. He is dangerous and unpredictable. Instead, dial 999 immediately and wait for the police to handle the situation."

The room fell silent, the gravity of the situation sinking in.

CHAPTER THIRTY-SIX

Frederick's heart pounded in his chest, his pulse quickening. He had always been one step ahead of George, but now the detective was closing in.

Then again, it was clear to Frederick the police were always going to get his DNA from the scene, and Freddie had resigned himself to his fate.

The taste of fresh blood from the artery had been worth it.

George cleared his throat, the tension in the room ratcheting up another notch. "We are seeking witnesses who might have information about these crimes. Your assistance could be the key to bringing this dangerous individual to justice."

"Is the murder of Jacqueline Bell in Bradford connected to Frederick Harman?" a journalist asked.

George thought back to earlier and the discussion he had with DC Jay Scott. "Boss," Jay had said, "I think you should only mention the three murders tonight at the press conference."

"Why?" George had asked.

"Because if we play dumb and pretend we don't know Freddie was Bell's killer, he may expose himself, boss."

George remembered nodding as he said, "So, make him think we believe Bell's murder was the work of the copycat?"

"Aye, boss, that's right," Jay had said.

George looked at the journalist. "No, there's no evidence to suggest Frederick Harman is involved in any of the Bradford murders."

As George concluded the press conference, Frederick sat in the darkness of his flat, contemplating his next move. He was now not just a criminal but a hunted man. The game had taken a darker turn, and he knew that his survival depended on his ability to outwit the relentless Detective Inspector George

Beaumont.

Little did anyone know Frederick Harman had no intention of becoming another statistic in the relentless pursuit of justice. He had a plan, and it was time to set it into motion, especially as they didn't know he'd murdered Jacqueline Bell.

* * *

That night, back at home, George couldn't switch off. He needed to know what happened to Freddie, Joanne and Benjamin, so he took copies of the therapy reports home and read them once Isabella and Olivia had gone to bed.

Setting up all three sets of reports side by side, Freddie's Bridge House reports from when he was seventeen, Joanna's therapy reports from the same time, and Freddie's hospital psychiatry reports, George found it wasn't long before Joanna pushed Freddie past the point of no return.

With deft manipulation, she got him to spend less time with his father by justifying her separation from him with the same pseudo-medical language that had driven Benjamin insane. Without anyone offering any rationality, the topic of poisoning was covered in great length, and she continued to present the same proof as always. However, the so-called symptoms he had been trying to ignore his entire life started becoming more noticeable after spending more time at his mother's house. Still, Joanne persuaded Freddie that these symptoms resulted from his father's continuous attempts to poison him.

But Joanne didn't stop there; no, she repeatedly pressed Freddie to decide between the father who had beaten him since he was old enough to remember and the mother who had loved and cared for him his whole life, the man attempting to poison him in an attempt to rob him of the life that she, with her own feeble body, had given him.

Naturally, Freddie chose to stay with Joanne, but his symptoms never really improved. He hardly attended college, saying he was too ill or tired to attend, and was eventually kicked out. The same excuses meant his social life was a complete mess. Elsie also stopped visiting him, and his mother spent most of her time in her room.

As such, the strings that had kept Freddie attached to reality were being cut, leaving nothing except Freddie and his illness in their wake.

With nobody to care for him, Freddie became gaunt. Instead of looking for solutions in his behaviour, he started believing the falsehoods that his hypochondria whispered in his ear. Daily, he'd plug his ears with his fingers and listen to the beating of his heart, convinced it was slowing, and that was the sole reason for his demise.

Everything else was illogical. So, he had a choice to make.

Would he lie there and wait for it to stop beating, or take action because the skipping beats of his heart explained everything that was wrong with his life? His faulty heart was why he couldn't love people. It was why his cock wouldn't harden, because of the lack of blood. It was why he was so pale all the time. But why was his heart killing him?

He asked the therapist why, and she, assuming he was talking in metaphors, reflected the question at Freddie.

In his hospital sessions, he admitted to blaming his mother. It was so apparent to him then that his heart had been faulty his entire life. And who had given him that heart? His mother. She was to blame. He saw it so clearly. She had been murdering him all his life, but he had been too enamoured with her to realise it, poisoning him while teaching him to trust no one but her.

* * *

Whilst DI George Beaumont was at home reading into Frederick Harman's past and who he murdered as a teen, Freddie was also thinking about that fateful night.

That night, all those years ago, Freddie had decided not to let his mother win. And so, he decided that if he could strengthen his heart, all his problems would disappear. But how could he do that?

By ridding himself of the poison. By getting rid of his mother.

It was the only thing that made sense to seventeen-year-old Freddie.

And so, that night, when she was asleep, he snuck into her bedroom, got on top of her naked form and closed his fingers around her neck.

Fury grabbed him, and strength rushed back into his fingers. He refused to allow her to take his life. He refused to remain here and allow her to poison him. She needed to pay for what she'd done.

Her face went red, then purple. He began to cry as she struggled against him. He was killing the one woman who cherished him. But it needed to be done. She was intentionally harming him and had been since he'd been born. At least his father had given him days off from the beatings.

And to think he'd taken her side over his.

She'd caused everything. Right from day one. It explained why he'd set fires, murdered animals, soaked his boxers with his cum most nights but couldn't get it up when around a woman he fancied. It explained why he was the shrivelled, miserable shell of a man. It explained why he was hard as a rock right now, the throbbing hurting him as he squeezed tighter and tighter.

It was too late when he crept back to his mother, sobbing and pleading for forgiveness two hours later. She was already gone. Dead. Murdered. The cause of all his issues was now gone.

Despite the purple bruising on her neck, she looked happier than Freddie could ever remember.

That last smile was an insult to Freddie, so he packed up his belongings and headed for his father's place.

He never wanted to see that smile ever again.

Chapter Thirty-seven

Friday morning arrived, casting a pall over the Incident Room at Elland Road Police Station, Leeds District Police HQ. As the morning sun cast long shadows through the windows of the Incident Room at Elland Road station, the weight of their pursuit bore down on Detective Inspector George Beaumont and his dedicated team. The hunt for Frederick Harman had intensified, yet their progress remained maddeningly slow.

They had a name, a face, and a horrifying victim selection, but they were still no closer to capturing the elusive Frederick Harman, nor could they provide a motive.

George gathered his team around a cluttered table strewn with case files and half-empty coffee cups. Constable Candy Nichols, Detective Sergeant Yolanda Williams, Detective Constable Jay Scott, and Detective Constable Tashan Blackburn all listened intently, their expressions a mix of disgust and outrage as George relayed the grim details he had uncovered the previous night.

"Seventeen-year-old Frederick Harman," George began, his voice heavy with emotion, "murdered his own mother. He believed she was the cause of all his problems, and he thought getting rid of her would solve everything."

George could see the frustration etched on the faces of

CHAPTER THIRTY-SEVEN

his team as they absorbed the grim details of Harman's latest atrocity. The murder of Freddie's own mother had only added to the darkness that shrouded their investigation. But George knew that this darkness could be their greatest asset, for it drove them to press forward with an unwavering determination.

Tashan spoke up, frustration etched across his face. "We're still hunting Harman, sir, but it's proving to be a real challenge. We don't have a known fixed address for him. According to the DVLA, he doesn't own a vehicle, and his bank cards haven't been used recently."

George nodded, his jaw tightening. They had all the pieces of the puzzle, but the pieces refused to fit together. George couldn't help but share in their frustration.

"And the facial recognition software we've been using hasn't picked him out yet, sir," Tashan added with a sigh.

The lack of progress gnawed at George, but he knew he had a relentless team at his side. Still, Tashan received a nod of appreciation from his boss. "Keep at it, Tashan. We need a breakthrough. We've been in this situation before, and we've always found a way to get one step closer to our suspect."

George turned to Yolanda, hoping for a glimmer of hope. "What about the CCTV we managed to obtain in Manningham, Yolanda?"

DS Williams shook her head in frustration. "No luck, sir. The prostitutes know about the cameras and avoid them, working in the blind spots. We're coming up short every time."

Jay Scott chimed in with equally disappointing news. "The door-to-door uniform team hasn't yielded anything either. People are either too scared or too tight-lipped. People keep saying, 'It's happening again, and you useless bastards aren't doing anything about it.'"

George ran a hand through his blond hair, his frustration mounting. It felt like they were chasing a ghost, and he hated that feeling. "We can't let up," he said, his voice unwavering. "Harman may have evaded us so far, but we'll find him. We have to."

The team exchanged determined glances, a silent pact forming between them. They were in this together and wouldn't rest until they had Frederick Harman in custody. The hunt continued, and with each passing moment, the noose around the elusive killer drew tighter.

* * *

Just as Freddie expected, no one, not even that idiot Detective Inspector Beaumont, was aware of his most recent murder. It helped that the West Yorkshire Police had attributed the murder of Jacqueline Bell to somebody else, a Yorkshire Ripper wannabe who was going around attacking prostitutes with a hammer.

It also helped he killed Jacqueline in Bradford rather than Leeds. And that she was a prostitute.

But the attack on the prostitute hadn't satisfied Freddie one bit, and he wondered what Sutcliffe saw in them.

What Frederick didn't know, however, was that George Beaumont and his team had linked him to the Bradford murder because the serial killer, who had dedicated his life to evil, had made a mistake.

* * *

CHAPTER THIRTY-SEVEN

"It's him, isn't it?" DI George Beaumont asked Mark Finch that morning.

"Aye, George," Mark replied. "And now you have the DNA to prove it."

George nodded.

The pair, at significant cost to DCI Atkinson's budget, had reviewed the data from all the crimes, concluding that Frederick Harman was Jacqueline Bell's killer and most likely their Ripper copycat by piecing together a composite profile of Frederick Harman from the different accounts by combining statements from witnesses and interviews from the Bingley survivor that Mark had been allowed to attend.

Not only that, but Mark concluded that, even in cases where there was no indication of rape or sexual assault, the killings were motivated only by sexual desires. Mark believed that the killer's thoughts had switched from sexual acts in Leeds to violent ones in Bradford and that his actions were motivated by this perverted drive.

For George, the fact that a forensic artist had managed to draw a detailed image matching Harman from the Bingley survivor's description convinced him enough that they had their man.

Harman was their ritual killer, and their Yorkshire Ripper copycat.

Now, all they had to do was find him.

Chapter Thirty-eight

According to the post Nancy Claybourn had put up on Facebook, she was new to the area and seeking friends with whom she could play the latest Disney Lorcana trading card game. Freddie had no idea what that was, but he certainly wanted to become her friend.

Initially, Freddie wondered whether it was a trap, paranoid that the police were onto him, but looking at her picture, he couldn't help but want her. She had long, dark hair like his mother had, like Penny had, and like most of his victims had. But her eyes were a cold blue, darker than the ocean's depths and hopefully just as deep. He wondered how they would taste if he plucked them out and chewed on them.

She was new to Bingley, but Freddie was not. He logged into an old profile, one unknown to the police. He started chatting with the group, careful not to like Nancy's comments but to make himself known as a fellow Bingley Lorcana enthusiast.

Nancy slid into his DMs quickly, wanting to meet up at the 5 Rise Shopping Centre that evening before heading to the library.

That evening, the disoriented and confused Nancy stood outside the station, unsure how to find her way to the shopping centre. Unlike most people her age, she couldn't afford a

CHAPTER THIRTY-EIGHT

mobile phone with GPS, so she could not use it to get to her location. As such, she asked for directions from the Yorkshire folk, struggling with their broad accents, resulting in useless directions.

That was when an unremarkable man about her age with short, dark hair and a black beard approached her and volunteered to guide her towards the shopping centre, as he, too, needed to visit the library. Naturally, Nancy was suspicious of the man. Still, as soon as he pulled out a library-bound book from his backpack, she relaxed, followed him away from the station's more crowded section, and headed in what he said would be the shopping centre's direction.

However, as the crowds started to thin, her fear grew proportionally. She had heard all about the Yorkshire Ripper copycat who preyed on lonely ladies, and so she froze, therefore, when they came to Myrtle Park and the man attempted to guide her inside. She was sure from her cursory glance at her laptop that Myrtle Park was in the entirely opposite direction of the shopping centre.

The kind gentleman suddenly became pissed off and began yelling at her when she refused to accompany him into the park, telling her that if she weren't just some naive Southerner, she would know that it was a shortcut to the library.

Nancy, still frozen at the entrance to the park, was understandably shocked by the treatment she was receiving as the man went about his tirade and was considering following him—if only so she could shout for help if she saw somebody in the park—when a passer-by stepped in to help her.

"Everything OK, love?" he asked Nancy.

The younger man frowned, but instead of causing trouble, he turned on his heel and left without a word.

"Thank you so much, I think he was going to—to—"

"It's OK, love," the man said. "Don't worry, you're safe now." He offered her a smile that met his eyes, and to the naïve Nancy, it appeared genuine.

Yet to Freddie, it was his Cheshire Cat grin he'd offered her—his Tim Curry Home Alone 2 grin that matched the mischievous Grinch's.

"There are dickheads like that all around the world, but not many of them in Bingley," Freddie said. "I apologise."

"It's not your fault."

"Us Yorkshire people are usually lovely, but there's always the odd one who gives us a shit reputation if you excuse my French."

Nancy smiled.

"Where are you off to, anyway?" Freddie asked.

"The library in the erm, 5 Rise Shopping Centre."

"Ah, I know the place. It's just—"

"This might be forward," Nancy said, "but if you're not doing anything, would you escort me there, please?" She looked at the ground and brushed the mud around with one of her shoes. "With everything in the news, I'm a bit worried."

Freddie felt himself immediately harden, so happy he'd brought his bag with him to hide his excitement from his prey. My god, she was beautiful, he thought. Nearly as beautiful as his sister, Elsie.

He looked at his watch, then grimaced.

"Oh, I'm so sorry, you're obviously busy," Nancy said.

Freddie shook his head. "No, it's fine; I can help you get to the library," he said. "It's not far, so it won't take long." He held out a gloved hand, gloved for necessity and the fact that it was chilly. He was sure he'd left DNA behind at Jacqueline

CHAPTER THIRTY-EIGHT

Bell's murder scene, and he wanted to be careful. "I'm Peter, by the way. Peter Sutcliffe. Nice to meet you."

She recoiled at the name and Freddie said, "I know, right. I'm thinking of getting it changed." He sighed. "My parents hated me I guess."

She smiled. "Nancy, Nancy Claybourn." She held his hand longer than necessary, but it didn't appear to faze the handsome stranger. Nancy wondered whether she could get the man to get a coffee with her, pulling out her phone to text her date and cancel on him. But then she didn't want to be caught in a coffee shop by her date, so she figured she needed to ask Peter to take her elsewhere for a drink. "I'm a bit cold. Do you fancy a drink? On me, for saving me?"

Freddie looked at his watch again. He had all the time in the world, but Nancy didn't need to know that. "Where were you thinking?"

She ran a hand through her raven-coloured hair. "Well, I'm new to the area, so I was hoping you knew a place nearby?"

Acting, Freddie frowned. "Didn't you need the library?"

"I need to thank you for being such a gentleman, Peter." She shrugged. "I can go tomorrow. And plus, you look familiar. Have we met before?"

Freddie grinned that mischievous grin once more but shook his head. "I'd have remembered you if we'd met before." Silly girl. Don't you know a serial killer is wandering around? he thought.

She blushed, and it only made him harder.

"OK, this way then," he said. "There's a tea room just through the park and over the Beckfoot Bridge," he lied, hoping she was as naive as she appeared.

There, of course, was a tea room in the park, but he wanted

her alone.

As they sauntered through the park, Nancy laughing at every one of his shitty jokes and Freddie showering her with compliments and making her blush, they got closer and closer to the bridge, closer to Nancy's demise.

The fog assaulted them as they continued towards the bridge, a welcome accomplice to the crime he was about to commit. Freddie had always wanted to kill somebody by the beck and so had scouted the most deserted spot, out of sight and sound of any houses, a place where he knew no one would come across them because he'd gone on the route enough times now to know who would be out and where.

With every step they took together, the rustle of the trees and the lap of cold wind that gusted against him set his senses alight. The gentle babble of the nearby brook, hidden amongst the tangle of foliage, soothed the fire inside him. But it was the sharpened scissors in the large central pocket of his hoodie that relaxed him.

He had prepared. No one would see him. No one would catch him. Not now, anyway. He would kill her, and then he would disappear—just as he had done before.

But this time, no altar would be involved, and he wouldn't drain her blood. This time, he would remove her heart and take it home with him.

They crossed over the bridge that spanned the beck, and then Nancy faltered.

"Are you OK, Nancy love?" Freddie revelled in the flash of utter fear that flashed across her face.

"Are you sure this is the right way?"

"Of course I am, love," he said, licking his lips.

He saw her calculating as she glanced around, but they were

in a vastly wooded area now, with no one around and no CCTV.

No help would be coming if she screamed when she screamed.

Swiftly, Freddie grabbed her arm and pushed her through the foliage and against a tree.

Disgust replaced her fear. "What the fuck are you doing?" she spat. "Get off me, or I'll call the police."

Freddie grinned and shook his head. "You won't get any signal on that piece of shit out here, trust me."

Frederick Harman drew forward, his body pressing her against the tree and, she didn't realise, the sharpened scissors resting flat between them in his hoodie pocket against her stomach. She resisted him, but he was stronger. He was easily able to dominate her.

He backed up a step and pulled out the scissors. "Do you want to know a secret?" he asked.

But her attention was on the scissors and not on him; her eyes trained on the flash of silver as it reflected the dull light of the setting sun. "What secret?" she eventually managed.

"My name's not Peter Sutcliffe, I wish!" He snarled, "It's Frederick."

And that's when it hit her. Why he looked so familiar. He was Frederick Harman, the serial killer the West Yorkshire Police were looking for.

"You don't have to do this, Frederick," she pleaded. "Please don't hurt me. Let me go, and I'll forget all about you. I promise." She spoke quickly and breathlessly, her eyes never leaving the stainless steel blades. They were shaped like swords and ideal for cutting and penetrating. He knew from experience that they killed extremely well.

Freddie laughed.

Nancy went to speak again, but he shot forward, his free hand finding her mouth, silencing her.

And that's when he decided he would treat Nancy Claybourn differently from all the others. Before meeting her, he hadn't decided whether to be the ripper or the ritual killer. But he was going to be neither; he was going to be Frederick Harman. There was no point in hiding any more, not now they had people looking for him. His mugshot had looked glorious on the TV during the press conference, though. Freddie grinned.

He turned her around so she was facing the tree, and with one hand on the back of her neck, he used his other to pull down her jeans. Her knickers came with her jeans, getting stuck at her ankles.

Freddie was immediately hard, harder than earlier, and he struggled to pull down his jeans and boxers.

And with only one hand, he decided not to wear a condom. They knew who he was, anyway, so it didn't fucking matter if he left forensics behind.

Freddie removed both gloves and threw them into the foliage, using his left hand to push her back down, her face scraping against the tree, his right hand guiding his penis inside her.

Frederick Harman thrust and thrust, and whilst she bucked and struggled against his strength, he found that he could not attain climax without the violence. So he decided to pull his scissors out of his front pocket and stab the fuck out of her whilst he violated her.

But he'd made a mistake. He'd taken too long. The patter of paws against the path alerted Freddie to his senses. A bark followed those sounds, and Nancy started shouting.

Panicking, he fussed over her, pulling up her knickers and

jeans, dusting the mud from her knees, and even rubbing the blood from her scratched face.

Unable to comprehend what was happening, Nancy froze and stopped shouting. It confused her that the once sweet gentleman that had turned evil rapist had returned to his charming self.

He did nothing as she backed away. He even nodded at her as she approached the bridge, where she pulled out her mobile and rang triple nine.

But as soon as she had got through to the police, she noticed that once again Freddie was heading towards her, so she sprinted away, hoping to find somebody who would help her in the park, screaming down the phone that she was running away from Frederick Harman, who had just raped her.

When the operator asked where Frederick was and what he was doing, she explained he was standing atop the bridge over the beck, his scissors in his hand.

It appeared to her that the psychopath was going to commit suicide.

Chapter Thirty-nine

"DI Beaumont," George said. He was sat in his office when his internal phone rang.

"Can you repeat that?" he asked the woman.

"I've just spoken with a woman named Nancy Claybourn, sir," the operator replied. "She was sexually assaulted just now in Bingley. She claims it was Frederick Harman."

"Right, get uniform to collect her and take her to the nearest police station. Get them to lock the area down immediately, and alert forensics."

"Already done, sir," she explained. "She's en-route to Manningham Police Station as we speak."

"Thank you."

George cut the phone off, put on his jacket and headed towards the Incident Room.

* * *

The Incident Room at Elland Road Police Station hummed with a palpable sense of urgency. The Big Board at the front, worn by countless cases over the years, bore the weight of the Frederick Harman investigation. Case files, notes, timelines and forensic reports filled every available inch. Photographs of crime

CHAPTER THIRTY-NINE

scenes and victims were scattered about, each a haunting reminder of the heinous crimes they were determined to solve.

Thin red strings connected various elements, creating a complex web of connections. George often found himself standing before the Big Board, searching for patterns, any hint that could lead them to Frederick Harman.

Some detectives worked diligently at their desks, surrounded by stacks of evidence files and computers, whilst others were on the phones, tirelessly making calls. The clatter of keyboards and hushed conversations filled the room as they cross-referenced information and conducted online research. Every detective was committed to bringing Frederick Harman to justice.

The constant ringing and clacking filled the room like a never-ending symphony of hope and anticipation.

The DI's heart pounded as he processed the horrifying call. "Uniform's on its way to collect Nancy Claybourn," he said, informing them of the situation in Bingley by Beckfoot Bridge, his team watching with a mix of anxiety and determination as the DI explained the sexual assault. "She's being taken to Manningham Police Station. We need to lock down the area immediately and alert forensics."

Candy Nichols, Yolanda Williams, Jay Scott, and Tashan Blackburn sprang into action, their training and experience guiding them through the necessary steps. They knew that capturing Harman was now more critical than ever.

Outside, the streets of Bingley buzzed with oblivious residents going about their evening routines. But they had no idea that a dangerous predator lurked among them, and George couldn't let that continue.

Uniformed officers arrived at the scene and immediately

secured the area around Myrtle Park and the River Aire, cordoning it off from the public. Forensics experts were summoned, ready to scour every inch of the river path for evidence that might lead to Harman's capture.

George headed for Manningham, feeling a sense of urgency like never before. Nancy Claybourn was waiting in an interview room for him. Her brave call had given them a crucial opportunity; they couldn't afford to waste it.

* * *

The interview room where Nancy Claybourn had recounted her traumatic experience was now filled with a tense silence. Detective Inspector George Beaumont sat with his team, reviewing the details they had gathered from Nancy's statement. The atmosphere was filled with determination and apprehension as they considered their next steps.

George broke the silence, his voice steady. "We need to verify Nancy's account thoroughly, but I don't think she's lying. We've got to act swiftly and smartly."

Jay leaned forward. "Boss, if Harman's involved, he might have left evidence behind."

George nodded in agreement. "CSI is there as we speak. And poor Nancy has been in with the nurse."

Candy Nichols, fingers tapping away on her laptop, acknowledged George's instructions with a brisk nod. "I'll get in touch with them right away for an update, sir."

As the team split into action, Nancy was invited back into the interview room. "I can't believe it," she said. "You say he's killed four women already?"

George turned his attention to Nancy, his expression empathetic. "Nancy, we can't be certain it is Frederick yet."

"So it's that Ripper copycat, then?" she asked.

George didn't want to tell her they thought Frederick was the Ripper copycat.

"We'll see what we can find on CCTV, but if he's surfaced, which it appears he has, we need to do everything we can to catch him."

Nancy's eyes were filled with a mix of fear and determination. "I just want to do whatever it takes to stop him from hurting anyone else."

George offered her a reassuring smile. "Your courage today has already made a difference. We need your help identifying him, even if it wasn't Harman. Can you give us more details about his appearance or anything he might have said?"

Nancy nodded, her voice steadier now. "Yes, I remember he had short, dark hair, a dark beard and a moustache, and he first mentioned his name was Peter Sutcliffe. But then he said it was Frederick."

"What did you do when he said he was called Peter Sutcliffe?"

"Well, I recoiled, obviously." She closed her eyes. "He blamed his parents."

Sounds like Frederick, George thought.

With Nancy's additional information in hand, the team prepared to investigate the Myrtle Park and Beckfoot Bridge area. Meanwhile, Tashan Blackburn had discreetly coordinated with the local police to secure the vicinity.

The fog had thickened as they arrived at the park, lending an eerie atmosphere to the already chilling search. They could see their breath in the cold air as they combed the area meticulously. The detectives were cautious not to overlook any potential clues that might lead them to the truth.

Jay crouched down by the Beckfoot Bridge, scrutinising the surroundings. "This is where Nancy mentioned she resisted. If there's any evidence, it could be here."

Candy, with a torch in hand, was inspecting nearby foliage. "We should also check for discarded items, like gloves or anything he might have dropped."

Within five minutes, Candy had found the pair of gloves Nancy had said Frederick had discarded before raping her. Lindsey immediately bagged them, and George authorised them to be tested immediately. They needed DNA evidence to tie everything together.

Hours passed, and the team watched as Lindsey Yardley's SOC team combed through the area tirelessly. They bagged potential evidence and carefully catalogued everything. As the search intensified, the detectives couldn't help but feel the weight of the past crimes attributed to Harman bearing down on them.

Finally, as dawn broke, Lindsey called out to the team. "We've found something in the river!"

"What?" asked George.

"A pair of scissors."

George approached, scrutinising the scissors. "Bag them, Lindsey." Knowing they could well be the scissors that killed Penny, Joy, and Laura, he added, "This could be a crucial piece of evidence. Get them processed ASAP. I don't care how much it costs."

With the scissors secured, the team watched as the SOCOs continued their search, not wanting to leave any stone unturned. They were determined to solve this puzzle, determined to find Frederick Harman before he killed again.

CHAPTER THIRTY-NINE

***

Detective Inspector George Beaumont and Constable Candy Nichols sat in George's Mercedes as they headed towards Middleton, determined to follow any leads that might shed light on Frederick Harman's recent activities. The night was filled with tension and uncertainty, and now they were pinning their hopes on the possibility that Frederick's sister, Elsie, might provide them with crucial information.

The drive to Middleton was quiet, the night sky hanging heavily above them. Candy broke the silence, her voice filled with a mix of curiosity and concern. "Sir, why do you think Harman didn't go through with it? With Nancy, I mean."

George glanced at Candy before returning his focus to the road. "It's difficult to say, Candy, but I think something disrupted his plan."

Candy nodded. "Nancy did mention the sound of a dog, but I meant, why did he fuss over her as if trying to make everything OK?"

"Maybe Freddie was doing something he wasn't entirely comfortable doing?"

"The rape, you mean?"

George nodded. "Mark Finch has suggested the murders committed by Freddie so far have all lacked a sexual element. That also includes Jacqueline Bell in Bradford."

Candy nodded her understanding.

"So I think he was trying to act differently, but it didn't resonate with him if that makes sense?"

"I guess so, sir."

"Still, we need to consider all possibilities. And, regardless of what happened, we can't let our guard down. Harman remains a grave threat."

Candy nodded in agreement. "Right, sir. We need to be prepared for anything."

As they approached Middleton, they could see rows of houses and a community that seemed ordinary on the surface. It was difficult to imagine that a notorious serial killer's sister lived in the midst of this seemingly tranquil neighbourhood.

The address provided by Detective Chief Superintendent Mohammed Sadiq led them to a modest two-story house with a well-maintained front garden in the New Forest Village. George parked the car nearby, and they both stepped out. The detective inspector and constable made their way to the front door, their footsteps echoing in the quiet street.

George rang the doorbell, and they waited patiently, their senses alert for any sign of movement inside the house. After a brief moment, the door opened, revealing a middle-aged woman with a tired but kind expression. She had pale skin and dark hair and wore a plain, worn-out cardigan.

Elsie Harman looked at the detectives with a mixture of curiosity and concern. "Can I help you?"

After holding up his warrant card for Elsie to see, George spoke calmly and reassuringly. "Good evening, Miss Harman. I'm Detective Inspector George Beaumont, and this is Constable Candy Nichols. We'd like to ask you a few questions regarding your brother, Frederick Harman. May we come in?"

Elsie's eyes widened slightly, and she hesitated momentarily before stepping aside to allow them entry. "Of course. Please, come in."

As they entered the modest living room, George and Candy noticed the family photos on the walls, revealing a seemingly ordinary life. They exchanged a glance, knowing that appearances could be deceiving.

Elsie gestured for them to take a seat, and they complied. She settled into an armchair across from them, her hands folded in her lap. "What do you want to know about Freddie?"

George began the conversation carefully. "Miss Harman, we believe your brother, Frederick, might be involved in some recent incidents. We're trying to gather information to ensure everyone's safety. Have you been in contact with him recently?"

"I've seen the press conferences." Elsie's expression grew sombre as she nodded. "Yes, I've heard from Freddie. It's been a while, but he reached out to me a few weeks ago, apologising for everything. As you can probably imagine, I don't have much to do with him after what he did to Mum."

Candy leaned forward, her voice gentle. "Do you know where he might be hiding or where he's been staying?"

Elsie shook her head. "I wish I did. He didn't tell me much. Just that he wanted to apologise and needed some time away from everything; he's always been secretive, you know."

George pressed further. "Have you noticed anything unusual or any changes in his behaviour in recent years?"

Elsie hesitated again, her gaze dropping to the floor. "Freddie has always been... different. He had a troubled childhood, and it left scars. He contacted me when he got released, and he contacted me recently to apologise. I'm sorry I can't tell you more."

The detectives exchanged knowing glances. "Miss Harman," George said gently, "we need your cooperation to locate your brother. We believe he may be connected to some serious crimes."

Elsie's eyes welled up with tears as she nodded. "I'll do

whatever I can to help but the man is a stranger to me."

As the interview continued, George and Candy collected valuable information from Elsie Harman about her brother's recent activities and potential acquaintances.

* * *

Frederick Harman crouched in the shadows, his eyes fixed on Elsie Harman's modest house. His heart raced, and a wicked grin played on his lips as he watched Constable Nichols and Detective Inspector George Beaumont step out of the front door. They had just finished their interview with Elsie, and Frederick's curiosity burned to know what she had revealed.

The chilly evening air rustled the leaves in the trees, but Frederick remained hidden behind a thick veil of darkness. His tall, lean frame blended seamlessly with the night, a predator concealed in the obscurity of the suburban street. He had chosen his vantage point carefully, ensuring that he remained invisible to anyone who might happen to glance his way.

Through the dimly lit windows of Elsie's house, he could see the faint glow of lamplight. It cast eerie, elongated shadows that danced across the curtains. Frederick's attention was solely on the figures emerging from the front door, the officers who had come to question his sister about his whereabouts.

As Constable Nichols and Detective Inspector Beaumont exchanged a few words on the doorstep, Frederick strained his ears, hoping to catch snippets of their conversation. His sister had always been a weak link, prone to cracking under pressure. He wondered if she had spilt any secrets or revealed any damning information that might lead them to him.

The seconds felt like hours as he waited for the officers to depart. His gloved hands clenched into fists, hidden within his pockets, as anticipation coursed through his veins. He had to know what they had discovered, what they suspected.

Finally, Constable Nichols and Detective Inspector Beaumont retreated from Elsie's house, their footsteps echoing softly on the pavement. Frederick's eyes followed their every move, tracing their path as they walked down the dimly lit street. He waited until they got into the Mercedes and disappeared from sight before he allowed himself to exhale.

A sinister smile curled upon his lips as he contemplated his next move.

With a predatory glint in his eyes, he retreated from the shadows and walked up to his sister's door.

Pretending to be a detective, he pounded on the door and waited.

Chapter Forty

George had just settled into his office, preparing to dive into the caseload for the day, when the shrill ring of his internal phone startled him. He reached for the receiver, his heart picking up its pace. The early morning sunlight streamed through the windows, casting a warm glow over his cluttered desk, but the call brought an abrupt chill to the room.

"DI Beaumont."

"Morning, sir," the operator's voice came through the line, crisp and professional. "We've received a 999 call from a concerned neighbour regarding Elsie Harman. Dispatch advised that we contact you immediately."

George furrowed his brow, concern seeping into his expression. Elsie Harman had been their last lead in the hunt for Frederick Harman, and her recent interview had left him with more questions than answers. "What's the problem?" he inquired, his voice low and measured.

The operator continued, her tone slightly tense. "The neighbour, Erin Cooper, reported that Elsie Harman's front door was wide open this morning, which is highly unusual."

George leaned back in his chair, his fingers drumming rhythmically on his desk. "People leave their doors open by accident all the time," he mused, hoping for a simple explanation.

"I've just received some more information, sir; one moment, please." The operator hesitated for a moment before pressing on. "Erin Cooper also mentioned that Elsie's car is still parked in the driveway. According to her, Elsie works every Saturday morning."

A knot of unease tightened in George's stomach. The puzzle pieces weren't fitting together as neatly as he had hoped. "She could be on annual leave or taking a day off," he suggested, trying to quell the rising sense of foreboding. It wasn't working.

"More information is coming through as we speak, sir." And the operator's following words shattered his attempts at reassurance. "Erin Cooper decided to enter the house to check on Elsie, and she found a note," she said. "Forensics has been dispatched, and they're waiting for you to arrive."

George's heart pounded in his chest as he realized the gravity of the situation. He knew that the Harman siblings were deeply entwined in this dark web of mysteries, and if Elsie was missing or harmed, it could have profound implications for their investigation.

"I'll be there shortly," he replied, his voice firm and determined. He hung up the phone, grabbed his coat, and rushed out of his office, leaving behind the sunlight that had lost its warmth and replaced it with a sense of urgency.

* * *

Middleton lay still under the morning sun as George pulled up outside Elsie's house. He knew that this could be a critical juncture in their investigation, and every step he took from his car was laden with purpose. The quiet neighbourhood seemed oblivious to the tension that gripped him as he prepared to confront the unknown.

With deliberate care, he reached into the backseat of his car and retrieved a Tyvek suit, a mask, gloves, and shoe covers. The rustling of the protective gear seemed loud against the backdrop of the peaceful street. George knew that the sight of him dressing in such attire could only fuel the speculation and worry of the neighbours.

Police Sergeant Greenwood, a seasoned officer with a face that bore the marks of countless cases, was already at the scene. He coordinated the uniforms, conducted house-to-house inquiries, ensured every neighbour's concerns were heard and addressed and looked for witnesses.

As George approached the house, he could see Forensic Coordinator Lindsey Yardley standing nearby, her presence a testament to the seriousness of the situation. Lindsey was known for her meticulous attention to detail, and George trusted her expertise implicitly. Her blue eyes met his with a mix of anticipation and concern.

They exchanged a quick nod before George began to don the protective gear, layer by layer. The Tyvek suit clung tightly to his frame, shielding him from potential contaminants. The mask covered his face, obscuring his features behind a veil of anonymity. His gloved hands were steady as he pulled on the latex gloves and shoe covers.

Once fully suited up, George approached the front door of Elsie's house, his gloved hand resting on the doorknob. He took a deep breath, steeling himself for what they might find inside. This could be the breakthrough they needed or lead them further into the darkness of the Harman siblings' secrets.

CHAPTER FORTY

With a determined push, he entered the house, the creaking door echoing through the silent rooms.

Once a sanctuary of normalcy, the living room had been transformed into a hive of frenetic activity. Scene of Crime Officers bustled around, their white suits contrasting sharply with the ominous scene before them. A pool of blood, dark and foreboding, marred the floor, a macabre centrepiece in the room.

George's eyes darted to the source of the commotion as he entered, drawn like a moth to a flame. He could feel the weight of anxiety settling deep within him, but there was no turning back now.

Amidst the meticulous collection of evidence, he spotted the note. It lay on a nearby table, starkly contrasting to the gruesome tableau around it. He approached it cautiously, knowing that this simple piece of paper held clues to the unfolding nightmare.

His heart sank as he read the words, and a chill coursed down his spine. The note was a chilling message from Frederick Harman, a man whose morbid fascinations had turned sinister. The message was both a taunt and a threat, a macabre invitation into his twisted mind.

"I see you are still having no luck catching me. I have the greatest respect for you George, but Lord! You are no nearer catching me now than when I started."

George paused. That was another reference to the Yorkshire Ripper, this time a reference to Wearside Jack, the nickname given to John Samuel Humble, a man from Sunderland who pretended to be the Yorkshire Ripper in a hoax audio recording and several letters during the period 1978–1979. Humble sent a taped message in a Wearside accent and three letters, taunting the authorities for failing to catch him. The taped message caused the investigation to be moved away from the West Yorkshire area, home of the real killer, Peter Sutcliffe, not only helping the Yorkshire Ripper to continue his awful attacks on women but hindering his potential arrest for a further eighteen months.

"I've taken my little sister to where my morbid fascination with paganism and vampirism began," the note read, its words etched in ominous ink. "Find us, George, before I drain her of blood."

The implications were clear, and dread settled heavily upon George's shoulders. Time was of the essence, and the race to save Elsie Harman had begun in earnest. Frederick's obsession with the occult and violence had reached a dangerous zenith, and there was no telling what horrors awaited them on the path he had chosen.

* * *

Detective Inspector George Beaumont stood in the cluttered living room of Elsie Harman's Middleton home, his heart pounding in his chest. The chilling note he held in his gloved hand served as a grim reminder of the urgency of the situation. He needed to find Elsie before her brother, Frederick Harman, could execute his twisted plans.

The room buzzed with activity as SOCOs meticulously examined the evidence scattered throughout the house. Bloodstains, fingerprints, and any potential clues were being catalogued and documented. George watched them work, his mind racing.

Forensic Coordinator Lindsey Yardley approached; her white Tyvek suit was splattered with luminol, and her mask obscured

CHAPTER FORTY

most of her face.

"DI Beaumont," Lindsey began, her voice muffled by the mask, "we've gathered samples from various points in the house, including the pool of blood over there. It appears there was a struggle."

"Human blood?"

Lindsey nodded. "We used the Kastle-Meyer presumptive test first, which indicated it was blood, then used a Hexagon OBTI kit to ensure the sample was human blood."

George nodded, his eyes never leaving the ominous note. "Get it analysed ASAP; I need to know whether it's Freddie's, Elsie's, or somebody else's."

Lindsey said, "On it."

"Sorry we're late, boss," a voice came from behind. George turned to face Detective Constable Scott and Constable Nichols. "We erm..."

"Say no more, DC Scott." George turned and looked at Candy. "Glad you're both here," George explained the situation. "We need to find out everything we can about Elsie and Frederick's history. Any past associations, known hangouts, or connections he might have. We're racing against time."

Lindsey retrieved the note from George, placed it in an evidence bag, and sealed it carefully. "I need to interview Erin Cooper, the neighbour who discovered the open door and the note. She might have information about Elsie's recent activities or any encounters with Frederick."

"Want us to come with you, boss?"

"No, stay here, DC Scott. Constable Nichols will be enough."

As George headed toward the front door, he saw Police Sergeant Greenwood supervising the uniformed officers conducting house-to-house inquiries in the quiet suburban neighbourhood. George approached him, his sense of urgency palpable.

"Sergeant Greenwood," George said, his voice tight with concern, "have we found any witnesses who saw anything unusual in the vicinity this morning?"

Greenwood adjusted his cap and consulted his notepad. "Not yet, sir. People are still waking up, and it seems most residents haven't noticed anything unusual. We'll keep pressing on, but the lack of leads is worrying."

George nodded, his thoughts racing. Time was slipping away. He needed something, anything, to point them in the right direction. Elsie's life hung in the balance.

Chapter Forty-one

George and Candy arrived at Erin Cooper's, their expressions tense with urgency. They needed to gather more information from the concerned neighbour who had discovered Elsie Harman's open door and the chilling note left behind by Frederick Harman.

Erin, a petite woman with greying hair, welcomed them into her cosy living room, her hands trembling slightly as she offered them seats. The atmosphere was charged with anxiety, and George wasted no time in addressing the situation.

"Thank you for agreeing to speak with us, Mrs Cooper," George said, his tone reassuring. "We understand this is a difficult time, but your assistance is crucial in helping us locate Elsie Harman."

Erin nodded, her eyes welling up with tears. "I just want her to be safe. Elsie's always been such a sweet girl."

Candy placed a supportive hand on Erin's shoulder. "We share your concern, Mrs Cooper. Now, if you could please walk us through everything you observed this morning, starting with when you noticed Elsie's front door was open."

Erin took a deep breath, her voice trembling. "Of course. It was early this morning, around seven o'clock. I was on my way to the kitchen when I glanced out my window and saw

Elsie's front door open. It struck me as odd because she's very meticulous about locking up."

George leaned forward, his eyes focused on Erin. "What did you do next, Mrs Cooper?"

Erin continued, her voice wavering. "I called out for Elsie, thinking maybe she'd left in a hurry or something. But there was no response. I felt a bit worried."

Candy nodded, encouraging her to continue. "And then?"

Erin swallowed hard. "I decided to go over and check on her. I called out again as I approached her front door, but there was still no answer. That's when I entered the house."

George listened intently, aware of the gravity of the situation. "Can you describe what you saw inside Elsie's house, Mrs Cooper?"

Tears welled up in Erin's eyes as she recounted her discovery. "I went inside and called out for Elsie once again, but there was no sign of her. The house was very quiet. That's when I noticed the note on the table."

George nodded, his gaze fixed on Erin. "Can you tell us more about the note, Mrs Cooper?"

Erin's voice quivered as she described the handwritten message. "It was a handwritten note with dark, jagged letters. The message was chilling. It said something like, I've taken my little sister to bite her. Find us, George, before I drain her of blood."

Candy glanced at George, her expression grim.

"I've heard about Frederick but didn't for one minute think he was Elsie's brother. Please find her, detective."

George spoke gently, his voice filled with empathy. "Thank you, Mrs Cooper, you did the right thing by contacting us immediately. We're doing everything possible to locate Elsie and ensure her safety."

Erin wiped away a tear and nodded, her fear still palpable. "Please find her, Detective Inspector. I pray she's okay."

George and Candy rose from their seats, their determination unwavering. "We're doing everything in our power, Mrs Cooper. We won't rest until we bring Elsie home safely."

* * *

As the interview concluded, George and Candy left Mrs Cooper's house and returned to the Incident Room at Elland Road Police Station. The urgency of the situation weighed heavily on him. He needed to act fast and find any evidence that could lead them to Frederick Harman and his sister, Elsie.

Back at the Incident Room, George gathered his team for an update. Detective Chief Superintendent Mohammed Sadiq had been briefed about the situation and had granted them access to additional resources.

"Listen up, everyone," George began, his voice firm. "We have a crucial lead, but time is running out. Frederick Harman has taken his sister, Elsie, to a location related to his obsession with paganism and vampirism. We need to find them before he carries out his sinister plans."

Yolanda said, "DCS Sadiq has provided us with a team who is analysing surveillance footage in Middleton and the surrounding areas as we speak, sir."

George nodded as Candy raised her hand. "What about issuing a public alert with Frederick's description, sir? It might engage the community and increase our chances of spotting them."

George nodded in agreement. "Good idea, Candy. We'll

consider that if we don't make progress soon. In the meantime, let's keep monitoring CCTV. We still don't know how Freddie arrived in Middleton, nor do we know how he left. That's the priority. If he arrived on foot, it means they left on foot. That means they can't be far."

The DI turned to Tashan. "Any update on whether there's a stone circle in Middleton, DC, Blackburn?"

"I'm working on it, sir."

As the team dispersed to carry out their assigned tasks, George felt the weight of responsibility on his shoulders. Elsie's life was in danger, and he was determined to bring her home safely, no matter the cost.

Over the next few hours, the Incident Room buzzed with activity. Detectives, analysts, and officers worked tirelessly to gather information, track leads, and uncover any possible connections that could lead them to Frederick and Elsie Harman.

The CCTV footage from Middleton was carefully reviewed, but there were no immediate sightings of Frederick or Elsie. Uniformed officers continued conducting house-to-house inquiries, hoping to find witnesses who might have seen something unusual that morning.

Forensic Coordinator Lindsey Yardley's team continued their work, analysing the bloodstains and evidence from Elsie's house. Every piece of information mattered, no matter how small.

George sat at his desk, studying the handwritten note repeatedly. He couldn't shake the feeling that there was more to Frederick Harman's message than met the eye. The reference to Wearside Jack, paganism, and vampirism hinted at a deeper obsession that might provide a clue to their location.

CHAPTER FORTY-ONE

As the hours passed, George's phone buzzed with updates from his team. They were making progress, but time was slipping away. He needed a breakthrough, a lead that would take them one step closer to finding Elsie and stopping Frederick's horrifying plans.

The clock on the wall ticked ominously, reminding George that Elsie's life hung in the balance with each passing moment. He couldn't afford to fail her. He couldn't afford to fail anybody else.

With his hands on his head and his chin resting on his desk, the DI was struggling with what to do next.

That's when George's phone rang.

Chapter Forty-two

"Hey, Gorgeous, how are you?" a familiar voice asked.

Isabella.

"Stressed, Izzy," he replied. "How are my two favourite girls?"

"We're tired, but good. One of us is hungry, and the other is grumpy. I'll let you decide who is who."

That brought a smile to George's face.

"Can I help you at all?" she asked.

The DI explained the situation to his fiancée, providing a detailed account of the missing Elsie Harman and the note Frederick Harman had left behind.

"So, you're looking for a stone circle like in Stourton and Woodhouse?" Isabella asked.

"That's right."

Isabella Wood hesitated.

"What?" George asked.

"It might be nothing."

"It also might be everything."

"This is going to sound weird, but I was on Facebook today, right, and I was looking through my feed while Olivia was asleep."

"Right."

"And a post from the Middleton group showed up."

"I'm sorry, but is there a point to all of this?"

"Patience, George."

The DI said nothing.

"A man named Michael Gibson posted in the group, asking, 'What's the best rumour about Middleton that you heard and believed growing up?'"

"OK."

"Well, he gave an example. He said, 'In-between St George's Centre and the new secondary school, there was a circle that I was told witchcraft happened.'"

"What?"

"Exactly."

"What's this guy called again?"

"Michael Gibson. He's always posting stuff, but somebody asked him to clarify where the circle was, and he said it was before the centre was built, and the area was known as Preggy Pond." She paused. "He's even posted a screenshot from Google Maps, circling where the pond used to be."

George swiftly got up, put on his coat, and struggled to keep his mobile to his ear. He gestured to his team to gather in the Incident Room ASAP and put Isabella on loudspeaker. "You're on loudspeaker, babe. Explain to everyone what you've just told me."

Isabella went on to provide more details, describing a playground next to the pond and how the circle Michael Gibson referred to was once an old playground ride consisting of a concrete circle with a hole in the middle.

Isabella's revelation had sent a ripple of excitement through the Incident Room. As Isabella continued to provide details about the playground and its transformation into a concrete circle, Detective Inspector George Beaumont's mind raced. This was a significant lead, and it was their best shot at finding Elsie Harman before Frederick could carry out his disturbing plan.

The DI took her off loudspeaker and placed the mobile by his ear. "Thanks, sweet," George said, his voice filled with gratitude. "You might have just given us the break we needed. Thank you."

Isabella's voice held a hint of concern. "Just please be careful. That psychopath is dangerous."

"I know, and I will, Izzy," George assured her.

"Please, George, keep me updated. I need to know you're safe."

George smiled, his heart warmed by Isabella's love and concern. "I promise, Izzy. I'll keep you updated every step of the way. Now, I need to go. We have a young woman to find."

Candy Nichols and other members of the team had gathered around, their expressions filled with determination. They knew the urgency of the situation, and the possible location of the stone circle had ignited their hope.

George addressed his team, his voice authoritative. "OK, everyone, we have a lead. We need to get there as soon as possible. I need Detective Superintendent Smith or Detective Chief Superintendent Sadiq to take charge of the raid."

DS Yolanda Williams nodded and quickly began making the necessary calls. George could see the worry in her eyes, mirrored by the rest of the team. They knew they were racing against time to save Elsie.

The Incident Room buzzed with activity as his team prepared to head to Middleton and raid the potential location of the stone circle. Preggy Pond was now the focal point in the search

CHAPTER FORTY-TWO

for Elsie Harman, as the note left by her brother, Frederick Harman, suggested that he might have taken her to a location associated with his dark interests and potentially connected to their childhood memories.

The urgency of the situation weighed heavily on them all, but they were determined to bring Elsie Harman back safely and put an end to Frederick Harman's sinister plans.

***

Frederick Harman sat in the dense foliage behind the now-dried-up Preggy Pond, his heart pounding in his chest and his thoughts a chaotic whirlwind. He cast a sidelong glance at his sister, Elsie, who sat bound and gagged next to him, her eyes filled with a mixture of fear and anger.

"Look, Elsie," Freddie began, his voice trembling with a strange mixture of regret and desperation. He had never expected their reunion to take such a dark and twisted turn. "I'm so sorry about Mum. I never wanted to hurt her."

Elsie's eyes narrowed, her gaze locked on her brother, her distrust palpable. When the gag was finally removed from her mouth, she spoke, her voice laced with bitterness. "Sorry won't bring her back, Freddie."

Freddie's shoulders slumped as if the weight of his crimes bore down on him. "I know," he admitted, his voice barely above a whisper. "I'll never forgive myself for what I did to her."

Elsie finally found her voice, anger now evident in her words. "You killed her, Freddie. You strangled her with your bare hands. I saw you, remember."

Tears welled up in Freddie's eyes as he hung his head in

shame. "I know, Elsie. I know. I can't undo what I've done. But at least I kept your name out of it. I didn't tell them what you saw."

"No, but I had to live with it daily for the last sixteen or seventeen years, Freddie."

The silence that followed was heavy and suffocating, broken only by the distant chirping of birds. Freddie knew he had to explain himself, at least try to make Elsie understand the torment that had driven him to such horrific acts.

"Why, Freddie?" Elsie demanded, her voice shaking with a mix of fear and curiosity. "Why did you kill those women, Penny, Joy, and Laura? What the hell did they do to you?"

Freddie took a deep, shuddering breath, struggling to find the words to articulate the darkness that had consumed him. "I miss Mum, Elsie," he finally confessed, his voice raw with emotion. "I miss her so much it hurts. And those women, they... they reminded me of her. They had her warmth, her kindness, her beauty. I thought if I took them into myself, I could fix what's wrong with me."

Elsie's eyes softened momentarily, a flicker of understanding in her gaze. But it quickly hardened again as she retorted, "That doesn't excuse what you did, Freddie."

Freddie's voice grew more desperate as he tried to make Elsie see his point of view. "Isn't civilization itself responsible for creating individuals like me?" he argued. "I didn't ask to be this way, Elsie. The world moulded me into this monster through abuse, suffering, and neglect. I've lived in a personal hell, and if the world had shown me an ounce of kindness, maybe I could have been different."

"Fucking bullshit!" Elsie shook her head, her eyes filled with tears. "You're responsible for your actions, Freddie, not the world."

Freddie felt a surge of frustration and anger. "But the world made me this way!" he insisted, his voice rising. "It pushed me to my limits, made me feel like there was no other way out. It broke me and wouldn't help fix me. So, I took it into my own hands."

Elsie's voice was a whisper, barely audible over the rustling leaves and the distant sounds of the world beyond their hiding place. "You could have sought help, Freddie. You could have turned your life around."

Tears streamed down Freddie's face as he gazed at his sister with a mixture of desperation and despair. "I didn't think there was any hope left for me," he admitted. "I felt like I was drowning in darkness, and there was no escape."

Elsie's eyes softened once more, and she leaned closer to her brother, her voice filled with a profound sadness. "I wish you had found another way, Freddie. I wish you hadn't let the darkness consume you."

Freddie nodded, his head hanging low. "I wish the same, Elsie. I wish I could go back and change everything."

As they sat there, hidden away from the world, the siblings shared a moment of profound sorrow and regret. The sun dipped below the horizon, casting long shadows over Preggy Pond, and the world outside continued to turn, oblivious to the pain and torment that had brought them to this dark place.

Freddie believed that there were two possible outcomes for him: he would either be destroyed and forgotten or become a legend—a symbol of what happened when society pushed a man too far. Despite his deep hatred for the world, he saw himself as a creature of hate, with the world as his enemy. And in that moment, he and Elsie were two lost souls bound together by the darkness that had consumed them both.

* * *

Elsie's reaction to Freddie's confession was a complex mix of emotions. At first, she was filled with anger and disbelief at the horrors her brother had committed. She couldn't comprehend how the person she had once known could turn into a ruthless serial killer responsible for the deaths of innocent women.

However, as Freddie explained the deep pain and torment that had driven him to commit these heinous acts, Elsie's anger gave way to a more nuanced response. She felt a sense of sadness and pity for her brother, realizing that he had suffered greatly and believed he had no other way out. She could see the despair in his eyes, tugging at her heartstrings.

Elsie's empathy allowed her to momentarily understand Freddie's internal struggle, the feeling of being trapped in a personal hell, and the belief that the world had pushed him to this point. She recognized that he saw himself as a product of a harsh and unforgiving world, a world that had failed to show him kindness or offer him a lifeline.

Despite this brief moment of understanding, Elsie couldn't condone or excuse her brother's actions. She firmly believed that individuals were responsible for their choices and actions, regardless of their circumstances or hardships they had endured. While she could empathize with Freddie's pain, she couldn't absolve him of the crimes he had committed.

Elsie's reactions fluctuated between anger, sorrow, and disappointment as she grappled with the complexity of her brother's confession. Their conversation left her with a heavy heart, torn between the love she once had for Freddie and the horrifying reality of his actions.

The conflict she felt became worse when Freddie asked, "Tell me how I can fix this, sister?"

"First, you confess to everything, and then you give yourself up." She held out her wrists. "And untie me, for heaven's sake!"

He untied her and said, "I've killed somebody else, too. A woman named Jacqueline Bell."

Fear flashed across Elsie's eyes, and Freddie recoiled. "So you're the Ripper?"

"No, I only killed Jacqueline. I just pretended to be the Ripper."

"Why on earth would you do that?"

"I pretended to be the Ripper because I thought it would make me more powerful," he admitted with a heavy heart. "I wanted people to fear me, to see me as someone to be reckoned with. It gave me a sick sense of control, Elsie, something I've never had in my life." He paused. "Dad took all the control away from me, and the body Mum gave me did the same. But as the Ripper, I felt different."

Elsie's disbelief and fear were palpable as she tried to process her brother's words. She couldn't fathom the depths of his depravity and the lengths he had gone to for a sense of power and dominance.

She shook her head as he said, "Sutcliffe heard voices telling him to rid the streets of prostitutes. Well, I heard voices telling me the only way I could fix myself was to become powerful!"

When Elsie said nothing, Freddie continued, his voice shaking with remorse. "I know I can never truly fix the pain and suffering I've caused, but I want to make amends somehow. I want to stop hurting people and find a way to atone for my sins. I've lost myself in this darkness and don't want to be a monster any more. You've made me see that, Elsie."

Still in shock, Elsie whispered, "You need to turn yourself in, Freddie. Face the consequences of your actions and seek help. It's the only way to start making things right."

Tears welled up in Freddie's eyes as he nodded, realizing the truth in his sister's words. The path to redemption, if it even existed, was a long and arduous one, but he had to try. He had to face the consequences of his crimes and, in some small way, find a way to make amends for the lives he had destroyed.

That was when the pair heard the sound of boots on the ground, and a male voice scream, "Armed Police!"

Chapter Forty-three

Fear gripped Freddie and Elsie as they heard the voice and the approaching footsteps. Panic surged through Freddie's veins, and he looked around frantically, searching for an escape route, but they were surrounded by dense foliage and metal fencing. He gripped the kitchen knife tighter in his hand.

His eyes widened with terror, realising the dire situation they were in. Sensing Freddie's fear, Elsie turned to her brother, her voice trembling as she whispered, "Freddie, you need to surrender. It's your only chance at redemption."

With a heavy heart and a deep sense of resignation, Freddie nodded. He knew that resisting would only lead to more bloodshed and pain. "Give me the knife, Freddie," she said.

Freddie nodded, handed his sister the knife and slowly raised his hands in surrender. Tears still streamed down his face as he contemplated the consequences of his actions.

Moments later, Authorised Firearms Officers burst through the under brush, their weapons trained on the two siblings. The tension in the air was palpable as they ordered Freddie and Elsie to get down on the ground, their voices stern and unyielding.

As they lay there, surrounded by the AFOs, Freddie couldn't help but feel a strange mix of relief and apprehension. He knew that this was the end of his reign of terror, but he also understood that the road to redemption and justice was just beginning.

* * *

As the tension in the air thickened, George finally received clearance to enter the police cordon, bringing him face to face with the notorious serial killer, Frederick Harman. He cautiously approached, his every step calculated, as he prepared to apprehend the man responsible for the deaths of innocent victims.

Unknown to George, hidden from view, Elsie still clutched the kitchen knife. She had bided her time, waiting for the right moment to exact her own form of justice for all the suffering her brother had inflicted upon her.

With the sun casting long shadows over the crime scene, George stepped forward, his every movement deliberate and purposeful. He reached out, his steady hand placing the cold, unforgiving steel of the handcuffs around Freddie's wrists. It was a moment of reckoning.

"Frederick Harman, you are under arrest for the suspicion of six counts of murder and three counts of attempted murder," George declared firmly, his voice carrying the weight of justice served. "You do not have to say anything. But, it may harm your defence if you do not mention when questioned something which you later rely on in court. Anything you do say may be given in evidence."

But just as George believed he had the situation under control, chaos erupted in the blink of an eye. Elsie, her anguish and anger consuming her, launched herself at her brother, the knife gleaming menacingly in her grip. Her intentions were unmistakable—she sought to end the torment her brother had brought into her life, no matter the cost.

Panic rippled through the officers as they scrambled to react. George, trained to respond swiftly in moments of crisis, acted on instinct. He lunged at Elsie, tackling her to the ground with a forceful impact that knocked the knife from her grasp. It clattered to the floor; a deadly threat neutralised.

Elsie fought against George's grip, her cries a cacophony of anguish and frustration. The years of suffering and torment, the scars etched deep into her psyche, had culminated in this moment of reckoning. But with the assistance of nearby AFOs, George managed to subdue her, restraining her wrists with handcuffs.

Freddie, who had been kneeling calmly until that point, watched the scene unfold with a mix of shock and relief. He had expected his sister's anger and betrayal, but the abruptness of her attack had caught him off guard. He knew he deserved death, though. He even welcomed it, not blaming his sister, but blaming himself.

With both Harman siblings now in custody and safely restrained, George let out a sigh of relief. The potentially deadly situation was defused, and the immediate threat was neutralised. He couldn't help but feel a pang of sympathy for Elsie, who had endured unimaginable torment at the hands of her own brother.

Elsie, her initial burst of anger subsiding, began to sob uncontrollably. The weight of her actions and the traumatic experiences she had endured had finally taken their toll. It was a heartbreaking sight, one that served as a reminder of the profound impact of Freddie's crimes on the lives of those around him.

As members of George's team arrived to take custody of the Harman siblings, George couldn't help but reflect on the complexities of the case. While justice would now be served through the legal system, the scars left by Freddie's reign of terror would linger, a sombre reminder of the darkness that resided in people.

Chapter Forty-four

In the small, sterile interview room at the police station, Detective Inspector George Beaumont and Detective Constable Jason Scott sat across the table from Frederick Harman, the notorious serial killer who had terrorised West Yorkshire. The air was thick with tension as they prepared to delve into the twisted mind of a remorseless murderer.

George leaned forward, his voice steady but filled with a burning need for answers. "Frederick Harman, we are here to discuss the horrific crimes you've committed. We want to understand your motives, the gruesome details, and why you chose these victims."

Freddie, his eyes locked on the table before him, began to speak in an unsettlingly calm tone. "Penny Haigh, she was the beginning. I watched her for days, studying her routine. I needed to feel in control and powerful. Killing her was my way of reclaiming that control."

"So, it's all about power with you?" asked George, and Frederick nodded. "That explains the strangulation but not the stabbing to the neck."

"I needed Penny's blood, Detective," Freddie explained. George narrowed his eyes. "My mother and father created me, just as your mother and father created you. But unlike you,

I was born tainted. I needed that blood to feel whole again."

George felt tainted by the blood he shared with his father, not that he would admit that to Freddie. "How did you do it?"

"I knew she was shagging that lad, Peter, and knew she met him regularly in Stourton. I was hoping to get there first and kill Penny before Peter arrived, but he actually got to her first."

George nodded. He remembered the CCTV footage of the masked man vividly. "So, were you wearing the mask?"

Freddie shrugged. "I didn't want to kill Peter, so I had no choice, did I?"

Frederick continued, "Joy Pritchard reminded me of my mother, a woman who both nurtured and tormented me. I couldn't resist the temptation to end her life, to release my anger and frustration."

George said, "She had young children, Freddie."

"As if I cared about that. She was just a means to an end."

"Tell us about the note."

"I planted it after killing her, thought it was genius on my part. See, I wanted you to look into Peter, knowing it would let me kill more women." Freddie grinned. "You're all as fucking thick as you were back in the seventies. Nothing's changed."

"Except you only killed half of what Sutcliffe managed. That's progress, is it not?"

Freddie shrugged. "Maybe, but I still killed a lot of women."

George and Jay listened intently as Frederick went into detail about murdering Joy Pritchard, their expressions a mixture of disgust and determination. But there were still unanswered questions.

"What about Laura Bennett?" Jay asked, her voice unwavering.

Freddie's lips curled into a chilling smile. "Laura was an

CHAPTER FORTY-FOUR

experiment, a way to push the boundaries of my cruelty. She represented purity, something I wanted to corrupt, something I wanted to absorb into myself. That, and like the other two, she reminded me of my mother."

The detectives exchanged a look, silently acknowledging the depths of depravity they were dealing with. But there was more to uncover. "That's why you sucked the blood straight from her neck?"

Freddie's grin stretched even further. "I thought her purity would cure me."

"Why did you mimic the Yorkshire Ripper when you killed Jacqueline Bell?" George inquired.

Freddie's eyes glinted with a perverse pride. "Jacqueline was my homage to the Ripper, a way to cement my legacy. I wanted to feel the fear and fascination that surrounded him. Sutcliffe is my hero."

Looking at the man, George could see the homage immediately. The only difference between the two men was the fact that Freddie didn't have a gap in his teeth.

The room seemed to grow colder as Freddie confessed to his crimes. George, however, was determined to uncover the truth about the other murders.

"What about the other two Yorkshire Ripper-style murders?" he pressed.

Freddie's demeanour shifted slightly, a hint of defiance in his voice. "I may be a monster, but I didn't commit those crimes. Someone else walks in Sutcliffe's long shadow, trying to replicate his actions. I wish them well."

George and Jay exchanged a disgusted glance. If Frederick was telling the truth, then a copycat killer was on the loose, mimicking Sutcliffe's gruesome methods. If it wasn't Harman, then the puzzle was far from solved.

"And the attempted murder of Lauren Robinson?" Jay questioned.

Freddie leaned back in his chair, his eyes narrowing. "I've told you what I've done. The rest is not my doing."

"So you're denying killing Cosima Winfrey and Tabitha Arrand and attempting to murder Lauren Robinson?" asked George.

"That's correct, George," Freddie said. Sitting handcuffed to the metal table, Freddie seemed surprisingly calm, given the gravity of the situation. His eyes, however, betrayed a hint of unease as he listened to the detectives listing the evidence against him.

"We have your DNA on Laura Bennett and evidence of sexual assault on Nancy Claybourn," George stated matter-of-factly.

Freddie merely nodded, his gaze fixed on the table before him.

"As for Penny Haigh and Joy Pritchard," Jay continued, "fibres matching the rope used to restrain your sister, Elsie, were found embedded in their skin."

Freddie remained silent, his face impassive.

"Bradford," George pressed on, "your prints were found at both Jacqueline Bell's crime scene and on her body."

Freddie couldn't help but respond this time, his lips curled into a humourless smile. "Seems I'm not as good a mimic as I thought."

Lauren Robinson's identification weighed heavily on the detectives. "Miss Robinson positively identified you in an identity parade," Jay said.

Freddie shook his head slowly, his voice carrying a hint of bitterness. "I protested my innocence, but I suppose that

CHAPTER FORTY-FOUR

doesn't count for much."

A similar situation occurred with a witness in Bradford, further corroborating Freddie's presence near the crime scene. "CCTV footage from both Cosima Winfrey and Tabitha Arrand's murders aligns with your height and hair," George added. CCTV footage at both Cosima Winfrey and Tabitha Arrand's murder scenes shows the back of a man's head. From the camera angle and the street level, forensics were able to ascertain that the man was five foot seven, the same height as Frederick Harman. The man on the CCTV also had dark, wiry hair, just like Harman.

Freddie leaned back in his chair, his fingers tapping rhythmically on the table. "I didn't kill those two women."

"We found a ball pein hammer and a Phillips-head screwdriver in your flat that matched the murder weapon used on Jacqueline Bell," George said, his voice tinged with uncertainty.

"I'm not denying killing Bell," said Freddie. "Have you found the weapons that killed Cosima Winfrey and Tabitha Arrand?"

Observing from next to the door, DCI Alistair Atkinson interrupted with conviction. "Don't be swayed, George." What the DCI meant by that was they hadn't found the weapons that killed Cosima Winfrey and Tabitha Arrand yet. "The evidence, the CCTV, the witness testimonies, all point to Harman."

George contemplated the evidence, torn between his doubts and the weight of the case against Freddie. But the decision was clear. "The CPS advises charging you with six counts of murder and two counts of attempted murder," George stated, locking eyes with Freddie.

Freddie Harman, the man who had inflicted terror on the

region, simply nodded again, accepting the fate that had finally caught up with him. As the interview continued, George and Jay were left with a chilling realisation: they were dealing with a killer who revelled in his notoriety, a sadistic mind capable of unspeakable horrors.

"Frederick Harman, the threshold test has been passed, and therefore, it is my lawful right to charge you for the murders of Penny Haigh, Joy Pritchard, Laura Bennett, Cosima Winfrey, Tabitha Arrand, and Jacqueline Bell. I'm also charging you for the attempted murders of Lauren Robinson and Elsie Harman." He paused. "You will also be charged with the sexual assault of Nancy Claybourn, a woman over the age of eighteen. Is all of that understood?" George asked.

"No," Freddie said. "I had nothing to do with Cosima Winfrey, Tabitha Arrand, and Lauren Robinson." He turned to his solicitor. "Do something."

"We'll be fighting this," Freddie's solicitor said.

"Interview terminated," George said. They left the room. Two uniformed officers entered, handcuffs out, waiting. Harman would spend his time in Armley Nick before his trial. While they uncovered the motives behind some of his crimes, the search for the truth behind the remaining murders and the elusive copycat killer was far from over.

* * *

The squad room at Elland Road Police Station was abuzz with excitement and anticipation as Detective Inspector George Beaumont walked in. His announcement about charging Frederick Harman had sent ripples of excitement through the team, and it was clear that they were eager to hear the latest

CHAPTER FORTY-FOUR

update.

A burst of rowdy applause erupted from the back of the room, and George couldn't help but smile at the camaraderie and support of his colleagues. It was clear that Luke Mason, with his boisterous personality, had been the one to set off the applause.

George made his way to the front of the room, where a large screen displayed a re-run of the press conference the DI had just given. His team had gathered around, their faces a mix of enthusiasm and determination.

"Alright, everyone," George began, his voice carrying a note of pride and gratitude. "We've charged Harman for the murders of Penny Haigh, Joy Pritchard, Laura Bennett, and Jacqueline Bell, plus the attempted murder and rape of Nancy Claybourn. His sister won't press charges, so that'll be down to the CPS." He paused. "In terms of the Ripper case, we've made some significant progress, and it's all thanks to your hard work and dedication."

The room fell into a hushed silence as George began to provide the latest update. He went through the details of the Ripper case, highlighting the evidence against Frederick Harman, detailing Freddie's insistence that he didn't kill Cosima Winfrey and Tabitha Arrand and attempt to murder Lauren Robinson.

Detective Chief Inspector Alistair Atkinson, clapping his hands and smiling at George, stood beside the DI and addressed the Homicide and Major Enquiry Team. "As you all know, this case has been challenging," the DCI said, his gaze sweeping over his colleagues. "But we've worked tirelessly, and today, we've taken a significant step forward." He paused for a moment, letting the words sink in. The atmosphere in the room was electric, a palpable sense of achievement hanging in the air.

"We'll continue to follow every lead, leave no stone unturned," Alistair emphasised. "Our goal is to bring justice to the victims and their families. Together, we can make that happen."

A chorus of determined nods and murmurs of agreement filled the room. The detectives were more motivated than ever, united in their pursuit of justice. But George wasn't convinced. They had zero evidence linking Harman to Cosima Winfrey, Tabitha Arrand and Lauren Robinson. In fact, all they had were the similarities between the Winfrey and Arrand and Bell murders.

But it was out of his hands. He'd done his job and caught the ritual killer that had been tormenting Leeds.

So George concluded the meeting, his heart filled with pride for his dedicated team.

The investigation had reached its conclusion, but the healing process for the survivors and families affected by Freddie's actions was just beginning. And for Detective Inspector George Beaumont, there was the hope that, in some small way, justice could provide a sense of closure and a path towards recovery for those whose lives had been forever altered by Harman's actions.

But Sutcliffe's long shadow still lingered over Yorkshire and the West Yorkshire Police, and George didn't believe for one minute that everything was over.

About the Author

From Middleton in Leeds, Lee is an author who now lives in Rothwell, West Yorkshire, England with his wife and three children. He spends most of his days writing about the places he loves, watching sports, or reading. He has a soft spot for Pokemon Trading Cards, Japanese manga and anime, comic books, and video games. He's also rather partial to a cup of strong tea.

You can connect with me on:
- https://www.leebrookauthor.com
- https://www.facebook.com/LBrookAuthor

Subscribe to my newsletter:
- https://leebrookauthor.aweb.page/p/cfff8220-7312-4e37-b61a-b1c6c2d15fc2

Also by Lee Brook

The Detective George Beaumont West Yorkshire Crime Thriller series in order:

The Miss Murderer

The Bone Saw Ripper

The Blonde Delilah

The Cross Flatts Snatcher

The Middleton Woods Stalker

The Naughty List

The Footballer and the Wife

The New Forest Village Book Club

The Killer in the Family

The Stourton Stone Circle

Pre-order Shadows of the Ripper: The Long Shadow novella

Pre-order The West Yorkshire Ripper

More titles coming soon.

Printed in Great Britain
by Amazon